IGNITION

The legend awaits...
- Emma Shefford

ALSO BY EMMA SHELFORD

Mark of the Breenan

IGNITION

MUSINGS OF MERLIN SERIES

EMMA SHELFORD

IGNITION

Kinglet Books
Victoria BC, Canada

Copyright © 2015 Emma Shelford
Cover design by Christien Gilston

ISBN-10: 1511902817
ISBN-13: 978-1511902816

www.emmashelford.com

First edition: May 2015

DEDICATION

For Steven

My inspiration, my enabler, and my sounding-board

PROLOGUE

Time. It rules our lives, ticking away the seconds, minutes, hours of our days. It's time to get up, time to leave, time to return. Suffering can stretch minutes into eons, and happiness can exist for only a heartbeat, yet stay with us for all time. From a baby's first angry wail to an old man's last sighing breath, our lives are subject to the coursing river of time. The only certainty of life is that everyone's time on Earth will end.

Everyone, that is, except me.

Time passes for me as it does for everyone else. It's just that I have seen so much more of it pass. For over fifteen hundred years I've walked this Earth, never dying, never aging. I'm waiting for someone to return. He was first my student, then my brother-in-arms, and finally my friend. They say he'll be back one day when he's needed again, and I promised that I'd wait for him to return. He'll need my help when he arrives. I'm pretty useful.

My name is Merlin, and this is one chapter in the story of my life.

CHAPTER I

I'm at my psychologist's office for the first time. Yes, I just started seeing a shrink. I've tried everything else in this world—why not get my head examined? Of course, the poor woman won't know what hit her once I open up. She's used to dealing with divorcées and troubled kids, not centuries-old magicians with abandonment issues and more baggage than would fit in an aircraft carrier.

Of course, I doubt I'll fill her in on the whole story. She'd laugh in my face—I've seen it before—although she might hide it behind a professional mask of genial understanding. If she thought I was serious, she'd likely urge me to check in for psychiatric examination. I don't look centuries-old. Thirty, give or take.

More likely I'll give her a condensed version—just enough drama to comfortably fit into one lifetime. We'll see how much the woman can handle. My life can be too difficult for regular people. It can be too difficult for me sometimes, and I've lived it.

I wonder how long the sessions will last, since half the things I tell her will have to be fabricated. She even has problems right off the bat with my name.

"Please sit down, Mr.—" She looks down at her notepad, and pulls a lock of shoulder-length brown hair behind one ear with a nervous twitch. "Lytton. My name is Dr. Minnie Dilleck. May I call you—" She squints at her notes again. "Merry?"

She's definitely new at her job. That's my fault for picking the youngest, prettiest female psychologist in Vancouver, B.C. Not that it's a problem—I came for the experience of being in therapy, not to delve deeply into my

2

psyche. I might as well enjoy the scenery along the way.

"Yes, of course. And before you ask, yes, Merry like the hobbit." Although I came up with the name long before Tolkien ever dreamed of Middle Earth. I make it a game with myself to choose names similar to my true name. Depending on the country I'm living in at the time, this can be difficult or easy. Merry Lytton is my nom du jour. Given my tanned complexion and black-brown hair, cut short for this time, it's not difficult to fit in wherever I please. And I've always had a flair for languages, especially after centuries of practice. It's easy to slide completely into whatever persona I've chosen. I'm eminently adaptable.

"Am I supposed to lay down on the couch now?" I flop onto the surprisingly uncomfortable couch covered in gray faux-suede, swinging my legs up and resting my ankles on the armrest.

"If—if you're more comfortable that way, by all means." She looks a little flustered at my teasing. I take my fun where I can, so sue me. The experience will be good for her. Builds character, as my mother was fond of saying long ago. So very, very long ago.

"So, Merry." Dr. Dilleck smooths her pencil skirt over her thighs. The glass coffee table between us houses a bowl of oranges and a discreet box of tissues. "Let's talk about you. Merry is an interesting name. Is it short for something?"

"It's short for Marybel, actually," I say. Her eyes widen and her hand grips her pen more securely. I relent. "Only joking. Don't look so worried."

"If your name were Marybel, it would be perfectly all right with me," she says. I raise my eyebrows. Perhaps the little mouse has a spine. This might be interesting after all.

"So, Merry, what brought you here? Is there anything in particular you'd like to discuss?"

3

Hmm. Good question. Luckily, I have my answer ready.

"I fight off and on with depression, and I've never come to anyone to deal with it. I thought maybe it was time. I'm feeling good now, you understand, but it always comes back. I figure it can't hurt to explore a bit."

She's nodding before I finish.

"It's great that you're here, Merry. Good for you. It takes courage to face your inner demons. Now you have help—we can face them together."

I settle in for the hour. We talk for a while about what happens when I get depressed—I sleep, mainly, because it's not as if I need to worry about wasting my life away—and how I improve my mood. I don't have high hopes that anything will come of this. It's not depression as people today classify it, brain chemistry gone haywire. It's simply too many layers of loss, and sometimes grief gets the better of me. There's not much this doctor can do about it. That's okay. She has a very calming voice, and her eyes are large with pale gray irises—quite mesmerizing.

"Do you find there is a trigger, some way to release you from your depression?"

Air puffs out of my nose in a mirthless chuckle.

"I try to remember that someone might need me, someday."

"That's good. Try to hold onto that." She nods before continuing. "Do you have any family? A significant other?"

I stare at the ceiling. Did she really have to go there? I guess I should have expected it. Oh well, I can give her some real fodder to work with.

"Family long since dead. Never knew my father. No children. My wife," my most recent wife, that is, "died years ago also. Honestly, I'd rather not talk about it." There's the truth. It's only taken me thirty years to move on from

4

Josephine's death. I swear, each time a woman I love dies, it gets harder.

"Okay." Her voice is soothing and low. "Whenever you're ready. There's no rush." I glance over to see her biting her lip and looking down at her notes. She's obviously itching to ask more but is professional enough to respect my wishes. I almost feel bad denying her. Maybe I should throw her a bone.

"I guess I should tell you—I have very strange dreams."

She sits up straighter.

"Oh?"

I try not to smile.

"I keep reliving my past. They're very vivid dreams. More like memories, really." I used to dream properly when I was younger, the usual nonsense about talking horses and flying castles and other bizarre things. Now, though, I'm only visited by the ghosts of my past. The intense memories fill me with joy and plague me with sorrow and guilt.

"Dreams can be very important parts of our subconscious. Often our brains are processing things in the night that we don't want to deal with consciously. May I suggest you start a dream journal? In fact, journaling in general can be very beneficial."

She's about to ask more when I notice the clock strike three.

"Oops, looks like we're done here." I swing my legs to the ground and push to my feet with alacrity. That's just about enough soul-searching for today. Perhaps this wasn't such a good idea after all.

She almost looks a little disappointed.

"Yes, of course. Well, it was wonderful to meet you, Merry. I think we made some progress here today. I'd love to see you back here soon."

5

We'll see. I smile noncommittally and say goodbye.

***

A few hours later, I cross the quad at the university where I work. One would think I could retire after fifteen hundred years in the workforce, but I doubt social security has figured out the paperwork for an eternity of pension benefits.

And besides, what would I do all day? Play golf? It's not as if I need to rest. I have the body and vigor of a thirty-year-old man, and a brain filled with centuries of knowledge and experience. Honestly, it's a relief to do something. It helps me avoid long contemplative introspection. Makes me wonder why I'm starting these shrink sessions, although I do enjoy talking about myself, which I'm rarely able to do.

"Hey, Merry! Wait up!"

To my left, a pretty girl lopes toward me across the grass, her long, slender legs in their tiny butt-hugging shorts dodging the clusters of sprawling students in her way. Her black hair swishes around her shoulders and sweeps forward as she falls into place beside me, her face beaming.

"Hi, Jen," I say. Jennifer Chan took one of my classes a few years ago—a translation course focusing on Old English texts, mainly pre-Norman Saxon. She was by far the brightest student in my class, an absolute prodigy at languages of all sorts. She'd come with great questions, and we would often fall into long conversations after class. We struck up a friendship once exams finished and prying eyes in the department were satisfied that the teacher-student relationship was dissolved. Not that I feel anything more than friendship for Jen, surprisingly. She's a beautiful girl, all slender limbs without sacrificing curves in the right places, with a pleasant oval face from her Asian father and large, friendly eyes gifted

6

by her Danish mother.

If I do have a weakness, it's for women. It's got me into plenty of trouble in the past, more than I care to admit. I may have a centuries-old mind, but the rest of me hasn't caught up. But Jen feels off-limits, somehow. It's refreshing, actually, to be friends with a woman without lust taking the driver's seat. As far as Jen is concerned, I'm simply a young sessional instructor at the university who's not much older than her. Hah.

I'm still not sure why she befriended me so readily. Perhaps it was our shared interest in language and history, and she wanted conversations with a little more depth than her circle of friends could give her. Or maybe she can tell I'm different, and who isn't attracted to something new and exciting? Whatever the reason, I'm not complaining. Friends don't come my way often enough, and I don't want to analyze this one.

"You look pretty peppy for exam season." It's true—Jen always has a bounce in her step, a physical release of her natural joie de vivre, but today she is positively springy.

"All done! Mandarin yesterday and ancient Hebrew this morning. The rest were last week. I totally aced them all, of course." She winks at me. She isn't very good at winking— her eyes sort of squint simultaneously—but it's endearing, and I get the message.

"I would expect nothing less from my finest pupil." I give her a one-armed hug. "Nice work. So does this mean you're done? As in degree, long robes, silly hat?"

"You better believe it!"

"Well, congrats. That's big news. I, on the other hand, have a huge pile of marking to do. Where your work ends, mine begins."

"Poor, long-suffering Merry. All those terrible essays.

Never mind all that. You can buy me coffee tomorrow to celebrate my accomplishments and distract yourself from the drudgery of marking."

I laugh.

"I guess that's fair." We walk in companionable silence for a few moments until Jen checks her watch.

"Oops, got to run. I have an interview for an interpreter job that starts next week." She rolls her eyes. "My dad set it up. The firm is run by an old buddy of his, so I'll probably get the job no matter what. But it doesn't hurt to be on time." Jen's father is the CEO of a very large, very successful corporation headquartered in Vancouver, with satellite offices all over the world. I know it bothers Jen to take advantage of her father's position, but it's hard to turn down the opportunities she's afforded.

"See you tomorrow. Come by my office at ten," I say. She waves goodbye and strides across the grass to the bus loop. She doesn't notice that she's walking straight into the middle of a Frisbee game. When she reaches the center of the grassy boulevard, the whirling disk spins directly toward her head. Without thinking, I tweak the *lauvan* surrounding Jen. The Frisbee bounces harmlessly off the air above her head and skitters across the grass. Jen doesn't even break stride.

Soul-searching with the psychologist left a bitter taste in my mouth, only momentarily alleviated by Jen's buoyant presence. I'm tired, the weight of memories threatening to pull me under the surface. My face lifts toward the sun in an attempt to banish ghosts. I don't have much luck.

I continue to walk across campus, deciding against marking any more today, and enter an outdoor breezeway to get to the car park. On the right wall hangs a poster for a Harry Potter movie marathon at the campus theater. My head shakes and my mouth twitches upward involuntarily. People nowadays love the idea of magic, at least around here. It's all wands and sparks and mind control. No one believes it, of course, except maybe the hopeful kiddies jumping off their beds on kitchen brooms. It's simply blissful escapism. I can understand that. It's much better than the witch hunts in the sixteenth century, or the lynchings and burnings in certain parts of the world today.

The thing is, magic doesn't exist. Not like that, anyway. The only person I've ever seen do anything out of the ordinary is me. And it's not wizard fire and "you shall not pass."

What I do is more—how do I describe it? It's as if there's a layer of extra matter around everything that is invisible to everyone. But to me, the layer appears as a vast covering of translucent, interconnected threads woven around anything that has inherent energy. A fire has plenty of threads, as does a rock flying through the air. A rock sitting on the ground, though, doesn't have much in the thread department, although if it's an igneous rock it may have a few leftover threads from its fiery birth in a volcanic eruption. I call these threads *lauvan*, which means "rope" in my native tongue—a language nobody speaks anymore.

Living things, especially, have an abundance of lauvan. In humans, they're an extension of the body, but also of the spirit. It's complicated. If the human body is like Earth, then the lauvan are the atmosphere around it. The atmosphere can't be seen except by a precious few astronauts, but without it, the Earth would be a barren, lifeless void. So too with the lauvan. The lauvan help make us who we are, and when we die, our lauvan unravel and dissolve into nothingness. They are an extension of energy from the physical body, what gives it animation. The soul, if you will.

As I said, it's complicated. I've had centuries to think

9

about it, and that's the best explanation I can muster. It doesn't help that I'm the only one I've ever known who is like me, so there's no one to ask. I've certainly looked. Any vague rumor of magic or sorcery used to have me running to examine the hopefuls, but no one could ever see the lauvan. I gave up after the eleventh century.

Not only can I see the lauvan, I can touch them if I wish to. Manipulating the lauvan affects the physical world—when I pulled at Jen's lauvan, I prevented the Frisbee from slamming into her head. It's certainly useful, and I've had a lot of time to be inventive.

My car waits for me in the car park. It's a dark blue Lotus Elise. I should really have something more inconspicuous, although in a city rampant with Ferraris and Maseratis, mine doesn't stand out as much as one might expect. I've taken the glamorous route in the past, but the less noticeable I make my life, the longer I can stay in one place. I have the money—it's not hard to make it when you're as resourceful and experienced as I am—but to keep my cover, I can't show off too much. This city is comfortable for the moment, and I don't want to leave it right now. But the car was too hard to resist. I've always loved the rush of speed even from my days on horseback, and the luxury of a fast car is an indulgence I'm not willing to forgo.

The car purrs to life. I back out of the parking spot and the radio kicks in.

"...with their newest single. Up now, your quick-bit news bites, the quickest news so you can get back to listening to the music you love! The big local buzz is volcanic activity on Mt. Linnigan, just outside Wallerton, B.C. Hikers reported steam coming out of the mountain's peak. Seismologists say that this is unusual activity from a dormant volcano, but insist there is nothing to worry about. I say, time to get the *popcorn! We could have an awesome lava show in the near future!"*

I grunt and hit the "off" button. Typical. The announcer seems to know very little about his topic. It's doubtful we'd get much lava in this region. It's possible, but not common, given the geology of the tectonic plates here. When plate tectonic theory emerged a few decades ago, I read everything I could about it. I like to keep up to date, especially where the Earth is concerned.

After a short and blissfully quiet drive home, I pull into the underground parking of my apartment block. Perhaps it's an odd choice for someone who could live anywhere he chose. I could say that it's to keep my inconspicuous cover— what would a sessional instructor be doing with a house in this expensive realty market?—but, in truth, it's comforting living among so many people. I can hear their lives occurring through the remarkably thin walls, and I can chat to them when we pass in the hallways. Their lauvan also occasionally float through the walls into my apartment. Did I not mention? It's mostly peopled by the elderly. I'm pretty sure I'm the "youngest" person living in the complex by a wide margin. Older people often have a greater number of loose lauvan. I expect that it's a function of a slow release of life, letting go of the spirit from the body. They often also have more connections outside of themselves, more of their lauvan stretching away in connection with distant friends and relatives. It's comforting to touch the lives of others, however tenuous the association, however minor. It makes me feel connected, part of something.

Not just a spectator living on the fringes, a part of the world but not of it.

My own lauvan are much looser than anyone I've ever met. Years of living and loving and losing have ripped the lauvan away from my body. After every loss, they have a harder time tightening up against my physical form. Now, after so many centuries, they tend to wave around me in a wispy cloud of chocolate brown threads rather than the coils I see surrounding most people. I'm still here, though—my lauvan haven't left me yet.

The elevator takes me to the fifth floor where I step out to walk directly into a particularly strong lauvan floating by. I smile. Mrs. Watson is telling off her husband again. Annoyance vibrates through the lauvan when it hits my own, but an underlying affection hums below it. It's their ritual, one I can sense they've been doing for decades. Gary Watson usually turns his good ear toward me when we play chess together, but I gather that his deaf ear gets a lot of use too.

Key sliding into lock, bolt clicking open, hand twisting on knob. How many doors have I come home to? This door opens up to a fairly decent view, as far as my past homes are concerned. I've had much warmer and welcoming homes to enter in my time but also some far worse ones, so I suppose I can't complain. It's simple and clean, a one bedroom with a view of snow-capped mountains, providing a uniquely restful view in the city. A lone bookshelf hugs the living room wall. It's full of my eclectic collection of keepsakes—a group of holy objects from different religions that hum with lauvan, such as a folded bundle of Tibetan prayer flags, a shrunken head from the Shuar tribe of Ecuador, and a splinter of wood reputably from the Christian cross, among others. Although these items are neither moving nor living, they still have lauvan. Any inanimate object that is valued or worshipped for long enough will collect the lauvan of its worshipers. All the relics I own, whether or not they have any intrinsic value or truth, are imbued with enough lauvan to have worth in their own right. There's also my sketchbook, a few of my favorite weapons that I've held onto, as well as some musical instruments. One is a small fifteenth-century harp I was given by the blind harpist Turlough O'Carolan when we played together one winter in the hills of western Ireland, and I transcribed some of his original melodies for him. The décor in the rest of my apartment is minimal. After living for so long on the move, I've learned not to keep many possessions. Even my keepsakes are disposable, except for my sketchbook. That has too many memories to leave behind.

I flop on the couch, too tired to stay upright. My mind flits back to the memories my therapy session dredged up. Josephine's laughing blue eyes torment me behind my eyelids. It's been thirty years since she died, and still she haunts me. My mind travels back through time, flipping through friends and lovers and wives on the pages of the book that is my life, further and further back. I fall asleep, my thoughts filled with some of my first memories, from so long ago.

CHAPTER II

Dreaming

I lie stomach-down on a large flat rock on the banks of a sluggish river. The water is clear and the dark shapes of river trout move in the depths beyond my reach.

My mouth waters at the thought of fresh fish roasted over a crackling fire. It's been two days since I've had a proper meal—game is scarce with winter fast approaching. I curse my wanderlust. What madness compelled me to leave the south?

"Here we go," I say out loud, and slide my hands carefully into the water. The lauvan of the fish are barely visible in the clear water and I can't see any breaking the surface.

My hands tingle and bite with the cold almost immediately. I grit my teeth and feel for the lauvan.

"What are you doing?" A voice breaks my concentration. I drop my head in frustration and look up at my interrogator.

A boy of about ten stares at me with curiosity in his brown eyes. His dark curls are a tousled mess around a plain but pleasant face. He has an open, hopeful expression, as if he expects me to say something exciting that he can tell all his little friends about. His lauvan match his face, lively and a fresh spring-green at odds with the falling brown leaves of autumn surrounding him.

I'm too tired and hungry to pander to a child. I settle for the truth, and hope it will be boring enough to make him go away.

"Fishing." I turn away from him and plunge my hands into the frigid water again. I close my eyes to concentrate.

A few moments go by, and then close to my ear, "With your hands?" My eyes pop open. The boy is on his stomach

14

beside me, peering into the water.

"No, with my toes. Now shush while I concentrate." I close my eyes resolutely and find the lauvan of a particularly large trout swimming a few arm-spans out of reach.

The boy is perfectly still beside me, surprisingly. With the lauvan firmly between my fingers, I risk a peek at him to make sure he isn't jeopardizing my dinner. He watches my fingers intently with a curious frown wrinkling his brow. He senses my gaze and smiles hopefully.

Little squirt. I'll give him something to tell his friends. I find myself answering his smile with one of my own, suddenly eager to show off my skills. I don't let many people see—it's far too dangerous when the fearful can easily blame me for all their woes—but this is just a boy. Who would he tell, and if he did, who would believe him?

"Are you watching?" I ask. He nods vigorously. I turn back to the water and wind the lauvan around my fingers, slowly, so slowly. The fish moves imperceptibly our way, as if it were meaning to do so all along. I know better. My hold on the fish is tenuous, and if the fish startled I would lose it. But my pulls are more of a suggestion than a command, and as the fish comes closer I snag more of its smooth and slippery lauvan. I twine them together into a coarse rope.

The fish is almost within my reach. I keep my eyes on the fish, but say, "Are you ready?"

"Yes," the boy whispers.

I grip the fish's lauvan tightly and say quietly, "One, two, three!" On the third count I heave the lauvan up with a jerk.

The fish leaps into the air. Scales glint in the dull afternoon light. The fish writhes in fear and lauvan spasm around its body. I roll onto my back, away from the boy, and lift my arms.

Just as I'd planned, the fish lands exactly in my

outstretched hands. Feeling very pleased with myself, I roll over again and bash the creature's head against the rock until it stills.

I find myself breathing heavily from excitement and grinning broadly. I look to the boy, one eyebrow raised, looking for his reaction. His eyes are wide with shock and his mouth hangs open. He stares at me for a moment, before his face expands with a delighted smile.

"Wow, that was amazing! How did you do that?"

It feels good to be admired, even if it's just by a ten year-old boy. But I'm only twenty-three myself and appreciate an ego boost in whatever form it comes. I push myself up to my feet and hang the fish by its gills from my fingers.

"So, little squirt, are you joining me for dinner? Know that I make visitors collect firewood to earn their meal."

The boy considers this. His face brightens.

"You could bring your fish home with me, and eat with us tonight. Father loves having visitors, and cook made honey cakes today."

The boy's family is rich enough to hire a cook? Suddenly a solitary fish in the woods is much less appealing. I pretend to consider for a moment.

"I'd be happy to accept your offer, little squirt." The boy beams and starts down a nearby path. I sling my bag over one shoulder and grab my harp case in my fish-less hand. "Wait. What is it that they call you?"

The boy runs back and relieves me of my harp. His eyes are bright and eager and his lauvan dance around him.

"My name is Arthur."

***

I awake. My eyes are full, and drip out onto the pillow

16

when I squeeze them shut.

CHAPTER III

Jen sips on her coffee and smiles in satisfaction.

"Mmm, it's perfect."

Of course it is. I made sure that the temperature was just right before I handed her the drink. It was a simple matter of twitching the lauvan of the hot coffee to release a little heat, enough to avoid a scalding.

"Well, I do have excellent coffee-ordering skills. It must be that."

"No, it was definitely you flirting with the barista. She put in an extra effort for you."

I laugh.

"So, my master plan is working. World domination via seduction."

Jen bumps my shoulder with hers playfully, and her long braid thumps against my back.

"Don't forget about me when you're king of the world."

We walk for a bit along the boardwalk at Steveston, a neighbourhood south of Vancouver with a history of fishing. Seagulls swoop and cry in a frenzy at the scent of fish sold straight off the boats. Families out for the first real summer warmth swarm the docks, ice creams in hand. We stroll up a set of wooden stairs to emerge onto a dusty side street, neglected by the happy family traffic. Jen slows down to look in a window and I match her pace.

"Check it out, Merry. There're all sorts of weird crystals. Ooh, that one's bright blue."

I peer through the glass in the direction of Jen's pointed finger. On a midnight-blue velvet cloth is a collection of jagged quartz crystals of varying sizes and shapes, some with veins of milky-white bisecting their structure, some with brilliant colors embedded in their surfaces. All the crystals are writhing with lauvan, a sure sign that they are valued to have power. The crystals sit next to a small fan of books with titles like *The Modern Tarot* and *Spiritual Mysticism and You*. Sheer fabrics of many brilliant hues are artfully draped above the display. They provide color as well as prevent a peek into the rest of the shop.

"Hey, look, they have free palm readings today." Jen grabs my elbow and tugs me toward the door. Her golden lauvan dance, framing her eager face with color and energy. I love Jen for her vibrancy—around her, the burden of my years lightens. I hang back for a minute, resisting.

"Really? You want to go to a psychic? I can tell you your future." I grab her hand and flip it up so her palm faces the sky. I trace the lines and say in a deep portentous voice, "Your life line is long and your head line is short. But beware a dark-haired man who provides delicious coffee, for he will surely buy you an ice cream later."

Jen giggles and swats my hand away.

"It'll be fun. And then we can laugh about it later over that ice cream. Come on, I bet you've never had your palm read before."

In truth, I had my first palm reading courtesy of an old Gypsy woman in the side streets of Florence during the Italian Renaissance. She told me I had a very long life line. I said, "Tell me something I don't know."

I allow Jen to drag me across the threshold. We pass through an old wooden doorway painted a vibrant aqua, out of place alongside the metal and glass of the surrounding shops. It looks like a retrofit, and a DIY job, judging by the gouges in the doorframe where the hinges were misplaced. I glance around the small shop after the door tinkles closed with the sound of wind chimes. They make a jarring jangle when I have to shove the ill-fitting door closed with my foot, ruining the ethereal mood they were clearly placed there to create.

The shop is tidy with minimalistic displays on round tables of varying heights. Directed spotlights on the ceiling highlight the contents of each table, while the rest of the shop is kept in cool dimness from the partially covered window. The displays contain more of the same from the window, plus some other offerings—stylistically illustrated tarot cards, candles, statues. The perfume of incense lingers mildly in the air. A murmured greeting floats to us from the corner, and when my eyes adjust I see a woman standing behind the counter dressed in a long, flowing shirt of undyed linen. Her graying hair is held back in a loose braid and her manner is friendly but not effusive, confirmed by muted silver lauvan that swirl calmly around her torso. She isn't trying for the hard sell, in any event.

Jen wanders around the shop to glance at a number of the displays. I follow her, amused by her show of browsing for politeness' sake. I wonder if it's as obvious to the shopkeeper, but conclude that we aren't the first skeptics to enter her shop on a whim. I haven't been in one of these new-age spirituality-type shops before, and my fingers hover over the lauvan of the nearest crystals with real interest.

After a minute, Jen must feel that she's done her time and approaches the shopkeeper.

"Hi. I saw you offered free palm readings?" She holds out her hand tentatively.

The shopkeeper smiles.

"Of course. On the house. It's always nice to have a little forewarning, isn't it? Think of this as an insight into the weather forecast of your life. Of course, nothing as detailed as rain on next Tuesday, but the signs will all be there. The interpretation is up to you." She grasps Jen's wrist gently and stretches out the fingers with her other hand to search the palm intently. Jen glances at me and we exchange raised eyebrows. The shopkeeper stays intent on her task until we turn our attention back to her. I wonder how much of our reaction she saw or guessed.

"It seems that you are waiting for someone. Waiting for your true love to arrive." The woman frowns and glances up at Jen, whose wrist is still clasped in her hand. She smiles at Jen's confused expression. "Don't worry. It will take time, but you will recognize him when he finally arrives and your eyes are opened."

Jen smiles uncertainly when the woman releases her.

"Thank you?" It's almost a question. She turns to me. "Okay, Merry, your turn."

"No, seriously, it's fine. I like my future a little foggy." I don't think I can handle the future as well as carry around all this past.

"Oh, come on, Merry." Jen grabs my hand and slaps it down on the counter. "Let's see what's in store for you."

I acquiesce—it seems easier. The woman cups my knuckles in her own palm. Her fingers are cool and dry, and I let my hand relax while she pulls each finger away from the palm.

She takes a long time to examine my hand. I stare at the top of her head, and wonder what she thinks she sees. I've never yet met anyone who I felt was actually practicing real magical ability, except myself. Perhaps they are all really good at hiding. I certainly am, after all. My eyes travel down to her neck and I'm startled to see orange lauvan, quite different from the woman's own, swirling around a gold chain. Lower, pulses of orange lauvan emerge from under the woman's collar. I'm intrigued. Does she have a lauvan-embedded amulet on her? Does it somehow help her see the future? I've heard of such things, but they are rarer than hen's teeth, and I'm dubious that they actually work.

Jen kicks me and I jump slightly. The shopkeeper takes her free hand and carefully closes my fingers in a strange, somber gesture. It's as if she puts something precious in my hand, or rather, gently closes it around something she cannot bear to see.

She takes a while to raise her eyes. When they meet mine, they are filled with confusion and a little pity. I'm curious now. What does she think she saw? Or, with the help of the lauvan-infused necklace, did she actually see something?

The woman clears her throat.

"I saw a few things. First, you have a tremendously long life line." I try my level best not to roll my eyes at this, but it takes all the effort I can muster. She continues. "Second, you are also waiting for someone, but it is not your lover. You have been waiting a very long time. Know that your patience will be rewarded."

This startles me. It's not exactly a cookie-cutter response for a palm reader, and it's a little too close to the truth. I glance again at the chain and see the orange lauvan twining around her neck.

"Third and last, I see signs that are somewhat unclear." And the previous ones were crystal? I try to keep a serious expression on my face. "All I see is that you must be aware of the portents of doom that are presenting themselves to you. They must be heeded." She shakes her head briefly and swiftly, like a dog shaking water out of its fur. She takes both her hands and passes me back my own fist across the counter in a ceremonial gesture.

"Thanks very much. It was very enlightening." Jen grabs my elbow with strong fingers and pulls me away to the door.

The woman stares after us, looking pensive. I echo Jen's thanks and follow her.

Once outside and three stores down the road, Jen lets out her breath with a whoosh and laughs. I try to shake the lingering questions I have about the truth of the shopkeeper's warning. Normally, I would never take the word of a fortune-teller seriously—I've seen too many charlatans in my day. But that necklace makes me wonder, especially when she told me I was waiting for someone. And then the warnings about portents—what did she mean? I clench my teeth in frustration. Stupid fortune-tellers—always telling you just enough to be curious, but not enough to be useful.

"Well! Now I've got to wait for my one true love to come sweep me off my feet." Jen holds out her arms and mimes running in slow-motion. I laugh and try to forget the comments of doom.

"Yeah, that was pretty bog-standard palm reading tripe. Are you happy now? You've had the best of the stereotypical fortune-telling visit."

"Oh, it was fun anyway. She was so serious about it, too. But your fortune was weird—she was trying to branch out a bit with you. Maybe she was trying to distract you from looking down her shirt."

"Is that why you kicked me? What you must think of me! I was checking out her necklace, that's all."

"Sure, sure. That's okay, I don't judge. If you prefer elderly women, that's your prerogative." I mime pushing her shoulder and she ducks away.

"That's not the wisest way of needling an ice cream out of me, just so you know."

***

The sun is low in the sky, even with the ever-lengthening days of approaching summer. I'm cooling my heels in my office, biding time until my obligations here are done. I offered office hours for any last-minute questions before final essays are due for my classes. Two students came right at the start, but since then I've been swiveling in my office chair, lost to the world. I descend into this state at times—I faze out and hardly anything attracts my attention. A by-product of endless life, I suppose. I have to make it pass somehow.

A sharp knock wakes me from my reverie, and a young man peeks his head around the door.

"Dr. Lytton?"

"Come on in." I stop my twirling with a solid planting of my feet on the floor. "You're just in time. What can I help you with?"

"I'm writing my essay on the Taming of the Shrew. Shakespeare, you know."

"I'm familiar with it, yes," I say drily. He doesn't notice my tone, which is just as well.

"I'm confused about the part when Petruchio acts annoyed and angry in front of Katherina. He yells something about being choleric. What's that about? Shouldn't that be a bigger deal if they've all got cholera?"

I try not to laugh. He's referring to the part in which Petruchio berates the servants for serving "choleric" mutton to two "choleric" people.

"Petruchio is referring to the four humors, a popular medicinal belief during that period. The theory goes that there are four fluids within each person that regulate their health and moods—blood, phlegm, and black and yellow bile. Lovely, I know. Too much black bile and a person grows melancholic. Too much yellow bile and they become choleric, or irritable and quick to anger. Often certain foods associated with each humor were fed to the afflicted person in the hopes that they would address the imbalance."

I remember when my wife, Maria, died in 1553. We were living in Italy at the time and I grieved as I tend to do, by shutting myself in and sleeping for weeks on end. My landlady was certain I'd fallen prey to the worst case of melancholy she'd ever seen. She tried for weeks to get me to call the doctor for treatment, and eventually resorted to feeding me her own concoction of garlic-infused milk. I moved away quickly after that, so perhaps her treatment worked after all.

"So Petruchio is saying that they've got too much yellow bile? That's kind of disgusting."

"It was a different time, certainly. It's all about creating a balance in the body. If one aspect is out of sync and is overpowering the others, then the body cannot keep a straight course. A balance of power is essential. Without balance of the parts, the whole will be sick." Although I agree with the principles of balance, it's less to do with fluids in the body and more to do with the lauvan. I can see if someone is sick through a gathering of their lauvan in different places than in their center. Sometimes, I can even help fix it by manipulating the lauvan. Sometimes.

"Okay," he says. "I guess I'll write about how Petruchio is trying to show Katherina how irritating she is."

"Sure. But you'd better write quickly. The essay is due the day after tomorrow."

"Okay. Thanks, Dr. Lytton." He swings his backpack over one shoulder and hustles to the door.

"But not too quickly! I want it understandable," I say to his back.

His retreating footsteps patter distantly before the door in the far hall slams shut. The clock tells me it's definitely time to go home. I gather my coat and a stack of papers to mark from another class and move quickly to the door. I don't want to be waylaid by a tardy student.

Once home, I settle myself onto the couch and rifle through the pile to find an essay by one of my better students. It's too late to start reading a terrible essay. Even so, it's slow progress. At every page, I look at my watch and am surprised anew. Time never seems to pass so slowly as when marking.

CHAPTER IV

Dreaming

Arthur's father Uther places his drinking bowl on the table with a definite thud. His white hair glows orange in the light from the fire, and his eyes appear sunken in the shadows. I was welcomed as a novelty and news-bearer as Arthur predicted, and I spent most of the meal telling tales of events in the south where I passed the summer. Uther is keen to hear of developments in the east, where Saxons made a large raiding forage into the southwest in the spring and killed many people. Arthur keeps quiet but his eyes mostly stay on my face.

I use the brief silence to thank Uther for his hospitality.

"No need, no need. News is a valuable commodity, and I thank you for your tales." Uther pours himself more wine and offers some to me. I reach forward to give him my bowl, a handsome—and likely very valuable—vessel of pottery with distinctive markings indicating its origin in faraway Aquitania. My sleeve snags on the edge of the table and exposes my forearm. On the inner skin of my arm is a blue tattoo of an oak leaf. Uther finishes pouring and frowns. "Is that…"

I hold up my arms to display the tattoo and its twin on my other forearm.

"Initiate of the first order of the druids of Eire." I shrug my sleeves back down. Arthur gapes, and I suppress a smile. "I would have carried on further, but my wanderlust is strong. Besides, experience is the best teacher."

"The druids are renowned for their learning and wisdom, even from across the sea. You were fortunate to have an opportunity to study with them." Uther takes a sip of his wine and considers me.

"Indeed. And one of the most useful things I learned was music. It's how I make my way in the world—there's always someone willing to take in a bard for a time. Would you care for a song or two in exchange for your generous hospitality?" I pick up my case and open it to reveal my harp, fashioned out of wild cherry and carved with delicate knots. It's not my work—sadly my carving skills are minimal—but another initiate's, in exchange for introductions to a particular girl he had his eye on. I think I got the better end of the deal, since the girl was shrill with a very annoying laugh, whereas the harp is perfection itself.

"Please. It would be a gift to our ears." Uther settles himself lower in his chair. Arthur wriggles a little and leans forward to watch my fingers.

I sing a song I learned this summer from another traveling bard, about the exploits of the warlord Vortigern. Arthur remains fascinated throughout. Uther looks as if he ponders a weighty decision.

Near the end of the last verse, light footsteps echo in the hall and the door opens. I expect the cook or a slave to clear the empty platters, but instead am greeted with the sight of a girl—young woman, really—of about sixteen. Her long black hair runs down her back in a thick braided rope. Delicate features surround sharp and lively eyes of deepest brown, and her robes only partly hide a body just beginning to fill out into womanhood. Her lauvan glow with a ruby-red gleam. She pauses at the doorway, obviously wondering what she interrupted. Her eyes light on my face at the end of my song.

"Wonderful!" Uther claps his hands and Arthur jumps from his chair to examine my harp. I hand it to him. Uther spies the girl and beckons her forward.

"Morgan, my dear, come meet our guest. Merlin, this is

28

my daughter Morgan. She takes very long walks and tends to miss dinner. It is something I like to discourage, especially at this time of year." He frowns at his daughter in a resigned way, and she bows her head in a gesture that somehow does not indicate contrition.

I stand and sweep my hand out in a bow.

"It's a pleasure, Morgan."

She nods back but maintains eye contact. When she speaks, her voice is light and self-assured.

"Likewise. Please, don't let me interrupt you."

Uther raises his hand.

"Actually, I want to ask you something, Merlin. Although I have lands and a place on the war council, I am a simple man without much learning. I want more for my son. I want him respected, not only for his fighting prowess, but also for his mind. I have a proposition for you—stay with us for the winter and tutor Arthur, and in return I will provide you with comfortable living quarters and meals. What do you say?"

This is a development I wasn't expecting. I look at Uther, whose frank and open face seems to hide no ulterior motives. Arthur looks ecstatic and bounces slightly in his chair, his lauvan bobbing along with him. My gaze travels briefly to Morgan, who looks both amused and exasperated at her father's hasty decision. I look to the fire. If I leave, I travel through the coming winter in the lessening hope that a lord or chieftain will want a bard for the winter. If I stay, I take on the new and strange role of tutor—what am I supposed to teach him?—but I also have room and board for the worst of the cold. I can move on in the spring. Who knows what the winter will hold, but with this opportunity at least I'll be warm and well-fed.

"Add in two ounces of silver in the spring if you're satisfied with my work, and it's a deal." I hold out my hand.

Uther laughs.

"You're a man who knows what he wants. I like that." He grasps my forearm and we shake. I wonder what I've got myself into.

***

Arthur and I stare at each other. Uther's departing footsteps echo on the tiled floor in the hall. Tutoring seemed like a wonderful idea by the dim of the fire last night, but in the pale morning chill I am dubious.

"So, what exactly does your father want me to teach you?" I ask Arthur.

He squeezes his lips around and wriggles his nose in a show of thinking.

"Stuff," he says. I continue to stare at him. "Lots of stuff. What do you know? Teach me that."

I aim a gentle swat at his head which he ducks, grinning.

"Very helpful, little squirt."

Morgan pipes up from the other end of the table.

"He only hired you because Lord Aelius has a tutor for his sons, and Father doesn't want to look inferior." She piles the breakfast dishes together. "Just teach him what the druids taught you, or whatever you think is useful. Father isn't going to care too much exactly what you're teaching him."

"Whatever I want? Maybe this could be interesting after all."

Arthur leans toward me.

"You could teach me how to *fish*," he says.

I tousle the little squirt's hair. He's beginning to grow on me.

30

CHAPTER V

Late in the morning, feeling bleary and out of focus, I brew a strong pot of coffee to fuel my essay-marking. I plow through the first one doggedly, claw and scratch my way through the second, then give the third one up as a bad job and toss the pile onto my coffee table. I throw on some jeans and give my hair a cursory comb. Ten minutes later I'm driving down the quiet weekend road, and half an hour after that the car purrs to the top of Cypress Mountain. In the winter it's crawling with skiers and snowboarders, but by this time the snow has mostly melted. I pull into the empty parking lot and strike out onto a familiar trail.

A vigorous hike straight up rewards me with a spectacular view—the cloudless sky reveals a vista spanning muted farmland on the left, glistening ocean on the right, and the glittering city nestled in the center. The air is unusually still. It's the perfect conditions to test a few lauvan.

I like to come up here and feel the pulse of the world. It keeps my lauvan-manipulation skills fresh—here I can focus on them without distraction. But it also connects me to the intense energies of the Earth.

There's nothing quite like the rush from touching the very spirit of Earth itself. The immense power from the vast energies of this planet, the explosive strength of its molten core, the whipping winds that howl across its surface, the might of its swirling oceans—these all add up to a potent conglomeration of energy. The Earth is much like a living human being, surrounded by its own swirling lauvan.

But the immensity of energies involved means that the Earth is surrounded by an enormous network of lauvan. Different cultures have intuited the presence of this network.

Some have called them ley lines, some *feng shui*, these invisible lines of power across the Earth.

But if you're me, that network can be seen and felt.

Stretching across the city, and up the mountain to the peak where I stand, lies a solid path of lauvan. To my eyes it appears as a vast electrical cord, lauvan upon lauvan bundled together to create a massive cable. As with all lauvan, their otherness lends them a semi-transparent appearance, but their sheer volume makes the ground below difficult for me to see.

The cable weaves its way up the mountainside and meanders beside the promontory on which I stand. Its pulsating twists snake their way over the peak, and flow beside the path to disappear behind a swath of trees, the diameter of the cable taller than I am. It lies along the Earth as much as possible, since the Earth is what sustains it, connects it, and gives it form.

But a cable that size cannot contain itself. A mist spreads, resolving itself near me as a fine network of loose lauvan fanning out from the cable. They twist and wind their way slowly across the land, becoming less dense further away from the cable.

I crouch down and reach into the fine filigree of silvery-brown threads. It can be a jolt connecting to the Earth's network deliberately—the absolute power contained in the network is awe-inspiring—but when prepared, it is a pleasurable one. I remember the first time I worked up the nerve to approach a lauvan-cable. I was sixteen, walking along a path high on a barren ridge, and I plunged my hands straight into the cable there. I must have flown twenty paces through the air and was dazed for half an hour after, but it was an incredible rush. Now that I know what I'm doing and approach cables with more caution and preparation, I'm not blasted through the air.

It's still a rush, though.

"Ahh." I lift my chin and close my eyes involuntarily as the sensation takes over. It's a mixture of immense power flowing through me and filling me up, making me more than I am. It's intoxicating. I let myself revel in the feeling for a moment and allow my mind to go blissfully blank.

Then I pull myself together and start to examine the pulse of the Earth under my hands.

This examination keeps my lauvan-sensing skills sharp. In the nineteen seventies, after Josephine died, I spent the end of the decade sleeping through my grief and then experimenting with all the drugs I could find in order to escape from my memories. When I pulled myself out of the haze, I was horrified to discover that my control and sensitivity had degraded. I've been making these little practice expeditions ever since.

The lauvan in my grasp slide through my fingers, each one hitting my skin with a small zing. The corners of my mouth turn up slowly as I connect with the power of the Earth, even in such a small way.

I open my eyes and search the mountain below me. A large boulder rests on the slope a hundred paces away, perhaps an arm-span from the streaming flow of the cable. I let the translucent threads in my hand fall out, one by one, until I find what I'm looking for. With a short, sharp contraction of my fingers, I tweak the last lauvan in my grasp.

There's a crack like a gunshot. A small fragment of the boulder flings high into the air, twisting wildly, and drops to tumble down the slope between pine trees.

I lean back on my heels, grinning, and plunge my hands again into the writhing mass.

I pull them out again just as quickly when a sense of

vileness hits me. My heart pounds with the feeling that something is terribly wrong. More cautiously I slide my fingers through the flowing lauvan, searching. After a minute, I find it—a lauvan buzzing with the same uneasy energy that I felt before.

My stomach protests at the sensation, and I carefully lift it out of the mass to examine it better.

The usual silvery-brown of the Earth's lauvan is muted on this strand. Its pale shade is tinged with a sickly yellow, repulsive to my eyes. I grit my teeth and close my eyes to sense more.

I follow the lauvan with my mind, tracing its path back to the main cable and into the stream. It travels behind me, away from the city. I follow it, the sensation less a visual one than a sense of knowledge of where on the Earth this lauvan leads. I swoop down valleys and climb up precipitous slopes, following the repulsive sick lauvan.

The feeling gets worse, and I realize that my lauvan is not alone. Other sickly strands join my cable and the nauseating sensation only increases.

I begin to sense the presence of many cables nearby. A center must be ahead.

Every human has a central area where all their lauvan gather. There's been much debate over the centuries about the location of the soul—Egyptians thought it was the heart, Plato philosophized that the tripartite soul sat in the head, chest, and stomach, and modern people in this country, although they don't use the word "soul," consider the powerhouse of the body to reside in the brain.

Actually, it's none of the above. If lauvan can be considered our souls, our life force, that which drives our inanimate flesh, then they tend to congregate just above the navel.

34

Although each living person has a center where the majority of their lauvan coalesce, the Earth is too vast for that. Instead, a multitude of centers dot the globe. Each center helps to both strengthen and control the Earth's lauvan. The cables stretch across the Earth's surface and meet at the centers. Sometimes they are places of great physical power, like Iguazu Falls in Brazil. Other times, they are solid and unchanging like Uluru in Australia, but give off such an otherworldly aura that even the least sensitive people can identify them as exceptional. A minor center can be as simple as a crossroads of three cables at a natural spring, usually accompanied by a legend of a sacred well or waters of healing powers.

I reach the center in an overwhelming surge of power, almost too much sensation to bear. A mixture of thrilling pleasure and actual physical pain runs up my own lauvan to my body. Before I accustom myself to reaching the center I'm hit with overpowering foulness. Imagine a sulfurous, rotting low tide assaulting your nostrils, the bite of earthy toxic mold filling your mouth when you expect fresh bread, a cankerous growth on an otherwise perfect apple.

The sensation is so disgusting that I pull my mind back to my body and find myself on all fours, retching. I release my grip on the offending lauvan and try to relax my shuddering body. A center that out of balance, that sickening, it shouldn't be possible. Surely a catastrophe is on its way.

I fear disaster may be sooner rather than later.

CHAPTER VI

I take the road down the mountain more quickly than I should, and pass dawdling tourist cars with plates from Washington and Alberta. My hand won't stop trembling on the gearshift and my fingers tap the wheel nervously.

I roll down the driver's side window and gulp in deep breaths of cool mountain air.

"Calm down, you idiot." I grip the wheel firmly to try and stop my finger-tapping. My encounter at the center rattled me. I try to think whether I've ever come across a center like that. Nothing comes to mind.

The fresh air helps, and I pull into traffic at the base of the mountain with more composure than at the top.

I take a right and wind my way past townhouses and twee shops to the ocean. Of course there's no parking at my destination, but I slide in at the end of a row of cars anyway. Once out, I surreptitiously bend down as if to check my tires, and spit onto the ground. I grab the lauvan of my saliva and force them to stretch in a long line parallel to my car, and tweak them again.

A solid white line appears, identical to the others in the parking lot. I smile. Sometimes it's good to be me.

My destination is a little hole-in-the-wall coffee shop entitled "Bean There," tucked between a high-class seafood bar and a musty secondhand bookstore. I have no idea how the café manages to pay rent on ocean-side property, and I expect this complex will be torn down shortly to make way for pricey condos. Not much makes me feel older than seeing a forty year-old building slotted for demolition, as is common on this side of the Atlantic. At least in Europe many of the buildings are old enough that even I have a hard time remembering their origin.

But until this shop winks out of its brief existence, it's a good place for a coffee.

The girl behind the counter greets me with a smile of recognition and reaches for the size of mug I always order. I stop her.

"I'm going to need a larger one today, thanks."

She grins at me, showing off the dimple in her left cheek. Her blond ponytail swings when she turns to the coffee machine.

"Long hike today?" The machine whirs to life and I wait to answer. She beats me to it. "Hey, have you heard about Mt. Linnigan? Scary stuff, eh? You think it's going to blow?" She grabs a saucer and tucks a chocolate cookie next to the cup. "Wouldn't want to be living in Wallerton right now."

"No," I say. A thought strikes me, an unwelcome, disturbing thought. "You grew up around here, didn't you? How far away is Mt. Linnigan?"

"Well, the news said if it blew it wouldn't be so bad here, just some ash maybe. Wallerton is probably a four-hour drive from here, heading north up highway one. I went camping there once—there's a great lake for swimming nearby."

"I've never been camping around here." Not in your lifetime, anyway. I smile at her when she hands me the coffee. "Sounds like fun." Our hands touch on the saucer. She keeps her smiling face steady, but her auburn lauvan squirm. I make eye contact. "I see you're encouraging my chocolate addiction. Good girl." I give her a conspiratorial smile. Her cheeks color and she giggles.

Feeling better already, I weave through the tables to slide into a prime seat in the corner of the balcony. It's free today, but sometimes I have to persuade interlopers to vacate. Usually a slight increase in the wind does it, although I once

37

had to be particularly aggressive with a young couple who were mooning over each other, oblivious to all else. I made the nearest seagull fly low and take aim. The resulting white smear on the girl's perfectly curled hair did the trick. Her shrieks of disgust had me biting my tongue to stop myself from laughing out loud. I reasoned that this was an excellent test of their relationship. If it couldn't survive the shame of seagull excrement, then it wasn't worth continuing.

Really, though, I just wanted my seat. Is that too much for an old man to ask?

Before checking out my hunch, I take a moment to savor the sun, sip my coffee, and let go of the last of the lingering jitters from the mountain.

The coffee helps. These days it's strong and smooth, not much relation to the swill they served in the Parisian coffeehouses where I first tasted it. My wife at the time, Celeste, was a real dynamo who was always in the thick of things. She loved the vibrancy and intellectualism that flowed freely in the coffeehouses, much freer than the expensive new drink did.

I dig out my phone and connect to the café's Wi-Fi. Only those of us who grew up in a village where the most advanced technology was a three-legged stool can understand how much I love the modern world. I thought I was well-connected all these years, but anyone with fingers and some money can access the world, right here, right now.

I do a quick search for Mt. Linnigan and get a whole collection of news articles. I open one with a map and study the mountain's location. It's suspiciously close to where I think I traveled along the lauvan-cable, to the foulness. Are they connected? I stare out to the ocean, frowning, and sip my coffee.

In what seems like a few minutes later I feel a hand on my

shoulder for a brief moment, like a fluttering bird. I look up, jolted out of my reverie, and see a whole new clientele surrounding me. The coffeeshop girl stands before me looking concerned.

"Are you okay? You look—" She pauses, as if searching for the word that will least offend. "Lost."

"Lost," I repeat, still a little dazed. My brain is slowly clicking away, and suddenly the word holds more meaning than I'm sure the girl intended. I think I know where to go to figure out where the foulness is. "Yes, I am lost, and—I need a map." I push back my chair with a sudden motion, and she takes a small step back.

I reach for her hand, the one that's not holding my empty mug, and bend over to kiss it.

"*Merci beaucoup, ma cherie,*" I say, and leave her pink and smiling.

* * *

At home, I breeze past Gary in the hall with only a simple "hello" instead of the chat he's obviously itching for. I need some answers about the foulness. I need to find a map.

Among the diverse items on my bookshelf are a sheaf of maps drawn on vellum and varied qualities of paper. I pull the sheaf down carefully and cart it to the dining table. My fingers flip through the pile as I go.

For centuries now, I've been following the cables and plotting centers around the world. I did my homeland first, and even today the European maps are the best documented, with almost every center accounted for and all the maps covered in spiderwebs of interconnected lines.

I put the maps of Europe aside. The South American maps slide out next, the continental sketches covered in far fewer

39

lines. Although I'd heard rumors of the Americas from the Norse, I didn't make it over to explore until much later, by which time everyone else in Europe had already barged in. I simply haven't got around to filling in the gaps yet. I go through bouts of industry as my interest waxes. When I'm busy with living a life or am in a funk, my map-making lapses.

My shuffling has finally produced the map I'm looking for—Western North America. I spread it open and lean over it. Maybe now I can figure out which center has the foulness. If I can just trace the cable from Cypress…

A sharp rapping on the front door jolts me upright. I rub my face in my hands on my way to the door. I don't feel like shooting the breeze with Gary right now.

Jen's beaming face greets me when I open the door.

"Hi!" She holds up a bag of sushi takeout. "You bored? I thought it seemed like a good movie night, and my roommate is out of town."

I look at Jen's hopeful face and push my worries to the back of my mind.

"*Mi casa, su casa.* I suppose I should be satisfied to be your backup plan? You're too magnanimous, my lady, gracing me with your presence."

"Hey, I brought food."

"She doth honor me too much. There'd better be Tobiko Nigiri in there."

"Oh, Merry, you act like I don't know you at all." Jen shakes her head. I head to the kitchen to grab some plates and drinks. I should really keep looking at the maps, but it's against my nature to refuse a woman an evening of entertainment, in whatever form. Moments later, a rustling noise emerges from the living room. A sense of foreboding creeps over me and I move to the other room.

"What're all these maps?" Jen leans over the table. Her long fingers leaf through my papers. My hands clench on the plates and I rack my brain for an explanation, but outside I remain calm. The best way to distract someone from a secret is to pretend there isn't one at all.

"Oh, they're old maps that the dean wants me to catalog." I'm a pretty smooth liar. I've had a lot of practice.

"Wow, some of these look ancient." Jen holds up an early map of Scandinavia I charted in the ninth century on scraped goat hide.

"Yeah, and I'll thank you not to paw them with your grubby fingers. I thought you were choosing us a movie." Jen drops the map and sidles over to the couch. Blame and distract—works a charm.

Quickly, I bundle the maps into their folder and shove it back on the bookshelf. I'll figure out the center tomorrow.

"Do you remember that manuscript you brought in for English 341?" Jen asks.

"Sure." I settle onto the couch and start opening containers. "The fragment of Beowulf I sweet-talked the curator of that traveling exhibit for." The curator was a mild-mannered woman in her early forties with a decidedly and unexpectedly wild approach in the bedroom. It's always the quiet ones. She had handed over the manuscript in its Plexiglas carrying case with a stern warning to bring it back promptly after my class, her sternness somewhat diluted by her parting ass-squeeze. God, I love women.

I brought the fragment into class and the students politely examined it, a few even lingering for a closer look. But Jen was drawn to it like a moth to a candle.

"*Scealt nu dædum rof, æðeling anhydig, ealle mægene feorh ealgian; ic ðe fullæstu,*" Jen pronounces.

"'Your deeds are famous, so stay resolute, my lord,

41

defend your life now with the whole of your strength. I shall stand by you.' Very good." I'm impressed, but not surprised. "You remember after all this time."

Jen leans back into the couch, the remote clutched in her hand.

"My favorite class! Of course."

"Well, I can understand. You did have an exceptional teacher." Jen nudges me with her knee and flicks on the TV, then pauses. She turns to me.

"Do you think they were much like us? I mean, physically we're all humans. But," she purses her lips and looks pensive. "Did they *think* like us?"

"How do you mean?" I say, but I think I know where she's going.

"Life was so much more—brutal than today. Everyone in Beowulf knows how to use a sword or ax, and they quite happily chop off heads and arms and whatnot. They must have thought completely differently back then. I have no idea what kind of person I'd be if I'd been born in the past. How different would I be?"

Part of the reason I love Jen is because she has an old soul. Comments like this elevate her above her peers.

"Yeah, I suppose they would think a bit differently." I put my feet up on the coffee table and recline into the couch. "Even if you travel around the modern world you can find hugely different viewpoints. But at the end of the day, everyone wants similar things—life, purpose, community, love. You can find those common threads in any time."

Jen ruminates briefly.

"I guess that makes sense." She sighs. "I wish more than anything I could meet someone from the past. It would be so amazing, enlightening. I have so many questions."

I try to keep a smile off my face, but it's difficult.

Jen reaches for the plastic container. She jerks back.

"Ow!" She holds up her index finger. Blood starts to well along a nasty-looking cut. "The stupid container was broken and sliced me open." She bites her lip and holds her finger out to me with her eyes closed. "How bad is it?"

I take her hand and examine her finger. The wound is much deeper than I expect, and blood oozes out swiftly. Jen peeks through her closed eyelids.

"So? How bad is it?"

"Close your eyes while Dr. Lytton takes a look. You know you're no good with blood." She obediently closes her eyes tightly again. It's true that Jen tends to gag at the sight of blood, but it's more for my sake than hers that I make her close her eyes. I bring my other hand to hers and quickly unknot the lauvan entangled above the cut. The wound slides shut and the oozing stops. I leave a small gash for appearance's sake and dab at the excess blood with a napkin.

"You big baby." I stash the napkin in my pocket. "Getting overexcited about a glorified paper cut."

Jen examines her finger.

"Wow, it felt so much worse than this." She holds her finger up to see it better in the light, frowning. "Thanks, Merry. I'm always so much luckier around you. Remember when we had that terrible fender bender last year?"

"I don't need to mention that you were the one behind the wheel, despite your dislike of my driving abilities."

"Yeah, yeah, no need to be all smug." Jen prods my ankle with her foot. "I could have sworn that I banged my head on the sidebar, and fully expected whiplash for the next six months. But we walked away without even a scratch."

That's because I took the opportunity while she was unconscious to unknot all the lauvan that had tangled themselves from her injuries.

43

"I guess it wasn't as bad as all that."

"I totaled the car, Merry. My dad was furious with me—he'd bought me that car for my twenty-first birthday."

"Well, cars these days are made to crumple."

She shakes her head, but turns to the television to flick on the streaming video and select a movie.

"Oh, come on, Jen," I say. "You're not going to make me watch *The Notebook*. Again."

"I bought dinner, my choice," she says, staring at the television. I smack the back of my head against the sofa in a gesture of exasperation and defeat. She starts to giggle.

"You idiot. Of course we're not watching that. I'm not that cruel. I just wanted to see your face."

I snatch the remote from her unresisting fingers.

"Give me that."

CHAPTER VII

Dreaming

Guinevere sits upright on the cold stone bench, her feet tucked beneath her skirts. She's tall enough to look me straight in the eye sitting down, although I still have a handspan on her when standing. Her long braid, blond and gleaming in the afternoon sun, lies across one shoulder and down her front where she twists and fidgets with the end in her lap. She worries her bottom lip. I know she's searching for the right words.

"Oh, it's no use, Merlin!" she bursts out in Saxon, her native tongue. "I can't think of the words. I'll never learn this stupid language. Brythonic is impossible." She presses her hands down onto the bench and leans forward. Her head turns so I can't see the tears that threaten to fall.

I reach out a hand and place it on her cheek to make her face me.

"Look at me, Guinevere," I say in her own language. Her eyes remain downcast. "No, look at me. You started from nothing, and now we can speak together in Brythonic, and you understand so much when others talk. You're getting better every day."

She gives a small sniff and looks into my eyes with her gray-blue ones. I give her an encouraging grin. After a minute, she gives me a watery smile back.

"There we are." I remove my hand from her cheek and drop it to her own hand, which I briefly squeeze. "Take heart. You're getting there."

"I don't know what I'd do without you, Merlin. You're my only friend now that..." Her voice trails off and she looks down again into her lap. "I just mean, thank you for taking over my lessons. And helping me—with everything."

"I know you've been lonely since your father sent you here to marry Arthur. I know it's hard, very hard, to find yourself among strangers who can't understand you."

Guinevere sighs.

"I know the peace treaty is good, and necessary. Both our peoples benefit. My tribe was lucky to make a truce with Arthur. We didn't want to fight, we just wanted to settle. Arthur didn't assume we came as enemies, like the rest believe. We're lucky to have Arthur—many other Saxon tribes invade western Albion by force, and not many can see that we are different." She lifts her chin. "I am proud I can help bring peace to my tribe."

"Of course." I study her face. Her eyes dart to mine and look away. "But still. I understand that it is difficult nonetheless."

Guinevere's back is stiff. Her next words are halting, despite speaking in her native tongue.

"Do you think Arthur will ever forgive me?"

It is my turn to sigh.

"I don't think forgiveness is the problem," I say. Guinevere jerks her head involuntarily, but keeps her eyes fixed into the distance. I pause—should I say what's really going on?—and decide Guinevere needs to know.

"Honestly, Arthur just doesn't have much confidence in himself, at least not regarding women." Guinevere frowns. This is not the answer she expects. I continue. "He's gaining renown on the battlefield and respect from the chieftains for strategy, but he's still very young. When you turned to Lancelot for love and companionship, he assumed he wasn't worthy of your regard. He doesn't expect anything now. He only sees you hurt and in pain, and he doesn't think that he could ever change that for you."

Guinevere releases her breath in a rush and slumps, covering her face briefly. She looks at me for confirmation.

"Really? Is that what he thinks?"

I shrug.

"Not that he's told me as much. But I've known him a long time."

"I just wanted someone I could talk to. The loneliness was unbearable. I felt so lucky that Lancelot knew a little of my language and could teach me yours. Everyone was behind a barrier of words that I couldn't break through. Even my new husband only looked at me with worried eyes and made hand gestures." She gives a heartfelt sigh. "I wish you had been here then, Merlin."

"I'm sorry I wasn't. But those first few months of your marriage were so precarious in the north that Arthur had to send me to lead the defenses."

"Well, at least you're here now, and Lancelot is far away on the eastern borders." She bites her lip and nods decisively. "I am glad of it. I want to make this right. What can I do to fix this? Advise me, Merlin."

I switch to Brythonic.

"Let's work on your words. Communication is vital between husband and wife, or so I'm told."

Guinevere puffs out her cheeks in resignation and squares her shoulders, ready for her lesson.

***

It's a sweetly domestic scene—Arthur mends a belt as he sits on a bench in front of the fire, and Guinevere stitches the hem of a cloak beside him. On the surface they're the very image of marital comfort.

I play with the lauvan of the fire absently, making the

47

flames rise and fall at my whim. Guinevere catches me changing one of the flames a deep cherry-red and smiles. She likes my little tricks, thinks they're funny, and doesn't question much beyond that. It's not that she doesn't understand that I'm strange and different, it's that she doesn't seem to care. I'm just Merlin to her, her only friend in this new life.

Arthur clears his throat.

"Did I tell you, Merlin, that Morgan's husband Idris was at the conclave yesterday?" He eyes the new hole he made in the leather of his belt.

"What did he have to say? He's always plotting some big push to get the Saxons out of Gwent for good."

"Yes, and he always expects me to join him, as his brother-in-law." Arthur shakes his head. "My marrying Guinevere was a real blow to him. I still don't think he understands why I did it."

"I'm sure he doesn't," I say. Guinevere looks up at the mention of her name, but I know she's following the conversation.

"He's been traveling around the countryside, drumming up followers. He's making a big push to get all the Saxons as far away from the borders as possible, and people are starting to listen."

"But there are thousands of settlers already in the far east, and hundreds more on our borders. Some of them are the grown children of settlers. I understand wanting to defend against pillaging and destruction, but is he really planning on forcing the settlers out of their homes?" I shake my head. "At this point, it seems like a fool's errand."

"It's only talk at the moment, but people are starting to listen. By the end of the conclave two factions had emerged—mine and Idris'." Arthur sighs. "Hopefully the harvest will be good this year. Fear of another bad winter is what's driving some of the warriors to follow Idris, I'm sure of it. Everyone gets anxious when there's not enough food."

"Especially when there's an easy target to blame," I say.

"Excuse me, my lord," Guinevere says. Her cheeks are colored and her eyes dart from mine to Arthur's, as if she searches for her words in our faces.

"Yes, Guinevere?" Arthur says, his voice polite but distant.

"Morgan—sister Morgan—she is here, month before. Yes?" I nod at her encouragingly. Morgan and Idris visited Arthur's villa for the midsummer festival. Morgan sat with Guinevere and the other women during the day while the men hunted. She looked as annoyed as ever to be left out of the action. Guinevere continues. "She is to say all Saxon leave now, we are bad people. She say to all women. She think I do not know Brythonic. Women…" Guinevere nods vigorously in pantomime to indicate the other women's approval of Morgan's words. "She say Idris at Samhain to make Saxon go."

Arthur stares at Guinevere, a look of surprise and pleasure on his face. I don't think Guinevere has ever spoken so much Brythonic in his presence before. She blushes with pride and confusion, and looks to the fire to avoid his gaze.

When the content of Guinevere's words finally sinks in, Arthur's face becomes grim.

"So, Idris is planning a concerted attack at Samhain. Why doesn't that surprise me?" He clenches his fists in anger. "What is Morgan doing? I wish I'd known the way she treated you, Guinevere. I'm sorry for that."

Guinevere lifts her shoulders. I don't know if it's a sign of resignation in response to Arthur's words, or whether she just doesn't understand. Arthur turns again to me.

"There's trouble ahead, Merlin."

"And we'll be ready for it." I feign a confidence I do not feel. A sense of foreboding is growing in my mind. Things are coming to a head, and I'm not sure which path we should take.

Arthur smiles.

"Yes, we will." Arthur's confidence in me is gratifying. I hope I'm right.

Guinevere puts her sewing down on the bench and stands up.

"Good night, my lord," Guinevere says to Arthur. He nods in reply. She wavers on the spot for a moment, then bends down to kiss him on the cheek. She pulls back to search his face as if evaluating his reaction.

Arthur looks a little stunned. Guinevere turns to go, and Arthur grabs her hand.

"Wait," he says. She looks at him quizzically. He clears his throat then says in Saxon, "Good night, Guinevere."

Guinevere flushes with pleasure at hearing her native tongue on Arthur's lips. She bows her head and leaves. Before she passes through the doorway, she looks back at me with a question in her eyes. I nod at her and she smiles back. Of course I taught Arthur the phrase. Why shouldn't the learning go both ways?

I let Guinevere's footsteps fade across the courtyard before I speak.

"Arthur."

"Mmm?" He picks up his dagger with a pensive air and starts to sharpen it against a whetstone. The *snick* of the blade percusses our words.

"Are you ever worried I'll follow Lancelot's example? With Guinevere, I mean?"

Arthur lets out a bark of surprised laughter.

"No. Should I be?" He laughs some more and continues to sharpen his dagger.

I neither laugh nor answer him. He looks at me, a little confused, and puts down the dagger and whetstone.

"Should I be?"

"No." It's true. I would never touch Guinevere. I would never do that to Arthur. But I don't expect him to know that.

"Well, then." He picks up the whetstone again but only plays with it absentmindedly, passing it back and forth between his hands. "Why the question?"

"Surely once bitten, twice shy. And I don't have the best reputation when it comes to other men's wives."

"But I trust you, Merlin." He looks at me with frank openness. "I trust you with my life and I trust you with my woman. You're my most valued advisor, my old tutor, and my best friend." He leans back on the bench, propped up by his hands. "It's that simple."

I turn away and stare into the fire so he can't see my eyes glisten.

***

I awake to shaking.

"Merry. Merry, wake up."

I open my eyes, groggy and dazed. Jen's face is close to mine, her expression troubled.

I sit upright. The movie credits are playing in the darkened room. Night fell while I was asleep.

"You started twitching in your sleep—totally missed a great car chase, by the way—and then, well, you seemed really distressed. I thought I should wake you up."

Only then do I notice the wetness in my eyes. I dash the tears away.

"Sorry," I say. "I guess I wasn't that into the movie."

Jen looks at me with questions in her eyes, but says no more.

CHAPTER VIII

Up with the birds today. I have a hard time sleeping this morning, but can't place why. I finally roll out of bed and throw on a T-shirt and pajama pants. Maybe the newspaper has arrived. My slippered feet pad out the door on my way to the mailboxes. It's too early for anyone to be up and about, so my pajama bottoms should go unnoticed. Not that I really care—I lost modesty and embarrassment centuries ago—but Merry Lytton should care, and it's important to keep up appearances.

Maybe when I get back I'll give my friend Braulio a call. He's always up early and we're overdue for a chat. I've known him for years and years, but these days he doesn't get around much. We keep in touch via phone and my occasional visits to his home in Costa Rica. Yes, the newspaper and a chat with Braulio sound like a pleasant morning. It's far too early to start marking yet.

I only have time to flip through the headlines coming out of the elevator before I bump into Gary.

"Morning, Merry! Up early today, are we?" Gary pats me on the back.

"Yeah, well, early bird, worm, you know the drill. What's shaking?"

"Ho! What's shaking. Is that what you kids are saying these days?" He laughs heartily. Nothing seems to faze Gary—if you looked up genial old fart in the dictionary, his picture would be there. I admire his ability to not let trials in life bring him down. I've never been able to learn that lesson for myself.

Gary points to the headline below the fold of my newspaper. "Oh, have you heard the latest on the volcano?"

He jabs at the page when I flip it over to look. "It's looking bad. Them scientists, they don't even know what's going on. They says it's all a big surprise to them. But you got to believe your eyes, and I sees on the TV that there's smoke. And I guess when there's smoke, there's fire!" He laughs at his witticism.

I scan the article with a shake of my head.

"It says here that Wallerton might be on the path of the lava flow, if it erupts. Not just a bit of ash. They're comparing it to Mt. St. Helens in terms of ash input to the atmosphere. Maybe even global weather changes."

"It's a bad business, all right." Gary nods his agreement. He nods for a while before saying, "But life goes on. So, are you up for some chess later? What's shaking this afternoon?" He chuckles to himself.

I only manage a strained smile. My focus is on the newspaper article, and my mind whirls. "Do you mind if I take a rain check on that? There's something I need to look into."

"Oh, sure," Gary says. "I'll go bother the wife instead. I expect she can find something for me to do. She's good at that."

I laugh and say goodbye. Once inside I head straight to my bookshelf. Out come the maps, hastily put away last night after Jen's prying, and I extract the West Coast chart. My pulse races.

My eyes close for a brief moment to get into the headspace I need to retrace my journey from Cypress Mountain to the center. I open my eyes and focus on the map, where the start of the Coast Mountain Range is clearly sketched on the chart. Vancouver's distinctive geography makes Cypress easy to find, even though there are no towns or political boundaries marked.

I locate the lauvan-cable that travels up and over Cypress and trace its progress north with my finger. A few finger-widths along, my cable is joined by others to create a swelling of the line. The reference point helps—I remember at which point they joined. Just above, a thick black dot indicates the sick center I'm looking for. It's located on a peak in the middle of a mountain range. It's unnamed.

I pull out my phone and look at the map, still open from yesterday. Mt. Linnigan is central. I place the phone faceup on the map, gingerly. I almost don't want to know.

The maps are a match. The peak is clearly Mt. Linnigan.

I reach for a chair without looking and sit down slowly.

"Dammit," I say out loud. My voice sounds deadened and tired to my own ears. Mt. Linnigan is a powerful, potent center, and it is seriously out of balance. This isn't natural—I've felt the lauvan of natural disasters before and they never had Mt. Linnigan's horrible foulness, its palpable sense of imbalance. Scientists are bewildered because science has nothing to do with it.

I stare at the black dot, feeling very lost and very alone. I'm the only one who knows what's actually happening. I'm the only one who stands a chance at preventing this disaster.

There's just one problem—I have no idea how.

CHAPTER IX

I sink into the dining room chair, lost in a fog of dread and trying to consider my options. Nothing in my vast experience springs immediately to mind.

There's only one thing that's certain—I can't restore the center while sitting in Vancouver. I need to actually see and feel the lauvan in person. My trick at Cypress was no more than a viewing, a thumbnail of the file that is Mt. Linnigan. It's time to roll.

This conclusion is so obvious that I'm almost surprised to find myself still in pajama bottoms. I half-expected my thoughts to manifest themselves into a fully-dressed me. Unfortunately, that's a trick I haven't mastered.

Now that I've decided on a course of action, I move swiftly through my apartment—spare clothes and a toothbrush into my satchel, pajamas off and jeans on, keys in hand. I grab my lauvan map as a guide.

The pile of unmarked papers on the coffee table catches my eye, and I hang my head in defeat. When do I mark the blasted things? And I'm supposed to pick up the newly handed-in essays from my literature class today. They're in my mailbox and the admin assistant is sure to notice and report to my superiors if I don't pick them up soon. The admin's nose has been bent out of shape ever since he found me chatting up his girlfriend at the end-of-term barbeque.

But honestly, the girl mentions nothing about having a boyfriend and is *very* friendly, and he gets shirty with *me*? I think he's looking to the wrong person if he wants answers.

So, a quick stop at the university to collect the papers and then I'm off. Marking will have to wait until I'm done. Thousands of lives at risk, versus dozens of angry students?

I'll take my chances with the student mob when I get home.

The admin gives me the evil eye after I empty my mailbox, but says nothing. His lauvan wave menacingly at me. I'm tempted to tweak one and give him a fright. Before I can do so, my name echoes in the corridor.

"Merry!"

I leave the bristling admin to stew in his own agitation and step out into the hallway. Wayne, my fellow instructor in the department and sometime lunch buddy, saunters down the hall.

"Hi, Wayne." I greet him with a forced calm that I don't feel. I'm on a mission—it's a long drive to Wallerton. The floating strands of my own lauvan start to dance with impatience.

"I thought maybe you'd snuck away early after term ended." Almost, Wayne. Almost. "Lucky bastard, with no exams to invigilate. I've got three next week."

A thought occurs to me.

"Hey, do you know when we have to hand in our marks?" How long can I spend in Wallerton?

"They're due end of next week."

"Good." I shove the papers into my bag. "Then I have time."

"Time to do what?"

I clap Wayne on the back.

"Time to procrastinate, of course. See you next week."

***

The highway empties once I leave behind the busyness of the city, and it's just me and my car barreling up the two-lane road, occasionally passing other vehicles that obtusely go the posted speed limit. Once in a while, I drive by magnificent streams of lauvan-cables running alongside the highway. At one point a cable looms into view, crossing the road ahead.

"Uh oh," I mutter. I grip my hands tightly on the wheel and brace myself for impact. When it comes, my body twists spasmodically and my eyes roll back with the heady sensation, but I manage to avoid swerving into an oncoming car. I'm quite pleased with the miss, although from the honking, I gather the other driver isn't as impressed.

I roll into Wallerton midafternoon. Just past the town sign is a church. One block down is another, of a different denomination. Down a side street a synagogue stands opposite another church. I pull into the parking lot of the only decent hotel in town—as indicated by my phone, all hail the Internet—across from which is an Interdenominational Community Sharing Center, whatever that means.

I'm not surprised by the density of religious buildings here. People are sensitive to lauvan to different degrees but the closer they are to a center, the greater the sensations. Since no one knows about the lauvan, people chalk up their feelings to the religion of their choice and seek solace there. And who knows, maybe one of them is right. Just because I can see what's causing spirituality doesn't mean I know why.

My hotel room is clean and plain, and I only pause long enough to empty the contents of my satchel onto the bed. I put my map back in for reference and take the satchel back to the car.

***

It's a beautiful day. Sunlight beams down on grassy meadows of mountain wildflowers, cheery pinks and yellows making me smile despite myself. The grasslands are surrounded by dense forests which glow a deep opulent green in the afternoon sun.

I roll down my window, relishing the fresh mountain air buffeting my face. Even at these altitudes I can tell spring is on its way. A fly zooms into the car through my open window and bashes against the windshield in a frantic attempt to free itself. I sigh with resignation. I've learned over the years that there's no such thing as perfection. There is always something, however minor, to keep us from complacency. I try to embrace this fact, but sometimes I don't want a fly in my car on a gorgeous day.

"Out, you crazy thing." I search through the air for the fly's erratic lauvan with my free hand. When I have them between my fingers, I fling the fly out of the open window.

With the distraction of the fly, I almost miss the sign for the road to Lake Carnarvon. My car veers off the highway with a squeal of tires and some kickback of gravel from the shoulder. Honking bellows from behind me.

"Oh, lighten up," I say out loud. "You're fine. No one got hurt."

The lake is ten minutes down the road, which turns to dirt pretty quickly after I get off the highway. I'm driving a route that wraps around the Three Peaks Provincial Park, Mt. Linnigan being the disruptive peak in question. In this fashion, I should drive perpendicular to the majority of the lauvan-cables on their way to the center. I'll come across one sooner or later.

And here one is. The cable looms huge on the road ahead, and glitters in the sun with a thousand refracted lights.

I pull the car smoothly to the side of the road, then bump over hummocks of grass and narrowly avoid a large rock that presents itself out of nowhere. I turn off the engine and step out of the car. The sun instantly warms my bare forearms during the short walk to the cable. The only sounds are the

59

chortle of a solitary raven and the ticking of my cooling car.

It's time to examine the cable. The lauvan coil and twist sinuously around each other, but there are far too many sick lauvan among the healthy ones, maybe one in every twenty.

There's not much to gain from looking, beyond the extent of the infection. I need to feel out what I can. I need to plug in.

A deep breath, and I slowly insert the outstretched fingers of both hands into the swirling lauvan. Nausea hits me full force, but I'm prepared and swallow hard to control it. I close my eyes to find out what I can.

The cable takes my mind away toward the center. I float down the thousands of lauvan, doing my best to avoid the sick ones that are omnipresent. The center approaches, but before I reach it I am brought up short. My progress slows to a crawl and it's not hard to know why—the lauvan around me are horribly tangled and knotted beyond anything I've seen. There's a huge blockage of energy flowing to the center. If all the cables are like this one, it's no wonder Mt. Linnigan is unstable. There's no way I'm getting through this blockage any time soon. I pull myself back to my body, which shakes from the effort of holding back the nausea.

I breathe hard to stay in control. Once my stomach stops clawing its way into my throat and sits grumbling in my abdomen, I reach my hands out again, but not to the cable this time. My fingers reluctantly grasp a single yellow lauvan trailing out from the cable. I need to find out where these infected lauvan come from—maybe that will help me find a solution.

This lauvan goes no great distance. There's a certain distinct hum of energy in my fingers that I equate, through long experience, with a close origination point. I might as well follow it to the end in person. Maybe then I can figure out exactly why the lauvan are sick.

The glistening yellow thread leads me back past my car and across the dirt road. It loops around a pothole and over a large boulder on the side before it passes into the woods. I sigh and check the hum. It's only a little farther—I shouldn't have to trek for long.

As I suspect, the lauvan continues for twenty paces and then disappears. Leaf litter covers the end. What could possibly be under there? Given the foulness of the lauvan I expect a poisoned river or a burning oil streak, but nothing appears out of the ordinary.

I brush away moldering leaves, anxious to find the root of the infection. Once the area is clean, the lauvan clearly descends into—a flat rock. There's nothing remotely strange or terrible about the rock. It's simply a rock, part of the fabric of the Earth.

That can't be it. I fall to my knees and scrabble at the soil to dislodge the rock. Perhaps something terrible is hidden beneath it.

When I free the rock from its earthen embrace and shift it to one side, there is nothing but a depression in the dirt where the rock used to sit. The lauvan descends into the soil and disappears from sight.

I sit back on my heels, flummoxed. Unless there is a secret burial chamber filled with noxious gases deep beneath my feet, I can't account for the infection. And it's unlikely that every sick lauvan has a gas chamber at its end.

I kick leaves over the hole in a fit of petulance and storm back to the car. I don't understand anything. All I see are dead ends and unexplainable mysteries. I like being the one who knows everything—it's my constant state of being, after all. I'm not used to being stumped anymore. It's not a particularly pleasant state of affairs, not something I've missed.

I pull the car out in a cloud of dust and protestations from my wheel axle, and zoom off to find another cable. Maybe they're not all blocked.

Maybe Arthur will come back one day, too. I guess I'm a sucker for the long shot.

The next cable is just down the road. When I plunge my hands deep into the swirling lauvan and travel toward the center, my passage is blocked once again.

I try another cable, then another. Each time, I immerse myself wrist-deep in lauvan only to find knots near the center. When I come back to my body at the fifth cable I can't hold back the nausea anymore. I fall to my knees, retching, until my stomach empties itself and settles down.

This is ridiculous, a fool's errand. Every single cable attached to this center has a restricted flow of lauvan. I've established that now—there's no point in making myself ill over it. There's a small access channel to the center through each cable, but not much. I wish suddenly, painfully, for Josephine. She knew everything about me, and we used to discuss problems with lauvan together. It's been such a long time since I've talked in depth to anyone about my abilities— or just talked deeply about anything, really.

I lift my head and the setting sun blinds me momentarily. I raise a hand to my eyes. Is it so late already? I'll have to try again in the morning. Maybe over dinner I will come up with a plan.

Yeah, and look—there's Arthur now.

***

I'm starving. My lunch consisted of a limp sandwich on anemic white bread from a gas station near Hope, and even that came back up in the aftermath of my lauvan explorations.

I drive into town and roll through the main strip. It doesn't take long. If I blink I might miss it. There is a grand total of one bar cum restaurant with a flickering neon sign advertising "BEER" in blue capital letters. Further out on the highway I know there is the requisite row of fast-food chains, but that doesn't appeal now.

That narrows down the choices. I double back and slide in between a battered red pickup and the concrete wall.

Inside is lively, but many diners are on their desserts and getting ready to go. It's cute for a small-town restaurant—they've tried to bring it upscale with low lighting, trendy brick-red walls, and a proper dining area with comfortable chairs, but they've kept their small-town vibe with a discreet display of license plates on a wall beside the bar counter.

I sigh in contentment. This is better than I expected. Finally, some real food. Steak, I think, if the kitchen can manage it. Hopefully they don't supplement the meat with too many vegetables. I don't understand the current fascination with all foods green. I survived and thrived on meat for centuries—why would I eat vegetation best left for rabbits and deer? I'll take a stab at looking at my map, too, but the thought doesn't thrill me. I'm at a loss with this center. Tomorrow, I'll jump in and start hauling lauvan around, just to do *something*.

***

I throw my maps and scribbles down on the table after dinner, frustrated and tired. I don't know what's happening, and it doesn't look like the answers are going to appear to me tonight. I lean back in my chair and survey the bar. It's still early and I have no desire to retire to my cheerless, uniform

63

hotel room just yet. Perhaps there's some old farmer who wants a chat, or a bored barkeeper—

—or a solitary woman with long, curling auburn hair just brushing a gorgeously round ass accentuated by tight white jeans.

Maybe this evening doesn't have to be such a wash after all. I look the woman up and down appraisingly. She's dolled up with extra makeup and huge hoop earrings as if waiting for someone. Strangely, her posture and lauvan show no anticipation or tension. She's definitely out of place. I mean, who wears white jeans? In a town where the majority of people work in the local pulp mill, this woman wants to go places. My bet is on a steady diet of *Sex and the City* during her formative years.

She chats comfortably to the barkeeper while she finishes her martini. I gaze at her a moment longer, then make up my mind. I gather my papers into my satchel and casually stand. Ten steps take me to the nearly empty bar counter, a carefully considered distance away from the woman. Too close and it's too obvious. Too far and she might not hear me or feel comfortable speaking. I've played the game for a while now. Experience—also known as trial and error—is the best teacher.

I catch the barkeeper's eye.

"One more for the road," I say, then wince inwardly. What an old thing to say. No one drives after drinking anymore— that's a phrase from decades ago. I amend my words. "Got to have something to cheer up my hotel room. Why is it that all hotel rooms are the same, no matter where you go?"

The barkeeper chuckles while he draws my beer, but doesn't engage. Good. There's a space for someone else to speak.

The woman takes the opening.

"What brings you to town?"

I take a sip of beer. When I look at her, she's turned toward me with an elbow on the bar and a coy tilt to her head.

"Oh, just passing through on my travels. Thought I'd stop and see what this volcano was all about. See what passes for excitement in Wallerton on a Friday night." I look down at the woman's empty glass. "What are you drinking?"

"Dirty martini," she says, giving just a hint of emphasis on the word "dirty." Her lauvan start to coil around her body intriguingly.

Dirty martini. Just the sort of drink a small-town girl might order to seem sophisticated. Did I call it or what?

"Another martini here, please," I say to the barkeeper. I add to the woman, "Please don't make me drink alone."

She laughs, a deep, rich chuckle.

"Never fear. When tall, dark, and handsome buys me a drink, I know my manners."

Tall might be a stretch in this century. At best I'm average height—but I can take a compliment. I raise my beer and we clink our glasses together. It's funny how some customs last for centuries.

"So, what do you think of Wallerton and our famous volcano?" The woman takes a sip and adds, "I'm Anna, by the way."

"Merry. You have a pretty little town here. It reminds me of Selfoss in southern Iceland. The mountain views, the tiny main street, the glacier-fed river." As I suspected, Anna's eyes glow and her lauvan twitch with interest. I'm new and exciting and she wants to get out of this town, if only by proxy.

She takes another sip of her drink, feigning disinterest.

"What's Iceland like?" she says offhand.

She can't hide from me, though. Her lauvan are active,

65

almost reaching toward me with her yearning to know someone different, go somewhere different, be someone different.

"Everything is crisp and clear." I try to paint her a picture with my words. She leans toward me slightly, involuntarily. "The mountains keep their snow all year, and the summer sun glitters on the crystal-white peaks all night long. The glacial lakes are an impossible milky green, and underwater cliffs descend to unknowable depths. In the winter nights that last all day the stars burn brightly enough to see by. And the northern lights..." I sigh a little, and look into Anna's eyes. Her mouth is partly open and she gazes at my face, her eyes longing. She lays a hand on my arm. Her swirling lauvan immediately twine through my own and my breath hisses in with the sensation. Our eyes lock and I can see we're both thinking the same thing—*I've got you now.*

"That sounds incredible," she says. Her breasts rise with her breath and don't come down, supported by her arched back. I remember my third wife, Clotilde, telling me that a woman will position herself in that sensual way either involuntarily through desire or voluntarily to foster desire. Anna knows exactly what she's doing—she saw me looking and reveled in it.

"Have you traveled a lot?" Her fingers slide down my arm.

"All over." I grab her fingers and stroke each separately, one by one.

"There's one place you haven't visited."

I smile. I know where this is going.

"And where might that be?"

She leans in and whispers in my ear.

"My place."

The bar stools are still spinning when the door slams shut

behind us.

***

Anna's hair spreads across her pillow and her eyes are softly closed, lit by a streetlight streaming through the uncovered window. Her sleeping breaths are quiet and peaceful, lulling me. Something tries to keep me awake, something I forgot to do. It's fighting a losing battle. Sleep beckons, and I can't be bothered to figure out the mystery.

CHAPTER X

Dreaming

A young man bobs awkwardly before me, a shapeless fabric hood twisted in his over-knuckled hands. His eyes dart to my face before they find refuge in my scuffed leather boots. The lauvan around his guts writhe in nervous discomfort.

"Well? What is your name, and what can you offer us?" I try to keep my voice pleasant, but am inwardly exasperated by the man's—more a boy's, really—fumbling manner and lack of confidence. Arthur asked me to select a few additional servers and helpers for the Lúnasa celebrations in a few days. He invited many of his father's old allies, and wants to put on a good show of hospitality. He can ill-afford the expense, as the harvest is not shaping up to be as plentiful as hoped for, and his father's funeral feast was more extravagant than was truly necessary. But he can't afford to show weakness in front of the other lords, who are more than ready to write him off as a shadow of his father, despite his victories to date.

The poor harvest resulted in more hands than are needed to pull in the crops. My call for extra help in return for silver is well answered. The young man stands at the forefront of a ragtag group of about ten men and women at the gate to the courtyard, which is enclosed by a barricade of sharpened stakes. The old Roman villa that Arthur calls home lies within, surrounded by stone buildings for livestock and the people of the household.

"My name is Gower. I am strong, my lord," he murmurs to my boots. I sigh silently. He brightens and almost looks up. "I'm good with animals, too. Everyone says so." His face reddens and he returns to my footwear.

I scrutinize him with narrowed eyes for the benefit of the watching group of hopefuls. The man does appear strong, despite gangly arms sprouting from newly-broad shoulders. At the mention of animals, his lauvan relax and spread as if searching for the creatures that are not so complicated to deal with as humans. I give a small, sharp nod.

"Very well. You may tend the visitors' horses when they arrive, and help the swineherd until then." I point to a side gate leading to the barnyard.

The man's face flushes again, this time with evident pleasure. His lauvan glow briefly.

"Thank you, my lord."

He shuffles off and I continue my interviews. I deem a dour-faced young woman with tidy gray lauvan coiled neatly around her hands fit for the kitchen, and a pretty one with lively lauvan as a server for the feasting. I send an older but hearty-looking man to help with firewood collection and other odds and ends. Most of the rest are too old or feeble to be of much use, and I dismiss them via the kitchen. The cook is a kind, matronly woman, well used to providing scraps to local hungry children. The applicants will at least go home with some bread for their troubles.

The last of the group at the gate is a very pretty young woman. I look her up and down and am well rewarded. Her tightly laced dress accentuates a small waist and breasts curving in perfect globes that strain against the fabric, heavier and larger than I expect for a woman her size. Her long dark hair is loosely braided and coiled as is the custom, but she has allowed pieces to artfully escape and brush her smooth browned shoulders. Her richly colored lauvan of lavender coil slowly and smoothly in and out and around her body. I wonder if I have ever seen anything move with such sensual grace. When my eyes finally travel to her face, her eyes sparkle deviously with the full knowledge of her effect on me.

"So, my lord. Do you think you might find something for me to do?"

I answer her self-satisfied smile with one of my own.

"I expect I can make use of you. There is always a shortage of pretty faces around here—for serving."

"I live to serve, my lord." She curtsies. I reach out my hand to gently grasp her elbow and lift her back up. She makes no outward physical sign that shows her reaction to my touch, but her lauvan writhe with greater intensity and focus themselves in interesting places. I bite back a smile. It is always gratifying to see oneself through the eyes of attraction.

"Does my newest server have a name?" I keep my hand on her elbow much longer than necessary, and my own lauvan start to twist. I let her go slowly.

She meets my gaze once again and smiles, sure of herself.

"My name is Vivienne."

***

I'm restless. I've been here at Arthur's side for many months as he transitions through his father's death and into the responsibility of being the head of his household, a member of the war council, and the main benefactor of the surrounding countryside and its people. Uther and I have taught him well, but it's a lot to lie on the shoulders of someone who's only just barely a man. He's growing into the responsibility, thank the goddess, because I'm starting to go crazy staying in the same place for so long. I've spent winters at the villa since Arthur was a boy, but most summers take me far from here. It's been a long time since I traveled

70

anywhere, and I have a yearning to cross the sea and try my fortunes there for a while. I'll be back, of course. I always come back. What started as a tutoring job for one winter has turned into a permanent advisory role to a young lord. Arthur relies on me.

In fact, he relies too much on me. It will be good for him to function on his own for a while. He needs to make his own decisions, be his own man, take advice but not require it for every decision.

And if I stay here much longer, I might start growing moss.

I pace through the villa. My twitchy, restless lauvan touch the lauvan of everyone I pass, and briefly infect them with my mood. I sigh and head toward the great hall to leave the villa. Perhaps a walk in the hills will settle me.

I squeeze through the heavy wooden door, carved with a mixture of old Roman gods, the Christian cross, and the knots and twists of my people. This villa and the people living in it are a strange melding of Roman and Brythonic. The village where I was born is so far into the hills that the Romans never bothered to make their presence known, and traveling monks rarely visited. We didn't bother them, so they didn't bother us. Down in the south is another matter—it's been Roman here for centuries. Many men here consider themselves Roman citizens still, even with civil wars in the capital and the withdrawing of all garrisons many years ago. Despite this, they have never forgotten their Brythonic heritage. It results in a mixture that seems strange to me and perfectly natural to everyone born here.

I'm a bit of an outsider, with my darker skin and distinctly un-Roman nose. I'm known to be "from the hills," which seems to automatically inform everyone that I am likely not descended from Roman citizens, and therefore not quite as

71

worthy. Not that many people seem to care. Especially not the ones I care about.

I slip through the doorway into the cool of the great hall from the courtyard, where my eyes adjust to the dimness. There is movement at the far end of the hall, past the many trestle tables and long benches. A multitude of wooden candlesticks dot the tables, the expensive iron ones reserved for the head table.

The movement resolves itself as the form of Vivienne. She is on tiptoes, reaching up to hang a flower garland above the doorway. Her feet waver on a little three-legged stool and her bottom wiggles lusciously under her dress in her efforts. I could steady the lauvan of her stool, I suppose, and give her an easier time, but she's so lovely to watch that I can't quite bring myself to do it. Nobody has ever accused me of being a particularly good man.

I cross the room on silent footfalls to come up behind her. Her garland now placed above the lintel, she turns.

"Oh!" Her eyes open wide with surprise and she sways dangerously on her rickety stool. I anticipate this and hold out my arms to catch her when she topples toward the ground. Her weight in my arms is soft and conforms to my body. I wonder if that is not just luck, for she seems to take her time righting herself, and is in no hurry to extract herself from my hold.

She looks up into my eyes from under her eyelashes.

"Did you do that on purpose?"

She sees right through me.

"Would it be a problem if I did?"

She reaches up to trace a forefinger along my jawline. My body tenses in anticipation.

"Cruel man. Startling poor, defenseless girls like that." She turns her face up to move her lips close to mine. Her

72

breath is scented with the honey cake cook served after the midday meal, sweet and deep and rich. "Perhaps you should be punished." She moves to kiss my lips, and grasps my waist to dig her nails into my side. I would gasp with pleasure except her mouth occupies mine fully. My lower regions grow hot and my trousers are much too constrictive. My lauvan twist through the air until they meet her own reaching tendrils. They twine together deliciously when her physical body presses into mine.

A door creaks, sounding far away through the haze of my desire. Vivienne breaks away from our kiss and turns her head. I slowly follow her gaze.

Arthur stands silhouetted in the doorway to the courtyard, his messy brown hair a halo around his head. There is just enough light to see the look of confusion and embarrassment on his face. I give a small sigh. He's still so young, that coming across a couple embracing is a cause for consternation. I wonder if I can leave him quite yet.

Vivienne slides out of my arms and pats down her dress. She curtsies to Arthur.

"My lord." She gathers her basket of flowers and hurries from the room using a side door that leads to the kitchen. She keeps her head down, but gives a very definite look to the head table. All of her lauvan snap in a tremendous jolt. I frown and follow her gaze. Behind the table, affixed to the stone wall in pride of place, is the banner of Arthur's house. Its faded embroidery depicts the golden eagle of Rome and the winged serpent of a Brythonic tribe from which Arthur descends. It is a very old emblem of power and commands respect. In fact, the visitors arriving tomorrow for the feast will expect to see it there as tangible proof that Arthur is worthy of address, for those who have not yet seen him in battle. I briefly wonder why it prompted such a strong response in Vivienne, but put it from my mind when Arthur speaks.

"Sorry, Merlin." He looks around the room, as if hoping for a distraction. I take a deep breath to cool my frustrated desires and wait a minute to gain control over my voice. Arthur looks as if he doesn't know whether to leave or not. He stays. I am still his old tutor, after all, and he is used to deferring to me. I'll have to talk to him about that later. The other lords will want to see confidence and self-assurance. They are qualities that Arthur needs to work on—especially with women.

"It's fine. I expect she'll be back. Now that she knows what she's been missing." Arthur doesn't respond to my attempt at levity. I rub my face in my hands and walk between the tables toward him. "Arthur, what are we going to do with you? We have to find you a woman. The other lords now know you're man enough on the battlefield, but they don't expect to find a blushing boy when the bawdy talk starts flowing along with the ale."

Arthur sighs and his shoulders slump. I immediately regret my words, unfiltered as they are from the sharpness of my frustrated emotions. He feels the pressure of this feast celebration. Every eye will be watching him, comparing him to his esteemed father, measuring his worth. His three battles against the Saxons were excellent victories, but hearing the news from afar and seeing the man himself are two very different things. I can tell Arthur feels the pressure keenly.

I put my arm around his shoulders and walk with him to the outer door. He follows, unresisting.

"Never mind, that's what I'm for. You just stay quiet and laugh when everyone else does, and I'll handle the retorts." I squeeze his shoulder and he rewards me with a lopsided smile.

"It is what you do best."

I laugh and release him to push open the heavy double doors.

"Come on, it's a glorious day and your visitors won't arrive until tomorrow. What do you say to a run through the woods?" It's a pastime of ours, started early in our relationship. I twist our lauvan into the form of powerful deer, and we run and bound for miles through the woodland and over the hills. It's incredibly cathartic.

His eyes glow with excitement.

"Absolutely."

***

The feast is loud. The lords and warriors are boisterous and their wives fill the air with high-pitched laughter. The ale flows freely, and my eyes follow Vivienne on her weaving path between tables to refill goblets over waving arms. I sit at Arthur's right hand, a coveted spot that afforded me curious glances and surreptitious whispers at the beginning of the night, although everyone is too drunk to care now. I knew it would be controversial, but I counseled Arthur to place me there. Not out of ambition—I really couldn't care less what these Gwentish lords think of me—but it gives Arthur an excellent excuse to not single out a particular ally and risk offending the others.

Arthur is occupied with the man seated on his left, a neighboring lord who was good friends with Uther before his death. The noble seated beside me, while decent company earlier in the night, has succumbed to the mysteries of his goblet and now snores gently, propped up by his less-than-sober wife.

I slouch low in my chair, content for the moment to watch

Vivienne's form slide gracefully through the drunken rabble. The buzz of ale relaxes me and my lauvan hum gently. I pick one up and twirl it around my fingers idly, pondering the vastness of eternity, the meaning of life, the soft perfection of a woman's breasts...

As I reach this train of thought, I rise from the bench. My sleeping neighbor does not notice my departure and Arthur is engrossed in conversation. I sidle to the pillars surrounding the center of the hall and lie in wait.

My target approaches soon enough and I thrust an arm out to encircle her waist.

"Oof!" Vivienne gasps and then laughs. "I might have known." She offers the pitcher she carries. "Care for some ale, my lord?"

I grab the pitcher from her and drop it over the table next to me without looking. Under my direction, the lauvan of the table take the pitcher and maneuver it down gently. The table was once living wood and therefore possesses a rudimentary lauvan structure still. I focus on more important things.

"The lords have had enough ale. I think your job here in the great hall is done." I put my hand on her cheek and draw her face closer to mine. "I think you should take your pleasure, now that you have worked so hard."

Vivienne's eyes close and her breath quickens between parted lips curved in a smile. But through my half-closed eyes, I notice her lauvan do not tell the same tale. They writhe and twist with desire, certainly, but those movements are at war with tight, straight strands of fear and anticipation of conflict. There is something else Vivienne prepares herself for tonight, and it has nothing to do with me.

Let's see if I can win this battle.

I send my hand from her waist downward, and slowly reach around to cup her bottom in my palm, my fingers gently spreading. She sighs, and the sensual lauvan twist closer around the straight ones. Then her eyes flutter open and she straightens when the tight lauvan become dominant.

"I can't. Not right now. I—I still have work to do."

I tilt my head in amusement. Her eyes search mine.

"I am your master tonight, so I'll be the judge of when you are done work. And I say that time is now. If you're not interested in a little recreation, that's fine. Just tell me so." I keep my gaze level into her eyes. She stares at me and out of the corner of my vision the lauvan battle. A sigh of desire and a final twist of the curvy lauvan, and I know I have won.

I kiss her firmly on the lips and reach my tongue deeply into her mouth. I am rewarded by her body arching into mine. Without further ado, I pull her through a nearby doorway and out into the night.

CHAPTER XI

The late morning sun shifts through the open blinds to land on my face. I blink awake groggily. My hotel has curtains, not blinds. That must mean—I turn my head to look at Anna, but the bed beside me is empty.

The apartment is silent. Anna must have left early. How trusting of her to leave me alone. I stretch my naked limbs under the duvet and luxuriate in the satin sheets sliding over my body. Really, Anna? Satin sheets? They're obviously a carefully chosen splurge in this rental apartment with an old radiator and nondescript white walls.

Gradually, I remember in reverse the chain of events that led me here—the frenzied undressing at the door, the flirting at the bar, the frustration at my lack of conclusions—and I groan out loud.

"Dammit." A leaden weight lands in the bottom of my stomach, previously held at bay by the pleasant distractions of last night, but returned and heavier than ever this morning. I still haven't figured out how to stop this volcano from erupting.

I roll out of bed and pad over to the window. Anna's apartment has a glorious view of the mountains, an agreeable surprise I didn't fully appreciate in last night's fumbling and unsuccessful attempt to shut the blinds. I look for Mt. Linnigan, but don't have to wonder where it is for long. A belch of steam hisses out of the top of the leftmost peak. Even from this distance I can see a trickle of rocks tumbling down the steep cliffs of the mountainside, likely loosened by a localized tremor.

A cold sweat breaks out on my naked skin. I shiver and turn from the window to look for my clothes.

My pants are easy enough to locate at the foot of the bed, although it takes some hunting to find my socks, one lodged under a pillow and another behind the night table. My shirt lies in a heap by the door. There's a carefully folded piece of paper lying on top.

It's a note from Anna.

Good morning, tall, dark, and handsome. Sorry I had to leave early. You can let yourself out whenever you're ready. Thanks for the good time last night, sexy. Your hands are magic.

Anna

The note brings a smile to my face despite my feeling of foreboding. I shrug on my shirt and tuck the note in my pocket. My eye catches an incense holder on the hall table, accompanied by a long-stemmed rose and a small mirror in a gilded frame. I frown. It looks like a shrine to something.

The coffee table houses a pile of papers, books, pamphlets, and various other items. I saunter over to the couch and sit, interested to learn more about Anna and prolong the moment when I have to face Mt. Linnigan.

Hey, she was the one who left me alone in her apartment. If she didn't want me nosing around, it was a silly move. I definitely can't be trusted not to pry.

A pack of tarot cards sits on top of the pile as a paperweight. I idly flip open the lid and slide the cards out facedown. I pick one and flip it over.

The Chariot meets my eyes. It's upside down. A warning of disrupted balance and loss of control? Suddenly irritated, I shove the deck back into its case and set it aside.

There's an envelope on top from a credit card company, addressed to "Anna Green." Interesting. Now I have a last name. I set it on top of the tarot cards and turn to the pile again. The next paper is an advertisement for a local store.

Obviously printed at home on brightly colored printer paper, its black text loudly proclaims the grand opening of "The Flickering Candle." The purveyors promise to help guide the reader to their "optimal spiritual well-being," with the aid of essential oils, healing crystals, and a choice selection of incense available for purchase. Promises of tarot card readings and monthly séances are also displayed.

I snort and set it aside. I find it hard to believe that a town of Wallerton's size can support this type of shop. The three churches I passed on my way into town indicate a brief existence for an alternative spirituality store.

I reach for the next paper without looking. A sizzle of sensation in my fingertips jolts me to attention. I snatch my hand back and shake it. What the hell just happened?

When I look to the pile I instantly understand. The large advertisement had completely concealed a small folded note on lavender stationary. But this is no ordinary paper—the entire surface is positively crawling with lauvan.

I'm fascinated. An immobile piece of paper should have little to no lauvan. Whatever lauvan the tree might have had in life should have been long since processed out of existence, and the paper should have very little potential energy sitting on a low table.

And yet, here it is. The only other explanation I have is that this note has immense value to a fair-sized number of people, and their lauvan have transferred to the paper.

I stare at it for a second longer, then gingerly pick it up. The note won't read itself, after all. Now that I'm prepared, the sensation of the foreign lauvan is bearable, even pleasant. In fact, the threads almost feel familiar, as if I have encountered them before.

That's doubtful. I would remember this funny little piece of paper with the extraordinary lauvan. Although, come to think of it, the lauvan on this note are all of one variety and color, as if from the same source. Objects of worship are generally surrounded by a multitude of different lauvan, the collection of their followers. This one has a layer of smooth, translucent lauvan of a deep, rich red that clashes horribly with the delicate pastel of the paper. I grin briefly, remembering Josephine's preoccupation with wearing shades of blue to match her lauvan so that she would look beautiful in my eyes. She needn't have bothered—she was always beautiful to me.

I puzzle over the uniform lauvan, but can't come up with a good answer. I open the note.

Dearest Anna,

The time is soon upon us. You must prepare yourself. On the eve of the new moon, at the sacred place, open the doors to the other plane just as I taught you. Use my gift to guide you on your way. Be strong, my darling. Once the deed is done, I will come and take you away from Wallerton forever.

The note is unsigned.

Curiouser and curiouser. I read the note again but don't understand it any better than the first time. Anna will be able to keep her secrets.

I put the papers and deck of cards back together and straighten edges until I recognize the signs of my own procrastination.

"Come on, Merlin," I say out loud. "Grab the bull by the horns. Bite the bullet. Eat the frog." Get my ass in gear, in other words. Who knows how much time I really have before Mt. Linnigan blows?

***

It's time to figure out this blasted volcano. I let myself out of Anna's first floor apartment and blink in the sunlight to get my bearings. Luckily, Wallerton is not large, and I strike out in the direction of my unused hotel and my car in the restaurant parking lot.

I turn the corner onto the main street and am confronted by "The Flickering Candle." The shop is trying very hard to develop its mystical aura, with the requisite colored scarves softening up the window display and sale signs in Papyrus font. It fights a valiant battle against the decidedly mundane Laundromat next door.

On a whim, I cross the road and enter. No wind chimes announce my presence—perhaps I should put these people in touch with the Vancouver shop proprietor so they can compare notes. A strong waft of incense pushes past me as if trying to escape the shop. I'm curious to know more about Anna and the lauvan-laced note. In a town this size, and with Anna's apparent interest in the occult, this shop seems like a sensible place to ask questions.

After this, I promise myself, I will go to the volcano and stop letting Anna distract me from my true purpose here.

As I enter, a woman leaps up from a stool in the only free corner of the crowded shop, where she has clearly taken up residence in the absence of any customers this morning—accounting papers and a calculator lie on the floor under the stool as if haphazardly shoved there during my entry.

"Good afternoon," the woman says. Her voice is deep and husky, almost too much so to be real. She has on a huge chunky necklace and flowing cotton shirt, but her brown hair is cut in a no-nonsense shoulder-length bob. She's trying for a look, but hasn't quite committed.

"Hello. Is it afternoon already?" I check my watch. It's just past noon. Dammit. I slept much later than I planned to.

"Can I help you find something today?"

82

"Actually, I was hoping you could help me find *someone*." I smile winningly at her. "Wallerton seems like such a tight-knit community, that I thought you might know." The woman's disappointment is palpable. I almost feel bad for not looking around first. "I'm supposed to meet up with a woman named Anna Green today, but I'm not sure where to find her."

The woman's face darkens unexpectedly.

"Yeah, I know Anna," she says. I raise my eyebrows. Apparently, Anna has a reputation. She continues, "She was originally my partner in this store, but bowed out late in the game." She lifts her head proudly. "It's fine, though. I've managed quite well without her."

That explains the shrine and tarot cards. But not the lauvan note, not yet. This woman's lauvan are a mountain-lake green, not red. The woman continues.

"I'd steer clear of her, if I were you." Oh ho, small-town cattiness, or a real warning? "She's into some pretty dark stuff. Bad energies." I doubt that very much, but I wonder what makes this woman say that. "I pity the poor guy she just got involved with. She's going to infect him with her dark aura, mark my words. You know," here the woman leans toward me. Her huskiness is replaced by a high, breathless stage whisper. "I live next door to her, and the racket those two were making, oh my word. I had to put in earplugs eventually."

I stare at her levelly. The ball finally drops and her face flushes a brick-wall red.

God, this woman is adorable. I could tease her all day.

"Well," I say. "I like what you've done with the shop."

The woman's face washes over with gratitude for the change in subject.

"Oh, thank you. Here, let me read your aura for you. As a

83

thank-you for coming in."

I don't really have the time or desire to have my aura read, whatever that means to her, but the woman is already rolling up her sleeves. I didn't realize aura-reading was so labor-intensive.

"May I?" She holds up her hands on either side of my head.

"Be my guest." Maybe it'll be quick if I acquiesce.

She lays her palms against my temples, her eyes closed. Then her eyes pop open.

"Sorry. I'm supposed to tell you my name. To foster trust, you know. My name is Sylvana." She gives this obviously false name an emphasis of gravitas.

"I'm Merry." I raise one eyebrow. "Sylvana?"

She flushes.

"Well, it's Jackie, really. But Sylvana's my inner-goddess name."

I nod graciously, as much as her hands will allow.

"Sylvana it is."

She closes her eyes again, and I study her features for a lack of something better to do. Her widely spaced eyes give her an open, honest-looking face, and her rosy cheeks are apparently prone to coloration.

Then I notice her lauvan changing. Where once only green lauvan swirled, now a mix of green and bright orange coil around her arms toward my head. They originate under the neckline of her shirt, where a fine golden chain descends out of sight. I'd missed it before, competing as it was for attention with the bulky beads of the other necklace.

Centuries without seeing an amulet of power, and then two in the same week? Where did these women get them?

"I can sense your aura," Jackie—Sylvana—proclaims. Both her lauvan and the ones from the necklace are tentatively touching my own. It's a very intimate connection, and I wonder how much she can feel. Perhaps it's just me.

"Your aura is very strong," she says in a dreamy voice. I don't know about strong. Tangled, maybe. She continues, "You have a very old soul." I smile since her eyes are closed. I wonder if she's actually getting something from using that necklace, or whether she was instructed to say that by whatever fortune-telling manual she memorized.

"Spirits!" Sylvana shouts out of nowhere. I flinch. "Speak! Fill me with your wisdom for this man!"

Whoa. This is going in a direction I hadn't anticipated. I consider my options for extracting myself from Sylvana's grasp, but stop when I see the lauvan of the necklace throb and twitch erratically. Something is definitely happening.

Sylvana's eyes open and immediately roll back in her head. I hear whispers in the air and freeze. What the hell?

Sylvana's head twitches back and forth for a solid twenty seconds. The whispers grow to a wordless murmur, then stop abruptly. Sylvana sags suddenly. I catch her and lead her to her stool.

"Are you all right?" Was that incredible acting, or did something really happen?

She takes a few deep breaths and looks at me.

"I'm sorry. It's not supposed to be like that. Normally I get very clear messages from the spirit world. But today, all I heard were angry mutterings and whispers about your father."

I stare at Sylvana, my mind whirling.

I know nothing about my father. He came to the Beltane celebration one year at my village and chose my mother to couple with that night. No one had ever seen him before, and no one ever saw him again. I don't even know his name.

I've asked and I've searched, of course, but my efforts have always been fruitless. I dwelled on it often as a young man, but eventually chalked it up to another mystery. I suspect the secrets of the lauvan and the mystery of my father are linked. How could they not be? The legends say that my father was a demon. I don't know what that even means, but I wonder sometimes whether that explanation is close to the truth.

Sylvana can't possibly know anything. She's talking of invoking spirits, for pity's sake. The druids spoke of a time when the spirits of the elements could be sensed, before I was born. Some of the older druids, even those I trusted and respected, spoke of hearing the spirits at ceremonies. Neither then nor any time since have I ever heard or seen any such spirits. I have my doubts they exist.

Still, Sylvana has the lauvan necklace. And something did happen.

"What did you hear?" I say.

Sylvana rubs her eyes.

"That's the thing. Usually it's clear. They'll say things like, 'His energies are strong,' or 'Her aura is sick and needs more fire.' It's never been like this. It's almost as if the spirits were angry, or frightened. All I could catch were the words 'His father.'"

I stare at her, trying to determine whether or not to question her further. She stares back at me with her wide, honest eyes. I sigh. She's told me all she knows. I stand up straight and offer her my hand.

"Are you okay?"

She takes my hand and hauls herself up. She's shaky and puzzled-looking, but stands just fine.

"Yes, thank you."

I turn to go.

"Wait." Sylvana grabs my arm. "Be careful around Anna. She's mixed up in something bad, something big. I can feel it. And I can sense you're not a part of it, so…" She pauses, then pats my arm and lets go. "Just be careful."

I nod.

"Thanks for the reading."

I exit the shop. Her eyes burn a hole in my back.

***

I only let myself dwell on Sylvana's curious "spirit summoning" for a few moments before banishing it from my mind. Despite wanting answers badly, I know it does no good to ponder my unknown father and heritage—I've done that too often in the past, with no reward. Right now I have more important things to focus on, like an imminent eruption that only I have a hope of preventing.

My pocket vibrates, and the screen says I have a text from Jen.

Where are you? I want to say bye before I head out on my first trip for my job!!!

I smile, but put the phone back in my pocket. I'll call her later—after I've figured out Mt. Linnigan.

It's a beautiful drive to the Three Peaks Provincial Park. Towering conifers loom over the road, interspersed with open areas of fertile wetlands where hundreds of birds swoop and twitter. I half-expect to see a moose in these prime locations, but no such luck. They're not as frequent as I remember from when I first explored these parts.

Mt. Linnigan looms up ahead of me after a bend in the road. It's steaming slightly and I wince, afraid of what I will find at my destination.

I'm too busy looking at the mountain that the road blockade takes me by surprise. A police officer in a reflective vest waves at me to roll down my window.

"You'll have to turn around," he says without preamble. "The park is restricted-access only."

"Because of the volcano?"

He nods, glancing at Mt. Linnigan which steams ominously.

"Best if you stay away. They're still figuring out how to predict when it'll blow."

I doubt they will. I have a flash of pity for the volcanologists on site, presumably pulling their hair out at this unexplainable activity.

The officer directs my turn and I head down the road with the mountain in my rearview mirror.

I don't drive for long. There is an overgrown logging road on my right—a perfect spot to park the car out of sight of the road. I'll need to hike into Mt. Linnigan if I want to find out anything.

My legs stride confidently into the undergrowth. I last about two minutes.

"Shit. This is ridiculous," I say out loud. The forest is dense and unyielding, and I'm traveling about twenty paces a minute. I pause to catch my breath, and close my eyes to feel for my own lauvan.

This particular trick of mine takes a fair bit of energy and concentration, although it's worth it to avoid tramping through the underbrush. I pull some of my lauvan tightly, some I twist, and some I stretch. It makes me a little dizzy, but I persist. Once everything is in position, I take a deep breath and give a final yank.

My body dissolves. At least, that's what it feels like. I would gasp or scream except there is no breath in my lungs. I'm not even sure if I have lungs anymore that would contain breath.

The sensation lasts for less than a second, and when it

passes my eyes open to a decidedly different viewpoint. A fern towers overhead and a line of ants crosses in front of me, huge and glossy black.

I try to smile in satisfaction, but my face doesn't move. Of course. I open and close my mouth, and my beak clicks together.

I have transformed into a bird of prey, specifically a *Falco columbarius*, also known as a merlin. What else would I be? I have a poetic soul. When falconry was popular, merlins were used frequently. The Book of St. Albans, a hawking manual published in 1486, carefully lists the merlin as the appropriate choice for both emperors and ladies. I thought that was apt.

My animal-transformation repertoire is limited, especially when transforming myself. It takes a good long while to learn the details of a creature well enough that I can manipulate my own form into its exact musculature, the precise layout of its fur or feathers, the motions of its eyes. It's a little easier transforming other people, but only if I have a version of the animal right in front of me to model the transformation after. Learning the ways of a bird was a useful decision. That this one has such a great name is a beautiful coincidence.

I spread my wings and push off from the ground. My powerful muscles transport me in a burst of motion, almost dizzying me until I grow used to the falcon senses. I tuck my talons into my body and let out a shriek for the pure joy of it. It echoes off the nearest trees. My flight is exhilarating, and I twist in a barrel roll to release my exuberance.

Now, this is living. Why don't I do this more often? Why do I contain myself on the ground so frequently? My stomach reminds me that it hasn't had breakfast yet, and my raptor senses narrow in on a twittering songbird, fifty wingbeats ahead and below. My instincts take over and I dive-bomb the unsuspecting bird. Two seconds later finds me perched on a nearby branch, where I nod my head in short, jerky motions to gulp down the inert form.

Oh, yes. That's why I don't transform more often. Control over my bird-form is limited at best, and once instincts take over there's not much I can do. My stomach is a horrible mix of revulsion and satisfaction. I finish swallowing and take off in a beeline for my destination. The longer I stay as a bird, the more susceptible I am to avian instincts and urges. Also, the strain of holding my lauvan in place is no laughing matter—after too long the effort is not worth the payoff.

I fly above the trees, dipping and skimming between treetops. I aim for the smoldering peak of Mt. Linnigan, the road to my right. The mountain grows larger and larger. It is an incredible sight, and not just for its rocks and trees.

Lauvan-cables spread out from the Mt. Linnigan center like spokes of a wheel. They glimmer and froth with multitudes of lauvan that glisten silvery-brown. Mt. Linnigan itself is the hub and it glitters transparently, magnificently, with the ends of thousands of lauvan dispersing at the foot of the mountain where the cables end to mingle together on the slopes. It's quite mesmerizing.

It would be more beautiful if my falcon's eyes didn't observe the hideous, sickly yellow lauvan that twine their way throughout the center, to crawl along the cables and spread their infection. I shriek again to express my frustration. This is bigger than I feared.

Close to the base of the mountain, the road ends in a large parking lot. The top of a white tent is just visible through the trees. I fly down for a closer look.

There's a bustle of activity around the tent. People scurry like ants, grabbing backpacks and equipment from the flatbeds of trucks, carting things into and out of the tent. A few police officers in reflective vests mill about, but the majority of the activity is from the plainclothes and uniformed park rangers.

This must be ground zero for the scientific base. It's as good a place as any to start gathering information. Anything I can get before diving into the lauvan would be helpful.

I land a short distance away and proceed to change back into a human. Fortunately for me, there isn't much manipulation involved, since my dexterity is severely hampered by my lack of fingers. My lauvan are practically itching to spring back to their usual form, and a quick shake of my feathers dissolves my bird-form and reassembles me into my usual shape.

I take a moment to gather my wits again after the transformation, and try to ignore the undigested weight in my stomach. I start walking to the camp, then look down at myself. My clothes need some adjustment. I take my lauvan in both hands and do some quick manipulations. A passable ranger uniform emerges. It will do.

I stride into the makeshift camp like I'm supposed to be there, and nearly get bowled over by a pair of women carrying a large surveying instrument between them. Looking around, I spot a man staring up at the mountain, a lone figure of stillness amid the hubbub. I make my way over.

"Hi there." I greet the man. He looks at me and nods, then shifts his eyes back to the mountain as if he can't bear to take his gaze away for more than a moment. Okay, first contact made. Let's get some info. "I just started my shift. What's the update? Any news yet?"

The man gives a very large sigh.

"The activity is only increasing. Since five o'clock this morning, there've been constant emissions and tremors every hour. We've been checking the spectrometers, and the gas composition is fluctuating like crazy." He sighs again. "And

91

what's worse, we've started to get readings from the other two, Mt. Vickers and Mt. Kullen. Nothing visible yet, but it looks like they're also getting ready to rumble."

"Any word on why this is happening? Why they're coming out of dormancy?"

The man shakes his head before I finish speaking.

"That's the thing. These mountains should be dormant. There's no indication of plate movement, hot spots, nothing." The man gives a bitter laugh. "Right now my money's on Hephaestus. Looks like he's waking up."

Hephaestus is the ancient Greek god of blacksmiths, fire, and volcanoes. This man is closer to the truth than he knows. The lauvan are about as scientific as a Greek god.

"Shit," I breathe out in reply.

"Shit," he agrees.

We stare at Mt. Linnigan in silence for a minute. The scientists and rangers run around and shout instructions behind us.

The ground rumbles under my feet ever so slightly. The noises behind us change in pitch, and the scurrying picks up pace. A large cloud of steam bursts forth from the peak of Mt. Linnigan.

"Thar she blows," the man says. He stands up straight. "I'd better go look at the seismometer. Not that it will say anything informative, but still. The motions need to be carried out."

I nod when he leaves, and reach out my fingers surreptitiously. I close my eyes and try to feel out the lauvan in the region. The air is practically thick with them here. I touch a sickly lauvan and fight the revulsion that threatens to bring up the contents of my stomach. The last thing I want is to vomit a half-digested songbird in front of everyone.

I plug myself into the lauvan and explore the region

briefly. When I pull myself out, I'm shaking. The man is right. The infection is spreading to the other two mountains due to their liberal covering of lauvan-cables. Everything feels so unstable.

I wipe sweat off my brow and make my way around the tent into the trees before I allow my disguise to revert back to my normal clothes. It's time to get closer and see if I can fix this. Somehow.

CHAPTER XII

The mountain is so close now that I elect to walk to the nearest cable. Anyone who sees me will likely take me for a scientist, since they're not allowing anyone else into the park. I grin briefly. I studied chemistry back when it was called alchemy—does that count?

Although the nearest cable runs straight through the bustling parking lot, I don't relish explaining my actions to the rangers. From this vantage point, the next nearest cable looks to be a few hundred paces to the east. I follow signs for the Michelson Lookout, surmising that a viewpoint will make it easy to spot my target.

A short climb through dense forest and multitudinous roots brings me to a rocky outcrop with a wide-open view that overlooks the narrow valley at the foot of Mt. Linnigan. I'm even closer to the mountain than at the parking lot, and the rising steam appears even more foreboding from this vantage. The sick lauvan are clearer here and cluster together on the mountain in large numbers, which explains how I am able to see them from a distance. A lauvan-cable snakes up the promontory, only paces from where I stand.

The mountain takes up most of my attention, which is why I'm caught off-guard when I hear my name.

"Merry?"

Anna sits on a wooden bench bolted to the stone under our feet, a backpack at her side and the cable glittering behind her. She looks as surprised as I am. She has a lot less makeup on this morning and her long curly hair is pulled back in a loose braid. A blouse of green and white stripes flutters in the faint breeze. The end result is fresh and clean, as if she's the younger sister of the woman in the bar. It's a good look on her.

"Anna?" I clear my throat. Do I have a feather stuck in there? "What are you doing here?"

"I could ask you the same thing," she says. When I don't respond right away, she gives a self-conscious laugh. "Never mind. Keep your secrets, mystery man. You might as well sit down and have some coffee, since we skipped the usual awkward breakfast dance this morning." She holds out a thermos.

I grin. We understand each other perfectly.

"Did you make it this morning? I didn't hear a thing," I say, sitting down and taking a sip out of the thermos neck. "Mmm, good."

"You were dead to the world." She leans back and gazes at the mountain. "I tried to be quiet but I think a bomb could have gone off and you wouldn't't've noticed. Sorry it's not very good—it's just instant."

"It's warm and wet. That's all I want."

She laughs.

"Spoken like a true man."

We grin at each other before Anna's eyes are drawn once again to Mt. Linnigan. I consider her profile. She hardly notices. She's completely enraptured by the sight of the steaming mountain, whose plumes rise to blend into the low cloud blanketing the sky.

She offers no explanation for why she's here, and I don't want to pry because I don't want her prying back.

"I met your friend at that new shop in town." I pass back the thermos.

Her face darkens. She takes the thermos, but continues to keep her eyes on the mountain.

"Jackie doesn't get me. She's so small-minded." She tosses her head defiantly. "What did she say about me? She's such a gossip. A frightened little mouse gossiper."

Well, that was a calm and unbiased analysis. There's no love lost between the two of them.

"Reading between the lines," if I'm being very generous, "I think she's worried about you. Something about a dark aura. I don't know what she meant. Maybe it means something to you."

Anna breathes out in a huff.

"No. You know what that means? All it means is that she's too much of a spineless chicken to grab opportunities right in front of her. And a hypocrite too. She has a chance to be part of something larger than herself, and she throws it away. Bah." She tosses her hand as if getting rid of something.

"Well, opportunities can look great to some and like work to others."

"Isn't that the truth? I just think it's a bit rich to be accepting gifts, and then turn around and not give anything in return." Anna absentmindedly touches her chest.

While I agree it is a very fine chest and should probably be touched more, I can't help but wonder at the gesture. My suspicions are awakened when I see a flicker at her shirt's neckline. Anna's lauvan are a rich purple, and I could have sworn I saw a flash of bright orange.

"Isn't it beautiful?"

I frown at the abrupt change of topic. Anna's eyes haven't left the steaming mountain for ages.

"I suppose. If you're into death and destruction." Although she has a point. The gently steaming peak of Mt. Linnigan has a certain majestic gravitas. I have a sense, though, that there's more to learn about our previous topic. I bring the conversation back to Sylvana.

"What kind of gift did Jackie get?" I ask. I'm not being

very subtle, but with Anna only half-paying attention it doesn't seem to matter.

Anna only shrugs. I pry a little more.

"Is it that necklace she wears?"

Anna starts and looks at me fully. I have her attention now. I hope that was wise. Her eyes consider me with interest but she says nothing.

"I just noticed that she touched it a lot when she read my aura, and—I got a weird feeling about it," I finish lamely, although truthfully.

Anna smiles then, a calculating rise on one side of her mouth that doesn't suit her fresh-faced demeanor.

"That's exactly what I'm talking about. You can't talk the talk and not walk the walk." She looks me up and down. She seems as interested as she did last night, but only says, "Can you give me your hand and close your eyes? I want to try something."

Bemused and really not sure either what Anna is talking about or planning to do, I hold out my hand, palm up. She takes it and lays it on her denim-covered lap.

"Close your eyes," she says, and I oblige.

Nothing happens for a moment, and then the strangest sensation runs along one finger. It's as if Anna is stroking my index finger with the lightest of feather touches, and yet the feeling runs so deeply that I can feel it pass all the way through my finger out to the skin on the other side. A sensation akin to pins and needles creeps up my arm.

The lightness of her touch is so sensual and the depth is so intimate that I am immediately aroused. My mouth opens in an involuntary moan.

How is she doing this? I ignore her instructions and open my eyes. Anna's eyes are on my face, and she smirks in a satisfied way. My eyes travel down to our hands. She strokes my index finger gently. Except she doesn't—her finger doesn't contact my skin in any way. What she is touching is my lauvan. And not just lauvan to lauvan, as usually happens between two people—indeed, as happened between us last night—but her physical finger is actually touching my lauvan. When she feels out a loose end and runs her finger and thumb up its length, my body shudders with a mixture of pleasure and pain.

This is unreal. Is Anna like me? I might hope that I have found a kindred spirit at last, except that her movements are clumsy as if she can't see what she does, only feel. My eyes move slowly to her face, but on the way I stop at her neck.

Spilling out from under her shirt is a huge amount of orange lauvan, the same color as the flicker I saw a minute ago, exactly like the ones on Sylvana. I feel a wave of crushing disappointment that Anna is not like me, and then indignant confusion. Really? Three amulets of power in one week? What are the odds?

Very low odds. Obviously these "gifts" are being handed out for a reason.

Anna must notice the changing expression on my face.

"What's wrong?" She continues to stroke my finger. "Don't you like it?" She looks down at my jeans and smirks. "Never mind. You've already answered that."

This is too strange, too much. I snatch my hand away and stand up, adjusting myself. I'm not sure I'm ready to be the recipient of lauvan manipulation just yet. I'm too used to being the manipulator.

"I have to go."

She considers me thoughtfully.

"There's something about you, Merry. Something different. You intrigue me."

Before I can answer—not that I have an answer ready—a

tremor shakes the ground beneath our feet. I stagger. Anna raises her arms as if in triumph, and the foreign lauvan around her neck glow brightly.

"Behold the power of the gods of fire!" she says. Mt. Linnigan gives a great belch of steam. Anna laughs exultantly. "Isn't it glorious?" She holds a hand out to me as if inviting me to revel with her.

I don't understand what's going on, not at all. I look into Anna's shining eyes and shake my head in bewilderment.

"I—I have to go. I'm sorry." I turn and walk quickly down the path, away from Anna and her mysteries and distractions.

I need to get back to work.

***

Examining the nearest cable would be difficult with Anna breathing down my neck, so I direct my steps back to the parking lot. I keep to the trees to skirt the busy base camp and circle around to another trailhead, this one marked "Eagle Creek Trail." The trees along the path are dense, but within minutes I know the next nearest cable is near. It's no Spidey sense—it's that the lauvan are getting thicker. Sick yellow threads gleam among the shining silvery-brown ones on their slithering path over dead pine needles that cover the ground.

I bend to pick up a sick lauvan, but before my fingers reach it my pocket vibrates. Relieved by the interruption—touching the yellow lauvan is no picnic—but feeling guilty for feeling relieved, I pull my phone from my pocket.

It's Jen. I suck in my breath. I haven't had a chance to come up with a cover story. Oh well, I'll have to wing it.

"Hi, Jen," I answer with as much composure as I can muster. My experience with Anna at the viewpoint has me still flustered.

"Merry! Where are you?" There's a roar of background noise behind her words. "I'm on the bus, heading to my new job."

"Hey, that's great," I say. I forgot she texted me.

"Where are you?" she repeats. "I tried to come by your office, but you must be slacking off." She makes a little tsking sound that's almost drowned out by the roar of the bus.

"Yeah, I guess," I say. "I took a little trip. Change of scenery to get the marking juices flowing. I just started driving and ended up in a little hole-in-the-wall town."

"You're so strange," Jen says, but laughs. "What's the hole called?"

"Wallerton. I think it's been on the news recently." Only everywhere. I doubt she's missed it. I expect Jen to be worried about my being in the town threatened by a volcano, or perhaps she hasn't heard of it. I don't expect the response she actually gives.

"Get outta here! That's where I'm headed!"

I'm shocked into speechlessness. What are the ramifications of Jen being in town? There's a lot going on here that she knows nothing about, that I can't tell her about. I have no good explanations to offer her for why I'm here and what I'm doing.

But despite this, my spirits lift. It'll be good to see Jen. This volcano business is starting to overwhelm me. It's hard to feel down with Jen around.

"That's crazy," I say. "What are the odds?"

"Yeah. I'm heading up to interpret for a businessman from Hong Kong, he's got money in a mining operation nearby. He wants to talk to the officials in person to find out how the volcano might affect him if it blows." She laughs. "Seems like a lot of effort for a few questions, but what do I know? Maybe it's a diamond mine, or maybe he's secretly a lava enthusiast. Whatever, it's my first job!"

"Sounds great." A thought strikes me. "Aren't you worried about the eruption?"

"It'll only be a few days. And I can deal with a bit of ash in my hair." The phone crackles. She says, "Hey, I have to go. There's a tunnel up ahead and I'll probably get cut off. But dinner tonight?"

"Sure. I'll call you," I say, and sign off.

Dammit. Not only do I have to figure out how to stop this volcano from erupting and harming thousands of people, my own friend included, but I have to do so while keeping my true purpose here a secret from Jen. And the mystery of Anna looms even larger.

One and a half thousand years, and life is as complicated as ever.

***

Jen's call paused me in the middle of the trail. I shove the phone back in my pocket and continue down the path. Ten paces later, a turn brings a glimmering wall into view. It's the lauvan-cable, where it bisects the trail on its travels through the forest to Mt. Linnigan. Its shimmering coils throw light on the path and surrounding trees, as if from sunlight dancing over water.

This cable is a good starting point for my attempts to fix this center. Any cable would do, really—they're all full of sick lauvan and all need healing equally.

The sick lauvan are getting thicker. To my left, where the cable stretches away from the center, sick and healthy threads lie smoothly together. To my right, the cable drapes across the path to the edge of the trees where it disperses into individual lauvan and creeps over the surface of the mountain. There, the healthy silvery-brown lauvan are wrapped around and entangled with sickly yellow lauvan. They should freely twist and spiral in a line toward the dispersal point. It's a mess to look at, like braided hair rubbed and tatted and covered in burrs.

I walk toward it slowly. The best approach that I can think of right now is to simply untangle the lauvan and hope that the center will heal itself. Because I don't know the cause, it's difficult to know the cure. I'm simply applying the principles of human healing to the Earth. A wound may be a mangled gash or a clean slice, but to me it's always the same—a tangled mess of lauvan, too knotted together to move freely. Parts of this cable appear just like a human wound. I really hope they act the same.

I take a few breaths to prepare myself, and reach out with both hands to the nearest knot. It's a complex twisting of silver and yellow a little larger than my head, each lauvan as narrow as a piece of fettuccini. Through my fingers, I feel less of the usual pleasurable sensations of the cable, and more of the nausea I now associate with the sick lauvan. My stomach roils and I think unhappily of my breakfast of songbird and instant coffee.

I grit my teeth and push my mind past the nausea. This will take a while, so I'd better get used to it. I grip two adjacent lauvan between my fingers, one healthy and one sick, and wiggle them slowly to tease them apart. At first they slide easily, then there is resistance and my progress halts. I work my fingers along until I find the source of the tension and set to work.

A few hours later finds me sweating and shaking, but with this section of cable clean and free of knots. The sick lauvan are still present, but bundled together separately from the healthy ones. I'm half-tempted to break them off entirely, to purge them from this cable, but I resist. The consequences of severing the connection between an Earth center and its parts could be catastrophic. I've seen unnaturally snapped lauvan on a person before. It can mean gangrenous digits, kidney failure, blindness—I've seen it all. Mt. Linnigan is already unstable, and I don't want to tip it over the edge.

The end of the cable, where the individual lauvan disperse toward the mountain, is much clearer and calmer now. Gone are the knots and tightness. Now the lauvan flow freely.

I sit down on a nearby mossy stump and hang my head. That was a huge effort. My arms shake as they hold my spinning head steady. My lauvan twich spasmodically at the edge of my vision. I groan.

"How many bloody cables are there?" I say out loud to no one in particular. I know the answer—far too many. But if this works, I will personally untangle every cable around this center. I still don't know what the hell caused the sick lauvan, but if I can prevent them from knotting up the healthy ones and doing any damage, maybe they won't be a problem.

I stand up slowly, clutching a nearby tree branch. When my tunneling vision clears, I walk over to the edge of the forest where the cable splits into individual lauvan at the base of the mountain. I look up.

The peak of Mt. Linnigan is empty of steam.

At first my mind is blank with shock. Then a slow smile creeps over my face. It worked. It actually worked. Do I even have to untangle the other cables?

But I will, I assure myself somewhat self-righteously. I'll untangle at least a few more, to be absolutely certain that Wallerton is out of danger. Tomorrow I will come back and focus on cables at intervals around the mountain.

Feeling buoyant, I step back toward the path with a bounce in my step. Then I notice the cable. The yellow lauvan are already spreading out from their bundling and wrapping themselves insidiously around the healthy lauvan. It's a slow creep, and I only see it on the section I completed first, but it's unmistakable—all my hard work this afternoon is coming undone.

At the rate it's going, I expect it will be back to its tangled self by this time tomorrow, and I'll be back at square one. Suddenly unreasonably angry at the inanimate lauvan, I clench my teeth and plunge my hands into the cable, intent on straightening out the lauvan once more or just teaching it a lesson—I don't know what I intend.

The sensation I feel makes me freeze on the spot. I don't know how I know, but there is someone on the other end of this cable.

As I say that, I don't even know what it means. On the other end? There is no other end of a cable, per se, it simply disperses into lauvan. But I feel the presence of another. And the other is aware of me. It's angry with me and my untangling—I can feel the fury radiating through my hands.

There's a crackling as if from a static charge, and I am thrown clear from the cable to hit a pine tree six paces away. My head bangs on the bark and I slither to the ground, stunned.

It takes a minute for my eyes to clear. When they do, the cable twinkles innocently at me. The sick lauvan continue to slowly unfurl from their bundling.

What the hell just happened? What was the presence in the cable, and how did it make me jump so far? I wonder if I would be able to do the same to someone else manipulating the lauvan. I've never tried because there was never anyone else.

I shudder involuntarily. Am I not alone? All these years I've searched for answers, searched for someone like me. I thought it was something I wanted. Now I'm not so sure.

My mind alights briefly on Anna and her lauvan-touching, but dismisses it quickly. The necklace she wore gave her lauvan-sensing abilities, but she was so clumsy that it was obviously a new skill. Whoever pushed me through the cable knew exactly what they were doing, and used the lauvan as if born to it. Like me. Or better than me.

I pick myself up off the ground and wince at my pounding head. This is no good. I'll never manage the transformation into a bird without being able to concentrate, and it's way too far to walk back to the car. I reach around to feel the lump on the back of my head. It's tender to the touch and dizziness threatens to overtake me when I press too hard. I lift my hand a hair's breadth and feel out the thickening of my lauvan that have twisted themselves together above my bruise.

I'm lucky—it's only a minor twisting instead of a knot. I would be at it for hours if there were a knot I had to untangle without looking behind my head.

I massage the lauvan gently until they loosen and release their tension. The pain in my head lessens considerably. My talents come in handy at a time like this.

Now that I'm not blinded by pain, I notice that the sun is slanting at a sharp angle through the trees. Tired and defeated, I prepare to transform. I'll have to regroup and try something new in the morning.

Before I transform, my phone rings. Jen's number is on the screen.

"Hello?"

"Merry! I'm in town! Where do you want to meet for dinner?"

My head is still foggy with the after-effects of my fall and distracted from all the questions before me, but my stomach hears the word "dinner" and loudly voices its approval.

"There's only one real restaurant in town."

"Yeah, I saw it. On the corner, green siding, lots of trucks out front?"

"That's the one. Meet you there in half an hour?" I need time to fly and drive. I look down at my dirty clothes, wet with sweat, and grimace. "Better make that an hour. I need a shower."

"Done," Jen says. "See you then."

***

My flight back to the car is uneventful. Thankfully, I encounter no prey on the way, as I don't think I can resist the urge to attack and fill my roaring stomach. Once in the car, I flip on the radio and turn the dial, trying to find a local station.

"...*and our correspondent on the ground reports a reduction of the seismic activity that has plagued the area around Mt. Linnigan for the past four days. Officials have declined to comment, but our sources tell us that scientists are unaware of what is causing this new development. Perhaps Mt. Linnigan is preparing to sleep again.*"

I grunt and hit the button to silence the announcer. I've given myself a brief reprieve to figure out how to fix this. I wonder if the presence will be there when I go back to untangle again. Perhaps I can reach out to it first. Fight fire with fire.

I'm heartened by this thought. Maybe there's a way out of this after all. I can incapacitate the presence, fix the volcano, and be the hero—to myself, at least. And then maybe I can find out where the presence is and finally get some answers. Is there someone else like me out there?

I gun it down the highway to Wallerton, take a quick

shower and change clothes at my hotel, and stroll into the restaurant at the appointed time. It took me a few lifetimes, but I'm now adept at time management.

Jen waits for me in a booth on the side. She gives me a hug which I gladly return. Her hair tickles my cheek.

"This is so bizarre that we're both here." Jen laughs.

"Funny old world," I say.

The waitress comes up then and gives us menus. She looks at me askance. She must have seen me leave with Anna last night, and now I'm chatting up another woman. I smile blandly at her.

"Two lagers, please."

She nods, gives me the most insincere smile I've seen in decades, and leaves. It's moments like these that make me remember why I love living in the city—the anonymity afforded there is a welcome relief from the nosiness of small-town life.

"So, what *are* you doing here?" Jen selects a piece of bread from the basket the waitress left and tears it apart with her long, thin fingers. She looks good—fresh-faced, eyes bright, a cute red sundress under a black cardigan. No wonder the waitress looked at me funny. Jen is quite the contrast to Anna's tight white jeans. I feel old and tired compared to Jen. The Mt. Linnigan mystery weighs heavily on my mind. Lack of food and sleep don't help.

"Oh, I couldn't face marking any more essays on Friday, so I just started driving," I say. I grab my own piece of bread and pop it into my mouth. "Oh god, that's good," I say between chews. "I'm starving."

Jen stares at me with pursed lips and raised eyebrows.

"So you just—left? When are you going to mark?"

"Relax. Marks aren't due until next week." I take another piece of bread.

107

"What did you do here today, then?"

"Hiking, mainly. There are some great trails." At least this is partly true, as well as believable. Jen knows I go to the mountains a lot in Vancouver.

Jen's face lights up.

"Which trails did you hike? I used to come up here every summer with my parents growing up. My mom's parents used to own a cabin nearby. My brother and I would hike all over and swim in Lake Carnarvon."

Uh oh. The only trail name I remember is the Michelson Lookout, which is currently off-limits to hikers.

"Mmm, I don't remember the names. I drove west down a logging road and found a path somewhere there."

"Oh." Jen looks a little disappointed. I wish I could give her more.

"Hey, congrats on your new job, by the way."

Just then the waitress arrives with our beers. She places Jen's down in front of her with a smile, and drops mine none-too-gently in front of me before leaving. Her lauvan are all sweet curves toward Jen and sharp angles when she faces me. I try not to roll my eyes, and raise my glass in a toast.

"Here. To all your successes."

Jen's cheeks grow pink and she smiles. We clink our glasses and drink.

"When do you start work?" I ask once I've swallowed.

"Tomorrow morning, nine o'clock," Jen says. "A car's going to pick me up from the hotel, and my client and I will drive to the volcano site and talk to the officials and scientists there."

"You're going right to the mountain?" Now I'm worried. The base camp is really close to ground zero should an eruption occur. Given the rate the lauvan are tangling, I think it'll be okay until midday tomorrow. It should last. Probably.

108

There are a lot of knots in a lot of lauvan-cables, and I don't know if things are getting worse all over. I'll be out at first light tomorrow, but still. I don't want Jen getting hurt.

"Are you sure you want to do this? Mt. Linnigan is an active volcano, and the scientists don't seem to know what's going on or when it will blow."

Jen shrugs nonchalantly.

"I'm sure it's fine. There are a ton of people at the base camp, so it can't be that risky. Apparently they've set up shop on a ridge that would be somewhat protected if there were a lava flow."

I can see her mind is set, so I don't push it further. I just make myself a promise to be there first thing so I can get a handle on this before Jen arrives, or at least buy a little time until she's gone. I wonder a bit about myself—what about the other people at the base camp?—but there's no shame in some personalized motivation. I've been working hard on fixing this already—now I have some added incentive.

Jen goes to grab another piece of bread, then looks up to my right. I feel someone slide into the booth next to me and a hand touches my leg. Purple lauvan float in front of my vision.

"Hello, Merry." Anna's voice breathes into my ear.

Crap. This is a complexity I didn't anticipate. I should have—this is the only place in town worth visiting, and this is where I met Anna last night. I just wasn't thinking. I was too hungry, too flustered—I don't know.

Jen looks between me and Anna, back and forth, her eyebrows raised so high that her forehead wrinkles. Out of the corner of my eye I see the waitress snickering. In a flash of annoyance I find some lauvan under the table and tweak them. The next instant, a pitcher of beer tips over on the bar counter and the waitress scrambles for a tea towel.

The waitress dealt with, I turn to the situation at hand.

"Hi, Anna." I try to appear cool and collected. "Anna, this is my friend Jen. Jen, this is—" I flounder for what to say. "Well, Jen, meet Anna."

Jen looks confused, but sticks out her hand anyway.

"Hi, Anna. It's nice to meet you."

Anna languidly extends her own. At the same time, she caresses my leg. I tense, but try not to react. I move my hand slowly down to my lap to push her away without Jen noticing.

"Likewise," Anna says. She turns to me. "I just wanted to say hello." She finds my hand under the table and sits the heel of her palm on my wrist to trap it. I can't wriggle free without being very obvious, and Jen is already more than curious. Anna continues. "I also wanted to say that sometimes when you visit a new place, it can be even better the second time around." Her fingers pat the air above my hand until they find my lauvan, and she grips one between her finger and thumb and rolls it gently.

I can't help myself. My eyes close involuntarily and my breath sucks in as the sensation hits me, deep and far-reaching. Anna doesn't belabor the point. She removes her hand and stands up.

"I'll leave you two to your dinner," she says, before sashaying to the door.

Jen and I are silent for a moment. I'm disgusted with myself for acting like a lust-driven teenager in front of Jen. I'm too old to not be able to control myself. But that sensation is so new, so different, so tantalizing—I feel young again, experiencing something for the first time. It's been a very long while since I've had that pleasure.

"Well," Jen says after an awkward pause. "Umm..." She laughs with a mixture of embarrassment and humor. "I guess

I know why you came up here, then. Hiking? Really, Merry."

"What?" What is she thinking? "I didn't come up here to meet…" I sigh. "Sorry, Jen. That was—unnecessary."

"Whatever." She eyes me and bursts out laughing. "Oh, Merry, you should see your face. I don't think I've ever seen you embarrassed before." I don't respond, and she tsks. "So you're human, and I found out. No biggie." She chuckles again and opens her menu. "Come on. Let's order."

***

I walk Jen to the hotel after dinner and leave her at the lobby, citing the need for a walk. She punches my arm.

"A walk, sure. See you later, Merry." She wink-squints at me and turns to the elevator.

I really do mean to go for a walk. I need to clear my head. It was a very confusing day, with too many revelations and mysteries cropping up. I need to think, to plan for tomorrow.

That really is my intention, I swear. But after a few minutes of strolling, my mind buzzing with more questions than answers, I find myself on the road outside Anna's apartment.

I guess Jen knows my intentions better than I do.

I curse and do an about-turn on my heel. I try to keep my mind on plans for tomorrow, but now all I can think about is Anna. Her hair flowing down her shoulder and curling around her naked breast, her deep throaty laugh, her finger on my lauvan—it's no use.

I stop in front of the restaurant, thinking. Maybe this is an opportunity in disguise. Anna seems entangled in something strange. The lauvan-infused necklace, for one, is worth investigating. Sylvana has one too, and there was definitely something going on with that spirit invocation she did.

111

Anna's inordinate interest in the volcano is puzzling, too, and might be worth checking out. Maybe there's a connection that could prove useful for my inquiries.

The problem with having a fifteen hundred year-old mind is that I can recognize when I'm rationalizing bad decisions to myself. The problem with having a thirty year-old body is that I don't care.

I stride purposefully up the parking lot to the side of the restaurant where there is an attached beer and wine store. It's a bit gauche to turn up on Anna's doorstep empty-handed.

An electronic bell chimes when I enter, and a fluorescent light flickers above my head. Classy joint. Ahead of me in the tiny store are an empty shop counter and an open door behind it, leading to what looks like a hallway to a storeroom. I turn to the shelf on my right and quickly scan labels of the wine bottles stacked there. I select a French wine I recognize—it's a favorite of mine, partially for the flavor and partially because it's from the region I lived in for a number of years in the ninth century—and place it on the counter.

Before I need to look for a bell to ring, a man bustles in through the open doorway. He wears an apron and rolled-up sleeves. He's obviously doing double-duty tonight in the restaurant and in here.

"Sorry about that. Hope you haven't been waiting long."

"It's fine," I say, digging into my pocket for my wallet. He takes my credit card and rings the sale through.

"Are you staying for long in Wallerton? We're all in an uproar here, not sure whether to stay or go. This volcano business is nerve-racking, eh? In fact, tomorrow I'm driving the wife and kids to the in-laws in Kamloops for a holiday. Just until we know, one way or other, you know?" He hands back my card and bags the bottle. "Sorry, I didn't mean to alarm you. It's just all any of us can talk about these days."

112

"I understand. Have a good drive tomorrow." I take the bottle from him and make my retreat.

Come hell or high water, I will figure this out in the morning. This center has been unstable for long enough. Even if I have to untangle every cable myself and tie them up with my own lauvan, I will fix this.

At the entrance to the apartment, I search the list of buttons for Anna's name. Near the top is a Jacqueline Appleton.

"Sorry, Sylvana," I say quietly. "Looks like you'll have to break out the earplugs again."

Anna answers the buzzer after a few seconds' wait.

"Hello?" Her voice is pitched low and throaty in a come-hither way. She needn't have bothered—I'm already here.

"It's Merry."

A buzz tone answers for her and the door clicks. I walk through the hallway on my left, and remember the breathless roll of our bodies against the wall the last time I entered this threshold. When I knock on 102 it swings open, unlatched. I push it gingerly.

Anna perches on the arm of her couch, dressed in a red silk dressing gown that barely covers the tops of her thighs. I look her up and down approvingly. She smiles in satisfaction.

"Mmm, wine. Good. I was just heading to the shower. Make yourself at home." She slides off the couch and saunters to the bathroom. She leaves the door ajar and a minute later the water starts to run.

I shed my coat and hang it on a hook behind the door. The couch beckons, but my attention is distracted by movement in the bedroom. I look more closely. Anna's shirt is on the bed, the one she wore this afternoon when we met at the mountain. Its green and white stripes shiver and move in the dim light that streams onto the bed from a lamp in the living

113

room.

I cross the room to take a closer look. When I draw near, it becomes clear that the movement is not from the shirt, but from some loose lauvan that cling to the neckline of the shirt. They are fading already from being away from their source for too long, but they still hold traces of their original orange color.

These lauvan are from Anna's necklace. What a find—maybe I can finally get some information about these mysterious amulets that keep cropping up in my path. I carefully grasp the center of one lauvan and pick it up. It hangs limply in midair, wriggling in a feeble way. It's very fragile. I close my eyes and attempt to glean some knowledge of its origins.

I expect to get a sense of location, or a pull toward a certain direction. Even, if I were lucky and knew the originator of these lauvan, a sense of personality. What I get instead is blankness. Blankness, and a faint whisper of wordless murmuring.

What the hell? Maybe the lauvan is too far gone to be of any use. I toss it down in disgust. Anna will be able to keep her secrets for another night.

"Merry? Are you coming in?"

Anna's voice makes me forget my annoyance at the useless lauvan. I take a deep breath.

"This is your last chance to walk away from this bad idea, Merlin," I chide myself quietly. "You could go back to your hotel room, watch a movie, go to sleep, wake up nice and early for your work on the lauvan. It's not too late."

But it is too late. My breath comes more quickly at the sound of running water from the shower. Anna's lauvan-touching abilities beckon to me.

I want the novelty. I want to feel something I haven't felt

ten thousand times before. I want to feel alive and fresh, young and new, like the world is full of limitless possibilities and is waiting for me to discover them. For a moment, when Anna touched my lauvan, it almost felt like that again.

There's no choice anymore. It's too late.

I strip off my shirt, hop out of my pants and socks, and pad over to the bathroom. The shower stall is steamy but Anna's dark silhouette appears through the foggy glass. I slide in behind her so we both face the showerhead. The only thing she wears is her necklace.

I don't care what she's hiding, or how she's able to use the lauvan. I only care that she can.

"Touch me again," I whisper in her ear, and slide my hands down her hips. "Like you did at the mountain."

CHAPTER XIII

Dreaming

I awaken to a sharp pain when my back rolls over onto a stone. I gingerly shift off the stone and open my eyes. The half-full moon has almost set, and it filters through a swaying oak to fill the meadow with dappled light and shifting shadows. The wind rustles through trees in the forest behind me. I shiver in the coolness and look for my cloak to cover our naked bodies.

Or just my naked body. Vivienne is nowhere to be seen.

I flop back down to the ground in disappointment, only to be met by the same unyielding stone as before. I curse and sit up, reaching for my clothes which have seemingly scattered themselves far and wide. The search for my boot takes too much time before my ale-befuddled mind remembers to feel it out using the lauvan.

Where did Vivienne go? Did she sneak back to her temporary quarters with the other women? She certainly isn't the regretful type and she seemed to enjoy herself. The Roman custom of containing their women never really caught on in these parts, and she isn't one of the timid ones. I scuff my boot against the ground, sighing. Who am I to chastise Arthur for not knowing much about women? I'm not doing so well myself. The blind lead the blind nowhere fast.

I shake my head, trying to formulate a plan. Head back to my own bed, yes. Good idea. I latch onto the coherent thought and push through the grass in the meadow, its faint lauvan waving mildly in the moonlight. On the path to the villa, I brush against an errant lauvan. It jolts me to wakefulness and my nerves jangle. With difficulty, I focus and feel out the lauvan. Another jolt until I hold it firmly, and the sensation settles into wild fear and excitement. I know the owner of this particular thread. Vivienne passed this way, and discarded pieces of lauvan in her wake. It can happen in times of great emotion. The lauvan won't last long—they'll likely dissolve by sunrise—but they should last long enough for me to see where Vivienne went.

What happened to her? Now I'm afraid—did a wild animal scare her off? But then why the excitement? I pick up my pace and follow the lauvan fragments down the valley toward the villa. Each fragment I touch jolts me anew, and the last effects of the ale leave me.

The fragments grow more frequent on the approach to the villa, as if Vivienne were practically panting with excitement. I'm a little miffed—where were the lauvan fragments when I was pleasuring her? I don't remember quite this volume back in the meadow. I sigh and vow to keep my big bragging mouth shut around Arthur in the future.

The main door to the great hall is ajar. I slip through and survey the room. Many of the visitors have simply keeled over in ale-induced stupors and now lie on the floor snoring. The torches are all extinguished and the fire is low. I pick my way through the bodies to follow the fragments. Every touch of fragment causes me to wince, the jolts so strong as to be almost painful. They lead me directly to the head table and behind it. I notice with approval that Arthur is not sprawled on the floor behind his seat. Puzzled, I wonder what Vivienne was doing here. Until I look up, that is.

The banner is gone.

No eagle stares disdainfully down at me, no serpent hisses a silent warning. The wall is nothing but blank stone with two blunt spikes where the banner used to hang.

My stomach clenches in horror. With the banner gone, stolen in the middle of the night, no less, Arthur will look

117

weak and unprotected. The banner is validation that he is his father's son in spirit as well as in body, and that he comes from a strong Roman lineage. And to have it disappear during the feast—there's no way we can hide the fact that it's gone.

Why did Vivienne take it? I look for more fragments but the trail ends here. All her worries must have been in getting to this point. Once she had the banner in her hands, the worst part was done. I imagine a look of calm satisfaction on her face and I clench my jaw in anger. Now I have to find her, before dawn, and the trail of lauvan leads nowhere but here.

I have another trick up my sleeve, though. Because of our lovemaking, we forged a connection that goes beyond those moments. I look down to my chest and see the expected rope of lauvan that leads away from me, toward the door of the villa. The threads of intertwined lavender and deep brown that join Vivienne and me are frail and tenuous, but that's only to be expected from such a short-lived encounter where lust was paramount and love only a notion. I have seen the connections between two people truly in love—the lauvan-threads that span the distance between them are thick and solid, like knotted tree trunks or heavy rope. I pluck the lauvan connecting Vivienne and me. They will fade and dissolve over time without constant renewal. But today, they are enough.

And these tentative lauvan will lead me straight to Vivienne.

I pick my way through the snoring lords and their retainers, and slide out the door without moving it—I know from experience that it creaks dreadfully. Once outside, I check the lauvan—she's heading due west. My eyes close to concentrate. Slowly, I sense her distance from me. She's further away than expected.

Luckily, I know how to move fast when I need to.

118

Summoning my focus, I carefully touch my own lauvan with my fingertips. I manipulate them while I concentrate on the form I'm aiming to transition to. The transition is slow at first, but then with a rush my body melts into its new shape. My antlered form leaps in the air and springs forward to follow the lauvan toward Vivienne.

It doesn't take me long to overtake her. My keen ears hear her panting as she walks quickly along the road. The panting that sounded so lovely only hours before now simply annoys me. I allow my body to switch back to its usual form, which it springs into with a feeling of release. I quietly walk behind Vivienne until she is only ten paces away.

"Vivienne."

She whirls around in a panic, a short dagger held in her shaking hand. Her lauvan sizzle out from her body like a porcupine. A little tension releases when she recognizes me, but not much. She keeps her dagger pointed toward me.

"Merlin. How did you find me?"

"Does it matter?" I take a step toward her, and then another. She holds her ground. "The more important question is, why did you take the banner?" A thought strikes me for the first time. The damn ale must have sapped my intellect until now. "Who are you working for?"

Vivienne worries her bottom lip before answering.

"The lady Morgan. She has as much right to the banner as Arthur does. More, in fact, since she's Uther's eldest child."

"Morgan." I shake my head, baffled. "What does she want with the banner? And if she has so much right to it, why did she send you to sneak it out in the dead of night?"

Vivienne lifts her chin in defiance.

"She knew Arthur would never part with it willingly."

"Does she think it will give her power over the warriors? That they will somehow bow to her because she carries a moldy old blanket?" I make light of the banner, although I know its symbolism is important. But it's not as important as action. "Arthur has made a name for himself. He's won numerous battles, and has earned the lords' respect. The banner is only a symbol. In Morgan's hands, it would mean nothing."

Vivienne stares at me, her expression unreadable. She keeps her dagger pointed at me, but her lauvan start to dance in agitation. She knows our little conversation is coming to a head. She wasn't prepared to fight, only to run.

"She deserves it." Vivienne's voice is only a whisper. "She needs it."

"I'm sorry, Vivienne. I can't let you take it." I run my fingers through the trails of lauvan that dangle and swirl from the banner. It is made of woolen threads, ancient but still from a living creature at one point. The lauvan are weak but present. I keep my eyes fixed on Vivienne's, and my fingers gather as many of the banner's lauvan as I can manage.

With a swift yank, I pull the lauvan toward me. The banner sails out of Vivienne's startled arms and straight into my waiting hands.

Vivienne gasps with disbelief.

"The rumors are true. You do have magic."

I raise an eyebrow as I fold the banner.

"You could call it that, I suppose." I tuck the banner under my arm and wriggle a ring off the smallest finger of my left hand, a simple golden band with blue enamel worked into the surface. It was part of a larger gift of gold and silver from a grateful lord on the edge of the war council's range, whose homestead we protected last spring. The ring is no more than a bauble I took a fancy to, although it's worth more than my intended purpose for it. I offer it to Vivienne. "Here. Your wages for your work. I suggest you leave now and don't come back."

A long moment passes while she searches my face. She takes the ring without looking at it.

"You're going to let me go."

The memories of the last few days, and especially of last night, fill my head. I look down at the lauvan between us. How can I bring her to punishment when there is this connection between us, however ephemeral? What Arthur doesn't know won't hurt him.

I sigh.

"Call me sentimental."

CHAPTER XIV

I awake with only the foggiest recollection of where I am. I open my eyes and wait for them to focus on my surroundings. Before they do, my leg moves against the slither of satin sheets. Of course. I swing my legs to the ground and stumble over to Anna's bathroom.

On the way out, the green glow of the microwave's clock informs me that it's ten past four. I shiver. It's far too early to be awake, and far too cold to be out of bed. I take the last seven paces to the bed and slide in, intent on nestling over to Anna to find some warmth.

But the satin on Anna's side is cold, and I can't feel Anna's soft body anywhere in bed.

"Anna?" Where the hell is she? Does she ever sleep? There's no answer from the living room, not that I expected one. I didn't see her when I passed through.

I flop onto my back. Now I'm awake—curiosity and mild annoyance work like caffeine on my system. Where did she go? Yesterday morning she was at Mt. Linnigan when I found her. Would she go back?

And a better question is—why?

I jump out of bed, now too intensely curious to even consider going back to sleep. I throw on my clothes, neatly laid over the sofa arm since I undressed myself last night. The door makes only the slightest click when it closes behind me.

Outside, I pause to consider my next move. There are a few different ways I could follow Anna, but I recall my dream and decide to stick with the easiest. From my abdomen extends a thin rope of lauvan, heading northwest. The intermixing of Anna's rich purple and my own chocolate

122

brown is pleasing to the eye, and I admire it for a moment before focusing on my next task.

When I touch the lauvan connecting us, they tell me that Anna is some distance away. I'd better transform. No one is awake at this hour but I look around anyway, then gather the necessary configuration of lauvan and yank.

A few moments later, I'm soaring high above the roofs of Wallerton. The black tips of the Three Peaks are silhouetted against the cold light of the night sky. The Milky Way is clearly visible in this remote mountain town as a smear across the zenith. It's easy to forget just how big and endless the night sky is when it's always hidden by the lights of the city. For most of my life my sky looked like this—I don't realize until I'm out of the city how much I miss it.

The leftmost peak of Mt. Linnigan stands quiet and steam-free for now. I still have a few hours left before it starts up again, once the cable re-knots itself. I flap my wings to pick up speed. Since I'm up anyway, I'll quickly satisfy my curiosity about Anna and then untangle the cable again. Maybe it won't take me long. It will buy me more time, especially important with Jen visiting the site later this morning. I'll feel out the presence first, though. I don't like mysterious forces throwing me around without cause. Or with cause—no one tosses me around without retaliation.

The lauvan lead me straight to Michelson Lookout—no surprise there. But why is Anna so fascinated with the volcano? Is it just some sort of thrill-seeking urge? I find it hard to fathom why anyone would rise at four in the morning, hike into an off-limits park—Anna can't fly, after all—only to sit and stare at the now-slumbering mountain.

When I'm close—the lauvan vibrate with a higher frequency when I brush them with a wingtip—I dip down into the trees and glide silently to the clearing at the lookout.

I debate whether or not to change back to my human form—merlins are quieter with better hearing—but I don't want to be distracted by bird instincts I can't control. A great horned owl could make falcon-me zip away in fright.

A brief melting of my body and I crouch on the forest floor, breathing hard from the effort of holding my bird-form. Slowly I stand and creep forward on silent footfalls. I learned long ago how to move through the woods undetected. When you're hunting and all that stands between you and the meat you need to survive the winter is your ability to step quietly, you learn fast or perish. I'm a survivor.

I'm lucky—a few thick bushes stand between me and the lookout clearing, perfect cover to remain undetected. The lauvan pass from me directly through the bushes to the other side. Anna is straight ahead. I creep around the bush and peek from behind a thick-trunked pine tree.

Anna sits cross-legged on the ground facing the mountain, right in front of a bench and beside the glowing lauvan-cable. I'm positioned so I can see her profile—her uplifted chin, her raised chest, her unbound hair cascading in a glorious river down her back. Her eyes are closed and she sways gently from side to side, as if she is underwater and waves push her to and fro. Three candles in a triangle formation before her illuminate her face.

I notice all this in the second before my eyes are drawn to the object between the candles. I stare, fascinated, captivated.

Anna's necklace lies in a bundle on the ground. Last night I had glimpses of it in the dark, but my preoccupation didn't allow for a close inspection. Now, however, it is clearly lit by the candlelight.

Or, it would be visible if it weren't completely and utterly covered by lauvan. Bright orange strands lie so thickly over the surface of the amulet that it appears to me as a ball of orange twine. I have no idea what the pendant is—it could be a diamond or a locket or a plastic rhinestone for all I know. A thin stream of lauvan connect the necklace to the adjacent cable. Lauvan surrounding the necklace writhe and twist with great agitation. At least, if the lauvan were attached to a person I would say the person were agitated. I don't know what it means for an object. Generally, object-lauvan calmly swirl unless they are being worshiped. I look sharply at Anna. Is that what she's doing? Is this what Sylvana was warning me about?

I don't have to wonder for long. Anna keeps her eyes closed but speaks in a powerful, authoritative voice.

"Spirits! Come forth! Anna Green invites you!"

Invoking spirits? That's what Sylvana did. What the hell are these women playing at? Do they think there are actually elementals on some other plane of existence that will answer them? I shiver, remembering Sylvana's strange reaction and words. I've never seen any tangible evidence of a spirit world, although I've known many fine men and women who swear it's there. Surely I would have seen something by now, after a millennium and a half of life on this earth. The memory of Sylvana's invocation springs to my mind. What did she hear? Why did she mention my father?

At Anna's words the lauvan of the necklace pulse three times, giving off a brilliant flash of silvery light each time. Anna doesn't notice, of course—her eyes are closed, but either way it's the action of lauvan, invisible to all but me.

My jaw drops. This is bizarre. I've never seen object-lauvan act like this. It's as if they are alive.

In the ringing stillness after Anna's invocation I begin to hear a whispering sound, like wind through leaves. Or like the quiet murmurings of a large crowd of people some distance away. Anna must hear it too, because her mouth parts in a wide smile.

"Welcome, spirits."

The whispering turns to murmuring then to indistinct muttering. I'm forcibly reminded of the sounds I heard during Sylvana's spirit invocation. But it doesn't stop at muttering. The lauvan ball gives a final pulse and starts to bloom. It writhes and wriggles upward and outward, growing huge and distorted. The lauvan gather themselves into three indistinct shapes.

Cold sweat trickles down my back. Lauvan don't move of their own accord like this. They don't create shapes, with rounded tops and long slender protrusions that a fanciful man might call arms, and a narrowing that could be construed as a neck...

"Greetings, Anna Green." A bland, androgynous voice emerges from the central lauvan-shape. My heart stops, then stutters back to life, three times faster than before. The lauvan in the front of the shape's—head?—twitch and writhe in an approximation of a mouth.

"How does your task progress?" Anna says, her eyes still closed. It's clear that she can hear the lauvan-shape but cannot see it. I notice with shock that two purple lauvan twist among the orange of the lauvan-shapes. Another of Anna's lauvan detaches from her body and floats to the shapes, where it is sucked into the wriggling mass.

Now I'm even more worried than before, if that's possible. Are the lauvan-shapes taking pieces of Anna? What does that mean?

And when am I going to stop calling them lauvan-shapes, and admit to myself that spirits might be real?

The central spirit responds to Anna's question with a flickering near its mouth region.

"Progress is slow but steady. Energy to the mountain is all

but blocked. We have needed to exercise caution on our end—we are being watched, and punishment would be severe if we were found out."

"Yes, I understand." Anna's tone hints at impatience, not understanding. "But when will it be done?"

"There is one on your side who thwarts us. Already this one has undone some of our work. But we will be ready for this one if there is an attempt to slow our progress once more. We anticipate completion after the second sunrise."

"There's someone else?" Anna's smooth forehead wrinkles in confusion. "I don't know who else could. It's certainly not Jackie or Bethany. And the others—they wouldn't." She lifts her chin higher. "It doesn't matter. You deal with this intruder, and the event will go on as planned. Then we will all benefit."

"Indeed. You can tell your people that the plan will proceed on schedule."

During this exchange, Anna's lauvan detach themselves from her body in a slow but continuous parade of purple. Her lauvan blend in with the spirit lauvan. I'm horrified to see the spirits becoming more formed with every purple lauvan they incorporate. Instead of blank expanses of lauvan, depressions form where eye sockets should be. The central spirit's mouth grows more distinct, almost forming lips.

Are the spirits taking Anna's life force, her lauvan? Are they harming her?

Anna seems to notice nothing, although her chest rises and falls with greater frequency than before and her cheeks are pale.

"Until the morning, spirits," she says. "Keep your end of the bargain, and we will keep ours."

The spirits begin to swirl together above the amulet. Faster and faster they turn, until they become one twisting mass of lauvan that shrinks and grows still, calmly twining around the necklace as before. The connection between necklace and cable severs, and orange lauvan slink back to the necklace.

Anna sways for a moment. Her limbs move as with a great effort and she fumbles around for the necklace to drape it over her head. Then her eyes open and roll back. She slumps boneless to the ground, clearly unconscious.

I'm by her side in an instant.

"Anna," I hiss. "Anna."

She's out cold. I check her heartbeat in the pulse of her neck, and her airway by her breath on my cheek. All is normal. Her lauvan are sluggish, but no more than when she sleeps.

I shake my head at her unseeing form.

"Anna, what have you got yourself into?" I pass my hands over my face. They're shaking.

After all these years, it turns out that the druids who schooled me were right. The spirit world is real. It can be contacted. I search my memories for what the druids taught me so long ago. It's all pretty foggy. I dismissed lessons about the spirit world early on as superstitious stories inspired by hallucinogenic herbs used in ceremonies.

Think, Merlin, think. What do I know? According to the druids, there are spirits in charge of each of the old-world elements—earth, air, water, and fire. They exist on a different plane from our world—one reason I dismissed them in my youthful arrogance. I thought I could see that plane in the lauvan, and laughed at those who believed that there were spirits when there were clearly not. They govern the elements and make sure none are out of alignment, that the scales of the world are balanced. The druids put a lot of stock into balance, and I certainly agree with them of its importance.

128

But the notion that there are beings that maintain the balance of the world, that surprises me.

Although, apparently not all spirits are interested in balance. These spirits have been deliberately knotting the lauvan around Mt. Linnigan to cause an eruption, for what purpose I'm still not clear. It sounds as if they are renegade spirits. If there are real, honest-to-goodness spirits controlling this volcano, things may be more dire than I thought. It certainly explains the presence I felt in the lauvan-cable. Now they're onto me. And they're not fans, according to Sylvana and the psychic punch I received from the presence in the cable earlier. Do they know who I am? Do they know what I am? Do they have the answers about myself that I long since gave up hope of ever finding out?

There's also another interested party—whoever Anna is working for. Some person or persons unknown are directing Anna's movements, undoubtedly the author of the note covered in red lauvan. It seems to me that Anna is in way over her head with whatever this is all about. She obviously knew nothing about the lauvan-stealing that took place while she and the spirits spoke. It cost her her consciousness this time—what will happen next time?

I stroke Anna's soft cheek. She looks so young when she's asleep, so vulnerable.

"Time to take you home," I whisper to her. She doesn't respond. I feel around in her coat for her keys and shove them in my pocket. Her car surely isn't far—I can't envision her hiking for hours in the middle of the night. I look around and spot a faint trail of purple lauvan glowing dimly to my left. Ah ha. Thank you, Anna, for your excitement in this early morning. Glad you had some left over from last night.

I blow out the candles, shaking off the wax and stuffing them into my pocket. That done, I bend down and gently slide my hands under Anna's body to pick her up. Her limp form hangs loosely between my arms. I try to tuck her head into my chest to avoid it flopping around on her neck. The car had better be close.

When I get Anna back to her apartment, it's time for answers. And now that I know what I'm facing, it's time for action.

CHAPTER XV

Anna's car is parked in a clearing of an abandoned logging road near the edge of the park, close enough that the journey is mercifully swift. I fish the car keys out of my pocket and unlock the backdoor of her cherry-red Acura, black in the dark. Carefully, I pick her up and lie her down on the backseat. She doesn't stir. Losing some of her lauvan sapped her energy, and now she needs time to recoup. I look at Anna's limp body and feel a pang of fear. I hope that's all it is.

The sky begins to lighten as I turn the key in the ignition and reverse the car out of the clearing. By the time I roll into town and wheel into a free space on the street in front of Anna's apartment, the sun has risen and glints off curtained windows up and down the street.

With Anna in my arms, I fumble for a minute with the keys in the door until the right one successfully turns the lock. I bang the door open with my foot, eager to get inside and put Anna down.

In the hallway, I walk past 102 with my cargo in my arms and stop in front of 103. My knuckles rap loudly on the door, despite my awkward hold on Anna. A light appears, filtering through a gap between door and floor.

"Sylvana," I hiss. "It's Merry. From the shop yesterday. I need your help. Anna's in trouble."

The door opens a crack, as far as the security chain will allow. Sylvana's wide eyes peer out from her sleep-puffed face. She takes a moment to absorb the scene. I pause to consider how it must look—me, tousle-haired and puffing with exertion, Anna a deadweight in my arms. Sylvana, to her great credit, doesn't hesitate.

"Oh my god." The door slams and a rattling chain precedes the door flinging open. "Come in. Lie her down on the sofa." Sylvana runs to reposition tasseled cushions and I maneuver Anna onto the couch. We stare at Anna in silence for a moment until Sylvana turns to me.

"What happened?" She looks back to Anna. "Should she go to a hospital?"

"No. Look, Sylvana, I need to ask you a few questions. Anna will be fine—I hope." I move to the table in the kitchen area and pull out two of the chairs. "Come sit."

Sylvana looks a little taken aback by my taking charge, but she comes and sits down gingerly.

"What is this about?" She looks at me warily, as if only now realizing the situation—a strange man barges into her home at sunrise, carrying her unconscious neighbor, and now wants to talk? I try to appear as unthreatening as possible, and try for a weak smile. It doesn't seem to help much. Sylvana's body is tense and her lauvan more so. I sigh.

"I'm sorry for bursting in like this. I need your help. Anna needs your help. Am I wrong in thinking you and Anna used to be friends?"

Sylvana lets out an explosive sigh.

"Yeah, we've been friends forever. We grew up together. It's just recently that..." She stops.

"Yeah. About that. I need you to tell me everything you know about those necklaces you and Anna were given."

As I expect, Sylvana's face blanches.

"What—how do you know about those?" She searches my face. "What did Anna say?"

"Look, I don't have much time. Just know that Anna is in deep, over her head, and I might be able to help. If you tell me what you know."

Sylvana worries her lower lip for a minute, and then

132

words burst out of her like water from a breached dam.

"We got them from my aunt when we were visiting her in Vancouver. Aunty Bethany was all excited, she'd met this guy who was really skilled in the divining arts. This was before we opened the shop, but Aunty Bethany knew it was in the works, she was helping us buy inventory and all that. The guy, this divination guru, he came into her shop one day and chatted with her, then gave her a necklace to try."

"Why did he do that?"

"He told her something about wanting to share the knowledge—that the more people who could see into a person's heart, the better the world would be. He just sounded like he wanted to spread his wisdom. I guess we should have known better, but the community is very tight-knit, very friendly, and I just didn't expect anything. Anna knew better."

"What did Anna know?"

"That there would be a price. 'You don't get something for nothing, Jackie-bird,' that's what Anna said, and she was right. After Aunty Bethany tried out the necklace—I think she read a lady's tea leaves, and she said the images practically leapt out of the teacup, with the meaning so obvious—she called me right away, she was so excited. We were visiting when the man came back and he offered us two more—she'd told him about us, I guess—and we took them. And yeah, they are amazing. I can really *see*, truly get visions of people's hearts, and actually talk to the spirits that underlie everything. It's beyond amazing."

She looks wistful for a moment. "But then the man came back. We were visiting my aunt, like I said, and he turned up in the shop and asked us if we could help him. There would be great power, rewards far beyond what he had already given us, if we helped him with something. He didn't specify

133

what it was, but as soon as he started talking I got an overwhelming sense of darkness. I was wearing the necklace at the time, you see. I must have been sensing his true intentions, his true purpose. And whatever he wanted us to do, I'm sure it wasn't good.

"After the man left, I found out that Aunty Bethany felt the same, and she and I agreed that we weren't going to have anything to do with the man anymore. Anna, though, you should have seen her eyes light up when he started talking about giving us powers we could only dream about. She wanted it. She wanted it bad enough that the dark aura didn't even faze her. We had the biggest fight that night. I tried to convince her that it wasn't worth getting tangled up in that darkness, and she kept saying that it wasn't right to accept gifts and not give back. She left the next morning on the first bus, and we haven't spoken since."

Silence falls in the little apartment. A bird starts to sing outside and the sun's rays creep in the window.

"Do you know who the man was?"

"He called himself Drew. I never got a last name. He was probably mid-thirties, light brown hair, shortish. That's all I know, I'm sorry."

"It doesn't really matter right now. But thanks." I blow air out through pursed lips reflectively. "I guess that explains why these necklaces keep cropping up. But not how to fix this."

"How do you think you can help?" Sylvana looks at me with a hint of defiance in her eyes. She spilled out her story, and I'm still the dark stranger trespassing on her domain. "Who are you?"

I smile wryly. I don't think this is the time or place or person to get into the finer details of the answer to that question.

"I'm just someone trying to help. Anna's in trouble. She's delving into dark—energies—she can't control, that are tearing her apart and she doesn't even know."

Sylvana presses a hand to her mouth. I debate quickly in my mind what to say next.

"What if I told you that there are centers of power in the world, places where the Earth's energies coalesce? And that Mt. Linnigan is one of them?"

Sylvana nods before I finish speaking.

"I'd tell you that you're absolutely right. I've learned about the energies of the world before—that's common knowledge in the spiritual seekers community—but when I came home wearing the necklace for the first time, I *felt* it. I felt the power of Mt. Linnigan. My necklace practically hums when I'm close to the mountain."

"Good. That makes things easier." I gaze at Sylvana for a moment before saying, "The eruption. It's not due to geology. Anna is playing with fire, and she's going to burn herself and everyone else in this town if we don't do something."

"No," Sylvana whispers. She looks to Anna, still unconscious on the couch. "Oh, Anna, what did you do?"

"I don't know what she thinks she's doing, but that volcano will blow if she completes her task." I stand up. "Can I ask you to keep Anna here, take care of her, distract her if she wakes up? There are some things I need to do today to fix this."

"Of course." Sylvana looks confused. "But what can you do?"

I smile.

"I have a few tricks up my sleeve. Don't worry, we can make things right. I just need your help." I move to stand beside Anna, and bend down to unhook the necklace from beneath her auburn curls. The orange lauvan of the amulet start to twist through my own immediately. I hold it up to have a closer look.

"Ow!" I drop the necklace on the carpet, a sharp pain making my fingers sizzle as if held in a flame for too long. I shake my hand, glaring at the pile of lauvan now twisting slowly on the floor. I've never had a reaction like that from touching an object of power before.

"What happened?" Sylvana stares at me, at the necklace, then back to me.

"Damn amulet—never mind. Just—can you hold onto this for me and keep it away from Anna? I think it's a key piece in her dealings with the volcano, so let's make sure she doesn't have it." I nudge the amulet toward her with my foot, trying to minimize contact. The spirits must have a very close connection to the necklace, too close for them to tolerate my touch. I suppose I should be grateful I wasn't flung across Sylvana's living room. These ridiculous necklaces are becoming very tiresome.

Sylvana nods silently and picks up the necklace with finger and thumb. When nothing happens, she gives a barely audible sigh of relief and puts it on top of her bookshelf, out of sight. I rub my hands over my eyes. "Could I bother you for some water before I go?"

"Of course." Sylvana turns and rummages through a cupboard in the kitchen.

I swiftly move to kneel beside Anna on the floor. I don't know how long she'll be out, but her unconscious state is so convenient that I think I'll help extend it a little longer. I grasp a few of her lauvan and twist them together. That should keep her asleep for a few hours, at least. Hopefully it will be long enough to do what I need to do. When I finish, I gently stroke the hair off her forehead.

"Sleep, Anna," I whisper. "And stop making life so difficult for me."

I turn to get up. Sylvana holds a glass of water in her hand, an expression of shock and wonder on her face.

"What did you do?"

I don't know what she thought she saw, but I decide to ignore her words. I move to her side and take the water.

"Thanks." I drain it and put the glass on the table. "Please, just keep Anna safe, and keep her here. I'll do everything I can to make this right." I leave Sylvana standing in the kitchen, the sunrise bathing her in an orange glow of fire.

CHAPTER XVI

I let myself into Anna's apartment with the keys that I haven't yet returned. It's not as if Anna will need them in the next few hours. I, on the other hand, need a quiet place to make an important phone call.

I settle onto the couch and put my feet up on the table. Might as well get comfortable—I'm calling a rambler.

I find the number in my contacts and press "send." After three rings, a woman's voice answers in Spanish.

"Happy Valleys Care Home, Rosa speaking."

I answer in my rusty but serviceable Spanish. It's been a few decades since I've used it with any regularity, but I have a flair for languages and a long memory.

"Hello. May I speak with Braulio Fernandez? You can tell him it's Merlo Nuanez."

"I'll see if he's up already. One moment, please."

He'll be up. I remember him lamenting bitterly in the sixties when his sleep changed, from the up-all-night, sleep-all-day pattern of his youth to the respectable schedule of middle age. Idly, I look down to my center, where my chocolate brown lauvan twist together with Braulio's terra cotta-colored ones. The resultant rope drifts south through the apartment wall. It's a solid rope—we've been friends for a long time.

The phone clicks.

"Merlo, you old dog," Braulio says in English, his raspy voice filled with warmth. "You haven't frozen yet up in the Arctic?"

"Braulio," I say, my smile wide. "You've never understood. When the winter is cold, the girls need help warming up."

Braulio guffaws.

"Always the same. Do you remember that time on the beach near Puntarenas, with those two sisters?"

"What, when you tried to body surf to show off and almost drowned? When I pulled you out of the water like a gasping fish?"

"Yes, and the younger sister nursed me back to life. Lots of life." Braulio laughs. "Those were good times." There's a quiet pause before he adds, "But the ladies here outnumber the men ten to one, so it's not all bad."

I laugh.

"Rascal to the end. What is it now, ninety-five?"

"Ninety-six," Braulio corrects me, a trace of his old youthful cockiness in his voice. "I'm going for one of those records. The beer one, you know?"

"What, a Guinness world record for oldest man?"

"That's the one. I'll win, no problem."

"Cocky bastard." Braulio is in good health, or as good as can be expected at ninety-six. I can envision him flipping the bird at time and marching on for another ten years. "You'll probably do it, too." I switch the topic to the reason I called. "Braulio, I need your advice."

"Of course you do," he replies promptly. He's amazing—still sharp as a tack, and as arrogant as ever. I find myself missing forties-era Central America. We were such a good team.

"Well, I hate to admit this, even once, but—you were right."

"Of course I was," he replies. A pause, and then, "About what?"

"About the spirit world. It exists. I saw them."

"Ha!" If Braulio's legs could still carry him, I have no doubt he'd be jumping around in glee. "Ha! I've been telling you that for years!"

"Yeah, yeah, rub it in."

I called Braulio, not only because he's one of the few people alive who actually knows who I am, the whole story. I also called him because he's spent the last fifty years collecting knowledge, legends, traditions, and hearsay about the spirit world, from all different cultures and times. He says he was inspired by me and my powers. I've helped him out from time to time in his more far-flung pursuits, but I made it clear that I didn't think it existed. He always persevered, doggedly, stubbornly, with the complete conviction that he was right.

And now it seems he was.

"I'm never going to live this down, am I?"

"No," Braulio says. "This is a beautiful moment that I will never forget. You were wrong, *anciano*, and I was right."

"If you're quite finished gloating, I need to ask you something. There's a woman here—"

"Isn't there always?"

"Just listen. This woman, Anna, she has an amulet that somehow lets her communicate with the spirit world."

"What does it look like? The amulet, I mean?" Braulio's voice is eager.

"I don't know. It was covered in orange lauvan."

"Oh Merlo, you're useless."

"Anyway," I say, ignoring Braulio's comment. "Anna has, for some unknown reason, told renegade spirits to tangle and sicken the lauvan around a center here. The thing is, that center is now an active volcano because of their meddling. If I don't figure out how to untangle the lauvan and heal their sickness, the volcano will erupt and people may die."

"Hmm." Braulio's tone is contemplative. I was hoping he would attack the problem with a little more urgency. "Where

140

did this Anna get an amulet of power like that? How was it formed?"

"I don't know." I tap my fingers on the couch arm, willing myself into patience. Braulio is an old man, after all, and things never seem to happen at any great speed with the elderly. I can sympathize, but I can't relate. I'll never experience that phase of life. I drum my fingers, waiting for Braulio to think, and reflect on the upsides of immortality.

"You know," Braulio says. "What if you tried grounding the lauvan with a relic, or an object of power? Something elemental, that the spirits would recognize. I wonder—if these are renegade spirits as you say, and if my research is correct—as of course it is—then they may be of a certain elemental presence."

"Meaning?"

"The spirits are probably one of the four elements. Try something representing earth or fire, since one of those two is likely affecting the volcano. I would guess fire, given the orange lauvan, but find an object of power that will cover both, just to be certain."

"Huh." I'm thinking hard, trying to get my head around all this new information that is changing my worldview. "So I 'ground' the lauvan, somehow—"

"That's your department."

"True. And I use a fire or earth object—dammit, I wish I weren't so far from home, I have the perfect relic on my bookshelf—then what happens?"

"Then the presumably excess earth or fire energy that is making the lauvan sick will diffuse out into the Earth through the object. The lauvan should untangle and the pressure release."

"That's brilliant."

"I know." Braulio sounds pleased with himself. There's a

pause while I think through the implications of the plan. Braulio is obviously considering a different line of thought.

"Have you told anyone else lately?"

"About what, the volcano?"

"No, about you."

I'm silent. Braulio continues.

"You haven't told anyone since we met Josie." A Spanish "j" softens the pet name he gave Josephine. "And now she's gone, bless her soul, and I won't be around forever."

"I thought you were going to beat the records," I say, trying to inject a lighter note to the conversation, but Braulio is undeterred.

"Yes, of course I am, but after that—you need to let someone else in, Merlo my friend. I know you. You need someone you can be yourself with. Otherwise, you get too moody. That's no good, and you know it." He pauses, as if waiting for an answer. When I don't respond, he says, "Do you hear me, Merlo? You won't let yourself get wrapped up in your own head?"

"Advice duly noted," I say, but I hear him. He knows me too well for me to not pay heed to his words. But right now I have more important things to deal with—Mt. Linnigan, for example. Before I can sign off, Braulio speaks again.

"This woman—Anna—is she a looker?"

"Oh, yes," I say without thinking, and then wince.

"You slept with her, didn't you? You sly dog. You never learn, do you?"

"I guess not."

"You stay away from her, *anciano*. You had your fun, and now be done. You need to find yourself another Josie."

My jaw clenches. It's time to end this conversation.

"Thanks for your advice, old friend. You're the best, as usual."

"As usual," he agrees. "Will you call me when you solve the puzzle?"

"Of course. And clear your schedule for the end of June— I'm coming to visit."

After we say our goodbyes, I hang up and stride to the door. I open it, turn left, and knock on 103. Sylvana answers it, now dressed in an oversized sweater and jeans.

"One more favor? I need to buy something from your shop."

Sylvana looks so confused and wary that I almost feel sorry for her, but I don't have the time or inclination to answer all her questions.

"What about Anna?"

"She'll sleep for a few hours yet. She'll be fine," I reassure her.

Sylvana just looks at me, shaking her head in bewilderment.

***

We're both quiet on the walk to the shop. I get the sense that Sylvana has so many questions that she doesn't know where to begin asking them. I'm okay with that, because I'm not sure what to tell her.

The deadbolt slides open with a loud clunk in the still morning air when Sylvana opens the door to her shop. The low angle of the sun slants in perfectly through the front windows, filtered only slightly by the colored scarves.

"What are you looking for?" Sylvana asks. She steps aside to allow me to pass into the shop, and jingles the keys in her hand nervously.

I step past her and pace around the room to examine its wares at each display. There are a lot of crystals which would easily work for the earth portion, but I need fire as well.

"I'm looking for an object that embodies or symbolizes both the power of earth and that of fire." I hold a crystal closer to my face to study it. It's not what I want and I place it back on its stand. "I need something of great spiritual value that you and others prize highly."

"Umm…" Sylvana thinks for a moment, then walks over to a display near the register. There are five objects carefully laid out on a tablecloth of crushed black velvet. Three of them are so thickly covered in lauvan that I can't even see their physical shape. Sylvana looks at me questioningly. "What about these?"

"Yes." I walk swiftly to the table and run my fingers over the nearest object. The vibration of a thousand lauvan hums on my skin and rainbow hues swirl over the surface of the crystal. I immediately dismiss the two I can see—agate and quartz, neither of which symbolize fire—and focus on the other three.

"What's this one?" I ask, pointing at the rightmost object.

"It's a rare raspberry-red bixbite," Sylvana says, a reverent hush to her words. "Very unusual, and used with great effect to recover from chronic illnesses."

Hmm. Not very fiery. I point at the middle object.

"And this one?"

She frowns at me.

"Surely you can recognize an amethyst when you see one? This one in particular is renowned for its spiritual cleansing properties."

I consider Sylvana for a moment. She looks uncomfortable with the scrutiny.

"I can see—" How can I put it so Sylvana will best understand? I continue carefully. "I see the energies around an object of power. It's an ability I was born with. And

144

sometimes when the energies are strong, I can't see past them to the object beneath."

Sylvana stares at me open-mouthed, an awestruck glint in her eyes.

"For real? That's incredible. That must be why I had such a strange reaction when I read your aura." She frowns as if struck by an unwelcome thought. "Does Anna know?"

"God, no. I don't go around telling everyone I meet."

"Well, I'm honored. What a tremendous gift you have."

"Yeah, well." I gesture at the table. "Sometimes it makes life difficult." I point at the leftmost object. "What about that one?"

"That's a fire opal. I wish you could see it—it's quite spectacular in the light." Sylvana picks up the opal reverentially and holds it up to the sun's rays. The lauvan glitter with all the colors of the spectrum. I sigh with relief.

"Yes. It's perfect." Stone of earth, lit with fire within, and spiritually valued by the multitudes that have owned it or been in contact with it in the past—if this doesn't ground the errant lauvan, nothing will. "I'll take it. How much do I owe you?"

Sylvana looks indecisive.

"You should just take it. Fix Mt. Linnigan. Save our town." She bites her lip and looks at the opal. It's obviously worth a lot to her, both monetarily and spiritually. I shake my head firmly.

"Don't be ridiculous. It's inventory you paid good money for, and I can afford it. Ring it up."

Sylvana hurries to the counter, trying to hide the relief in her eyes. Once my credit card processes, she hands me the receipt and the opal.

"You can really do this, can't you?" Her wide-set eyes are lit with hope and awe. She's not afraid or unsettled by me, and I now realize why—I'm a validation of her beliefs. She confirms my suspicions when she says, "You did something to Anna's aura, her energies, didn't you? I saw you hovering over her before you left." She smiles and shakes her head. "You're so fortunate."

I raise my eyebrow.

"I don't know if 'fortunate' is the word I would use." I slip the opal into my jeans pocket. "Wish me luck—I hope to have this volcano business in the bag by the end of the day."

"Good luck," Sylvana says, gazing at me with her big, hope-filled eyes. Then she frowns. "Wait, what should I tell Anna?"

"Say—say I found her stumbling into her apartment early this morning, just before she passed out. I had to go, but I asked you to look after her. Neither of us knows what she was up to." I fish out Anna's keys and hand them over to Sylvana. "You'd better put these in her pocket. Sound good?"

Sylvana nods.

"Good luck."

***

I pick up my car from the hotel parking lot. Its doors are open, and I retrieve the keys from their home in the glove compartment. I don't bother locking either this or my apartment, mainly because I never really got into the habit after centuries of not owning a locking door. It drives Jen crazy, but I rarely have an issue with break-ins.

At the trucker gas station on the highway I grab a muffin and gulp down coffee. I'm starving and the muffin hardly makes a dent, but it will have to do. Once my breakfast is down the hatch, I zoom out onto the highway in the direction of the Three Peaks, ready to take on the mountain.

Wisps of mist cling to the steep peaks of the three mountains before me, but quickly burn away with the rising sun. When I drive past the road that leads to the base camp, a van turns onto the main road. Inside are three sleepy-looking figures, obviously some scientists coming off the graveyard shift. I suppose the volcano never sleeps, so neither does the monitoring team. A pang of guilt hits me. I push it back with the justification that if I hadn't slept with Anna and got to know her, I'd still be in the dark as to the cause of Mt. Linnigan's awakening.

I can't lie to myself—I was lucky, not smart. But I can change that now. I can undo the spirits' meddling and stop the eruption.

I drive farther and turn onto an overgrown logging road that is half-hidden by a fallen tree. This is where I pulled out last night with Anna in the backseat. It will take me right to a trailhead, which leads directly to the main trail around the mountain. I could have flown, I suppose, but this back road is so convenient that I might as well use it. I expect today will be a tiring one, and I need to save my strength for dealing with the mountain. The car parked, I hike to the trail and strike out in the direction of the lauvan-cable I worked on yesterday. It's a mere ten-minute walk through the morning forest filled with birdsong. I pat my pocket nervously but the fire opal is still there, an unyielding lump at my hip.

Okay, it's time to wrap this up. I've had just about enough of Mt. Linnigan. I want to stabilize this situation, get out of Wallerton, and start studying everything I can about the spirit world. Maybe I can go see Sylvana's Aunt Bethany and examine this spirit-conduit amulet more closely.

In any event, it's time to end this. When I reach the lauvan-cable, I take off my coat and roll up my sleeves. The air is still too cool for shirtsleeves-only, but I know I'll get warm enough soon. I leave the coat hanging on a nearby branch and get to work.

The cable section I untangled yesterday is half-knotted up again as predicted. I avoid touching the cable, and walk to the edge of the trees where the lauvan fan out to extend across the surface of the mountain. I don't want to alert the presence I felt yesterday to my work here today. I reason that if I stick to touching individual lauvan, the presence will be less likely to notice me. That's the theory, anyway. But even if it does sense me, there's little it can do from a lauvan alone. Yesterday, the presence harnessed the power of the cable to push me away. It won't have nearly the same strength from a lauvan.

Here's hoping. This is all new territory. I'm outside my usual knowledge base, which is a distinctly uncomfortable sensation. I'm not used to it, and I'm not a fan. Braulio and I will have to have a long chat when I visit him in June, so he can teach me what he knows. He'll love that.

I squat and begin to pluck sick lauvan from the sea of glittering strands that surrounds me where the lauvan dissipate from the end of the cable. I keep them bundled in my right hand and select with my left. When my hand fills up, as it does all too quickly—there are so many sick lauvan—I twist one of my own floating lauvan around the bundle to keep it close to me and gathered together. The contact only intensifies the nausea I'm already feeling from handling the lauvan, but it's the easiest way to keep them from drifting away from their bundling.

It's slow, tedious work, and I'm appalled by the sheer number of sick lauvan piling up against my chest. By the time the cable is clean, I've collected eighteen handfuls of the yellowish strands. I swallow hard, try to ignore my roiling stomach, and wrap my arms around the bundle. I stand

148

straight and gently pull the bundle away from the cable. My aim is to separate the sick lauvan from the mountain, in a motion that reminds me of separating a lock of hair from a woman's ponytail. The lauvan ends are not attached to the Earth at the center as they are at their origination points—instead they twist and mingle together en masse—so it's possible to separate the strands. There is some small resistance, but for the most part the lauvan glide through my arms easily during my walk to the west, clockwise around the mountain. I look to my right at the sea of glistening threads and am pleased to see the long yellow lauvan in my area slither toward me and separate themselves from the healthy ones lying on the ground.

I hike along the edge of the trees until I spot the next nearest cable, just over a hundred paces from the first. At the edge of the cable I squat down again and carefully maneuver the lauvan bundle onto my back, out of the way. I pull the nearest sick lauvan toward me. It's time to begin the process all over again.

When I finally have the sick lauvan from the second cable under control, I wrap my left arm around the new bundle and gingerly transfer the one on my back to my right arm. Now I have two bundles and I can connect them.

I really hope this works. I feel the sweat beading on my forehead from a combination of my efforts, nausea, and the beating sun. I also hope no one is watching—this next step would be hard to explain.

I step forward on my clockwise path en route to the next cable. The lauvan bundles slide smoothly through my arms. Three paces from the cable I stop and bend over. My right leg lifts over the bundle in my right arm, and my left leg follows. That done, I twist my body around one entire turn until I'm facing my previous direction.

I look back at the bundles of lauvan behind me. They are now crossed in a humming twist.

Feeling immensely pleased with myself, I take five paces and repeat my climbing turn. I can't imagine what I must look like to a bystander. But as long as this works, I don't care what I look like. My plan for this mountain is to weave together all of the sick lauvan in a circumnavigating ring around Mt. Linnigan, and join the ends to the grounding fire opal. The extra earth or fire energies in the sick lauvan should release back to the Earth through the opal in a harmless way, and hopefully release the tension in the knotted cables. So far, my plan is working. I just need to gather and walk in my peculiar twisting dance around this center. It's going well. Two cables done. There can't be that many more.

CHAPTER XVII

There are fifty-two lauvan-cables connected to Mt. Linnigan.

Fifty-two.

By the time I reach my original cable, I'm shaking with exhaustion and my mouth is desert-dry. The sun has almost set, which is saying something only two months from the summer solstice. I've been at this since daybreak.

"Last one, Merlin. Come on, you can do this." I complete another ungainly turn. "It's only the most important part now. No sweat. Metaphorically speaking, that is." Sweat drips from my face onto the grass below.

The yellow cord of bundled lauvan from the first cable lies neat and tidy along the ground, running away from my feet. I breathe a sigh of relief. It's staying together as I hoped it would. Now I just have to complete the circle and ground the lauvan. I step over the bundle, dragging my cargo with me, and lie down on the ground. The old bundled cord lifts off the ground just enough for me to shimmy underneath with my new bundle in tow. I pull the new lauvan through, and carefully twist it so that it becomes a neat cord. Most of the lauvan finish at the same place, and I am left with a frayed yellow end of the bundle of lauvan in my arms. I encircle this with one of my own lauvan once again, sling the bundle to my back, and pull the fire opal out of my pocket.

The rainbow lauvan of the opal provide such a welcome contrast to the sickly yellow-brown I've been dealing with all day that I simply gaze at the opal for a moment, enjoying the sight.

But I'm too tired to spend much time delaying the end of my efforts, and I quickly scuff the dirt at my feet with the heel of my hiking boot. I want to make a small depression I can bury the opal in, so no one accidentally picks it up and wrecks all my hard work. It will never be hidden from me— I'll be able to see where the lauvan descend into the ground. It's probably best if I don't tell Sylvana what I've done with the fire opal. She might throw a fit if she knew I'd buried it in the dirt.

I kneel down and drop the opal into the small hole I've managed to dig. I reach in with both hands and gently pick apart the lauvan so that a few loose ends sway in the air. The sick lauvan need connection points to attach to. After a few moments, some of the lauvan begin to fumble their way into the dirt, as if reconnecting to the earth where the opal came from. Perfect. Before they all disappear into the earth, I grab the bundle on my back and shove the loose ends into the hole. A few minutes pass until the sick lauvan begin to mingle with the fire opal lauvan. Once every visible end is connected, sometimes twenty yellow to every opal lauvan, I release the bundle from my grasp and untangle it from my own lauvan. The bundle sways and falls to the ground, but its end remains in the depression. I fill in the hole so the fire opal is covered from prying eyes, and stand up.

"That's it," I say out loud. "I did it. They're all grounded."

I look up at Mt. Linnigan. All afternoon I've been working with regular tremors shaking the ground beneath my feet and the ominous cloud of steam an ever-present fixture in the sky. But now the steam has changed from a constant pillar to an ephemeral cloud that floats away from the peak, not to be replenished. The ground is still. The mountain slumbers once again.

I throw back my head and my arms come up in celebration.

"Yes! Woo-hoo!" I yell incoherently in my delight. I

finally did it. After false starts and dead ends and too many distractions, I finally solved this puzzle. I won. The unknown spirits and the people behind Anna's actions won't get the destruction they clearly pine for.

I hardly feel my exhaustion and aches through my elation. I start to run, gathering up the necessary lauvan, and when I leap off a small outcrop I yank hard to transform. A flight is just what I need. I shriek to release my euphoria, circling an updraft to soar high above the troublesome center of Mt. Linnigan. But not so troublesome that I can't deal with it.

***

I keep my flight short and land beside my car within a few minutes. Beneath my jubilation my exhaustion threatens—it's best if I don't delay my return to Earth. I don't want to drop out of the air just because there is no energy left to keep my falcon-form.

As I roll into town, I look at the vista of Wallerton with a fondness I didn't feel this morning—its glinting windows in the setting sun, its cars zooming along the highway, its fast-food strip with cheerful neon lights—I gaze at it all with a proprietary air and find it pleasing. On the main street a pizza shop greets my eyes, a mom-and-pop joint so common in these small towns. My stomach suddenly roars, a reminder that I've only eaten that one bland muffin after the sun rose. I park in the adjacent parking lot and pull out my phone.

It rings twice before Jen picks up.

"Merry!"

"Hey, Jen. You eaten yet? I can bring pizza to the hotel."

"You're an angel. I'm in room 215. Come by sooner rather than later. And don't forget the pineapple."

"Yes, ma'am."

I hang up and approach the pizza shop with light steps and a lighter heart. I fixed the volcano, I'm heading home tomorrow, and I'm staying away from distracting, disturbing, alluring Anna Green tonight and instead sharing a meal with Jen.

An electronic buzzer sounds when I open the door, and I'm hit by a waft of warm, spiced tomato breeze. I breathe in deeply and sigh in contentment. It was a glorious day for the cuisine of the world when Hernán Cortés stepped off his ship in 1521 carrying the first tomato plants to Europe.

I place my order—screw it, I'm getting two pizzas, I'm starving—and lean against the wall to wait. My eyes wander vaguely until they come to rest on a television screen flickering in the corner. It's tuned to a local news channel. With a start, I realize that they're reporting on Mt. Linnigan. The man I spoke with yesterday, the scientist from the tent, is speaking to the reporter. He looks tired and confused.

"We've had absolutely no activity over the past hour, which is unprecedented since we started monitoring the mountain."

"So has Mt. Linnigan finally fallen asleep again? Are we safe in our beds?" the reporter asks.

"It's far too early to be making any claims, but if these trends hold it would be an excellent thing."

Indeed, Dr. Pessimist. It would be an excellent state of affairs indeed.

I stand against the wall smiling foolishly at nothing in particular until my order is ready.

"Thanks very much," I say to the teenage boy who hands me my two pizza boxes. "You have yourself a great night."

"Thanks?" he replies, looking bewildered but gratified.

On my way to the hotel, I drive by Anna and Sylvana's apartment building. I debate whether to stop, and whose

154

buzzer I should hit if I do. After a moment of indecision, I park the car and walk up to ring buzzer 103. Sylvana answers right away.

"Hello?"

"It's Merry. Can I come in for a sec?"

"Sure." The door clicks. I push through it, and try to be as quiet as possible while passing 102.

Sylvana opens the door before I can get there. Her face is pale and her eyes search my face.

"So? How did it go?" She looks down at my grubby clothes and frowns in confusion. "Umm…"

"Don't worry, I'm not staying," I reassure her. "I just wanted you to know that I wrapped everything up at Mt. Linnigan, and it looks really good."

"I know, I saw it on the news." She covers her mouth with both hands in a nervous gesture before laughing in partial disbelief. "Wow. That was really you?"

"Seems like it." I smile back at her, my jubilation still making me buoyant. "It was a hell of a lot of work but if it really fixed the problem, I don't care." I remember my other reason for visiting. "How was Anna? Did you manage to distract her? I didn't see her at the mountain, so thanks for that."

"Well, I don't know what you did to her, but she slept until noon. When she woke I told her what you said to me. She was really groggy and confused for a while. When she finally woke up for real, she remembered to be angry at me, then only begrudgingly thanked me for looking after her."

I laugh.

"There's gratitude."

"I didn't expect anything better, honestly. She's still pretty sore at me from our fight. Anyway, I tried to tell her she needed to take it easy, and it seemed like she took my advice.

She rolled into her own apartment soon after and I didn't hear movement until about seven o'clock, when the mountain stopped steaming and rumbling. Then she hopped in her car and left, I don't know where. I'm sorry." Sylvana looks contrite.

"That's okay," I say. "Seven is when I finished. I don't think there's much she can do at this point. Everything is tied up pretty well." I turn to open the door and say, "I'd better go. Thanks for all your help today. You were great."

"Thanks for saving Wallerton," she replies, giving me a smile full of hope and admiration. It's been a while since I've let anyone in on the lauvan secret and they've taken it well. It feels nice to be admired.

"Sleep well. May you dream of cool water and fresh breezes, not lava flows."

Sylvana laughs.

"You too, Merry."

My dreams are preordained, so that's not likely. But maybe a happy memory can visit me tonight instead. Although even happy memories are tarnished by the grief of loss.

***

I quickly visit my own room to shower hastily before beating a path down the hall. Jen opens the door before I can knock.

"My savior. Bring those boxes of heaven in here right now." She swings the door wide with a flourish and steps back to allow me to enter. "I'm famished. My first day of work took it out of me."

"Yeah, how was that? Did you ace it like you do everything else?" I hand her the pizza boxes. Jen lifts the lid of the top box and takes a whiff.

"Mmm, lovely. Well, I don't know if I 'aced' it, but everyone seemed to understand everything, even when I had to translate random volcanology terms with my own descriptions. I mean, how am I supposed to translate 'correlation spectrometer?' I had to get him to translate into English first before I attempted Cantonese."

I laugh.

"Some science electives would have come in handy today, wouldn't they?" I sit on the edge of the bed. "Well, this is awkward. Where do you want to eat? I forgot this hotel has a minimalist approach when it comes to furniture."

"Just hop on the bed. We'll see what's on TV later. No sense not being comfortable."

I prop myself up on the headboard with the endless spare pillows hotels love to provide. Jen sits cross-legged on the other side of the bed, and we tuck in with gusto.

We're silent for a while. I'm mindlessly enjoying the flavors on my tongue and the sensation of my stomach slowly filling up. Jen finishes her piece and reaches for more.

"So, what did you get up to today, on your little hooky holiday?"

Holiday, my ass. I worked like a beast all day.

"Hiking again," I say through a mouthful.

"Man, you're fit. Do you remember where you went this time?" Jen tilts her head in my direction.

"Well..." I debate what to tell her and decide on a portion of the truth. "I may have snuck into Three Peaks Provincial Park to see this famous volcano."

"Merry! You didn't," Jen gasps. She smacks my arm. "You idiot. What if it had blown?"

Then I would have constructed the strongest lauvan barrier I could, and hoped for the best. I shrug in a sheepish manner.

"I wanted to see what all the fuss was about. It's pretty amazing to feel the Earth shake beneath your feet. Living on the edge, you know?"

"You'll be a daredevil until it bites you in the ass one day." Jen shakes her head and takes a bite of her forgotten pizza.

"Hey, you're one to talk. You're the one who took a job that went straight to base camp. You didn't even hesitate."

"I was surrounded by people who were monitoring every miniscule burp the mountain gave, with a fast car to whisk me away the minute things went south. Whereas you were traipsing around on foot on the slopes of a volcano. Point to Jen."

I lift my free hand in a sign of defeat and I pop the last of my crust into my mouth, then reach for another slice.

"Hmm, meat lover's or Hawaiian? It's a hard decision. Ha, just kidding. There's no decision."

Jen grabs my arm before I can take a slice of the meat lover's pizza, and flips it over so the pale underside of my forearm is exposed. She touches the small blue leaf tattooed there.

"I've been meaning to ask you forever. You've never told me—what's the story behind these?" She waves her hand at my other arm and its matching leaf when she releases me.

How long do you have, Jen?

"These?" I hold up my crooked arms to expose the tattoos. "They're the result of me not following through with my grand vision. Losing interest partway through."

"What was the vision?"

For an answer I lean over and grab the hotel's notepad and pen from the night table. I have to think for a moment—it's been a long time since I've dredged up memories of my brief

158

schooling with the druids. Quickly I sketch the outline of my oak leaf, then methodically trace out the other leaves, snakes, and knots that mark the different levels of initiation. By the time I draw the full tattoo of a high priest, the notepad is full of a mélange of figures and symbols. I remember seeing a high priest at a ceremony only once—the tattoos covered his entire forearms.

"There." I turn the notepad to Jen and push it over to her. She leans in to study it. "That was the vision."

"That's incredible. And so typically you, Merry. It's like a neo-pagan's fantasy. Have you always been interested in history?"

Neo-paganism, indeed.

"I guess." I look at the drawing thoughtfully. "I went through a phase. I wanted it, but I didn't account for my lack of follow-through and changing interests. It pays to know yourself. Although it worked out okay in the end." I trace an oak leaf with my finger. I would never have become Arthur's tutor without my druid training, minor as it was. And without Arthur—I can't even fathom what my life would be like. As tenuous and ridiculous as waiting for Arthur might seem, it has given me a purpose for my overlong existence thus far. It may be a silly purpose, a hope too faint to bother hoping, but it's mine. It's what I cling to and it's what makes me get out of bed in the morning, most days.

Jen looks at me as if expecting me to explain more. When I don't, she studies the drawing instead.

"I would have started with the snake," she says, twisting the paper to get a better look.

"Yeah, well, the idea was to do it all."

"You could finish it." Jen wraps the paper around my forearm and tilts her head to evaluate.

I smile, but my heart gives a pang for a past that will

never come again. I can never finish the tattoo in earnest, because there are no more druids. Not that I particularly want to, but still. The choice is no longer mine.

"I'm too old now, way past that phase. I'll just keep the leaves as a reminder not to get tattoos without careful consideration—they last forever."

Jen giggles and takes another slice of pizza. She fluffs and arranges the rest of the pillows I'm not using and flops down next to me.

"So, you're not seeing your new friend tonight?" Jen asks, peeking at me slantwise.

I groan.

"No, I'm done with Anna. She's bad news."

"I could have told you that." Jen tsks but softens it with a smile. "You should ask a woman for advice sometimes. We know things."

"Yeah, but usually I don't want the advice until it's too late."

"Ha. That I can believe." She picks at a piece of salami but doesn't eat it. I'm contemplating another slice when she speaks.

"Merry?"

"Hmm?"

"Why have you never—you know—tried to go for me?"

I look over at her sharply. She keeps her eyes on her pizza slice, trying to act causal, but it's disintegrating under her picking fingers. Her golden lauvan are not their usual lively swirls, but have slowed to cling closely to her body as if she's protecting herself, as if my answer matters.

I'm flummoxed. Where is this question coming from? A minute ago everything was easy between us, and now she wants to know why I haven't come on to her?

"Do you want me to?"

"No! No, that's not what I meant." Her lauvan twist in agitation and I can see she's telling the truth. I still don't understand what she's getting at. "No, I want you as a friend. I love what we have. I'm just—I just wondered—why *not* me?" She rubs her upper arm with her free hand in an unconscious gesture of protection from what I might say next.

It finally clicks. Jen thinks I'm not interested in her romantically because I don't find her attractive.

I turn to her fully, taking her mangled pizza slice and placing it in one of the half-empty boxes. I pick up both her hands in mine.

"Jennifer Chan, you listen to me. You are an intensely beautiful, incredibly intelligent, fiery spirit of a woman, and never forget it. I haven't pursued you because our friendship is vastly more important to me than trying for some half-baked hook-up. I love spending time with you, and I think everything is perfect just the way it is." She stares into my eyes for a brief moment, then her eyes crinkle in a smile and her lauvan relax. I shake her hands and release them.

"Thanks, Merry. You always know just what to say." She considers me for a moment, then punches my arm lightly.

"Besides, you deserve better than me." I lean back further into the pillows.

Jen looks shocked.

"Careful, Merry. That reeks of low self-esteem."

I let out a bark of laughter.

"I have an ego the size of a house, Jen. Don't worry about me. I know my demons and low self-esteem is not one of them. But I also know what kind of man I am, and I know there's someone out there who deserves you more than I do. You'll find him one day and then you'll see. And you'll thank me on bended knee for not sweeping you off your feet."

"Oh, and I'd have no say in this 'sweeping,' would I?" Jen's eyes flash, but a hint of a smile plays around her mouth.

"Nope. Very few can resist the magic of Merry Lytton."

"There's that ego I was worried about. I think it might actually be the size of an office building."

"An office building? How boring. I think the Eiffel tower would be a better fit."

Jen kicks my ankle, laughing.

"You would."

My answering chuckle is interrupted by an enormous yawn. Jen clears away the remains of the pizza and grabs the remote.

"I'm zonked. Let's find some terrible made-for-TV movie to vegetate to."

"Sounds like a plan."

CHAPTER XVIII

Dreaming

Arthur droops behind me on the last stretch of trail before home.

"Can't we just change into deer and run there? It'd be so much quicker and easier."

"Come on, lazy boy," I throw back over my shoulder. "We're almost there." Running as deer would be much quicker, but easier? It's been such a busy day. We were up before daybreak to catch the sunrise for direction reckoning, followed by arms practice with Uther's men in the courtyard, then deep into the woods to gather agrimony. I'm far too exhausted to find the strength to transform both of us, but I don't tell Arthur that.

"Keep up," I say. "You know your father doesn't like us to be late for supper."

Arthur trots to catch up to my long strides. He's grown like a weed these past few months, and I think he forgets sometimes that he can step farther than he used to. He's not quite as tall as me yet, but he's well on his way.

My words get him moving at last. Uther is a loving father, but as he ages his tolerance for things out of routine diminishes. Dinner at this time of the year is promptly at sundown.

The last few hundred paces last forever. Arthur is too tired to chat much. When the villa comes into sight across a small valley with its tiny burbling creek grown noisy with the winter melt, I pat him on the back.

"You did well today. Especially at the beehive—your technique for infiltration was very well thought-out."

Arthur smiles bashfully at the praise. It's not often I dole it out, after all. His eyes light up at the memory of the afternoon. I transformed him into a honeybee from a foreign colony and placed him carefully at the entrance of a hive embedded in the empty crevasse of a lightning-struck oak. His task was to make his way into the beehive and then escape unharmed. He had done so by cleverly finding some discarded comb near the entrance of the hive and rubbing his tiny bee body with the honey and wax in order to mask his foreign scents. Once disguised, he simply flew past the guard bees and waddled around the hive, his natural curiosity driving him to explore this new environment. I kept a watch on him by holding onto the lauvan that connect us. If he had ever been in trouble, I would have felt a change in energy. Then it would have been a simple matter of transforming him back into a human. It would have destroyed the hive in the process, of course, but the tree knot was large enough to support Arthur's size and he would have been unharmed, save for a few stings.

"If your father asks you what you learned today, what will you say?" I ask him this question every day in which the lessons include my special talents—which is often. Uther still doesn't know what I can do, and I'm perfectly content to keep him in the dark.

"Today we worked on navigation by the sun, healing techniques while on the march, and strategy when in enemy territory," Arthur recites. He's good at distilling our lessons into their essences, as well as knowing what his father wants to hear. Uther is never keen on the details but likes to know Arthur is progressing.

I reach over to ruffle Arthur's hair. I have to raise my arm quite high these days. He dodges my hand and grins.

As we approach, it becomes apparent that something is going on. Boys run around with reins of horses in their hands and dodge bustling men with swords at their sides who enter the great hall. The dim light makes it hard to identify physical features of the figures from this distance, but their lauvan glow despite the dusk.

"What's going on?" Arthur asks, squinting in an attempt to see better.

I narrow my eyes in thought when I recognize the lauvan of a few of the men in the doorway.

"I think the nobles have gathered. Yes, look, there's Lord Deverell." I point to a huge man wearing a short green cloak who leaps off his horse, his distinctive orange lauvan clearly visible.

"Oh, yes. But why? The Samhain festival isn't for weeks yet." Arthur looks to me in confusion, and his eyes widen. "Do you think there's trouble in the east?" He tightens his lips but can't hide the excitement in his eyes.

I repress a chuckle. Arthur wants desperately to prove himself in battle, even more now that his swordplay has progressed so far. Even today he disarmed the youngest of Uther's soldiers, a young man named Cadoc no more than four years Arthur's elder. Arthur was more astonished than anything by the win, but he graciously helped Cadoc to his feet. It was only later, when Arthur was alone with me, that he gloated about his victory.

"One day you'll get to see a battle firsthand, I have no doubt. The Saxons aren't going anywhere fast, and when they take a break the Angles push forward. We'll be fighting for years. Don't worry—you'll have your day for blood and glory, little squirt."

Arthur glowers at me.

"When are you going to stop calling me that? It's such a child's name."

"When I decide that a child no longer strides beside me." I

raise my eyebrow. "The precise day, well, that's up to you."

Arthur sighs in annoyance but makes no further answer.

By the time we reach the villa, the lords have already entered and the boys with the horses have trotted off to the stables. Arthur eagerly flings the door open and slips inside the great hall. I follow more sedately, but I'm no less interested than Arthur in the reason for the gathering.

A fire roars in the hearth against the chill beginning to seep in through the stone walls from the dusky autumn air. Candles in wooden holders dot the central table where eight men lean over a piece of parchment. These men are the local lords and warriors who make up a portion of the war council, those in charge of defending the region of Gwent from pillaging by Saxons from the east, or bandits from Eire over the sea. The men vary in age, from the son of Lord Deverell who is several years younger than myself, to a few strong but battle-scarred warriors, close comrades of Uther. Uther's white hair and moss-green lauvan are visible at the head of the table.

Arthur hangs back, reluctant to interrupt the men despite his eagerness for news. Uther looks up at the closing door and his head nods in greeting.

"Ah, there you are. Merlin, will you join us? We could use your knowledge of the southern kingdoms. Saxons have landed on the coast of King Marcus' lands and he asks for help, given our alliance."

"Of course," I say, and move to the end of the table. Arthur fidgets behind me.

"Arthur," Uther says. "You come and join us too. It's high time you should be listening to these talks. Soon enough you'll be taking my place on the council, no doubt."

One of the men next to Uther, a short man with arms like haunches of venison and a perfectly bald head that shines in

166

the candlelight, guffaws and slaps Uther on the back.

"Not yet, Uther! You'll be fighting Saxons until you're too old to walk, and then we'll carry you onto the field."

The men laugh and Uther smiles fondly.

"Only if you swing your ridiculous battle-ax beside me, Ector. Somebody has to make the enemy piss their pants in fear."

When the laughter dies down, I notice that Arthur has quietly inserted himself at my side. I nudge him with my elbow. When he looks up at me, I give him a wink. He smiles briefly, looking reassured.

Uther pushes the map in my direction.

"Penn, show Merlin where the Saxons have landed." To me he says, "This is the best map we have, unfortunately. It's rough, but will have to do. King Marcus' messenger here," he nods at a slender young man in a woolen tunic that I hadn't noticed before, "didn't bother to bring us a better one, and he doesn't know the lay of the land well enough to aid us." The messenger flushes and looks defiant but says nothing. His lauvan twist in annoyance.

I pull the parchment toward me, the ragged edges of the skin soft under my fingers. Penn points to a spot on the map near a lake.

"Here's Marcus' base, and here," he points to a promontory on the coastline, "is where the Saxons landed three days ago. The messenger left right away, but at that time he says the Saxons were setting up camp there as if getting ready to raid the surrounding countryside. King Marcus is the defender of these lands and has sworn protection for the people living there. He would deal with the interlopers himself, but his forces are stretched thin by invaders from the east."

"And they are Saxons," Uther says. "They won't be

167

satisfied with raiding that area alone. They will push farther inland, if they haven't already. If we let them gain a foothold, they will cross the Severn before winter, mark my words."

Arthur leans in close to me, studying the map before us. I point at a range of hills on the map, near the landing place.

"See this? There's a line of hills here. And here," I point to a blank space on the other side. "This is swamp land, impassable for an army or even a small group, unless they know the paths. There are villages here, here, and over here." I look at Arthur. "If you were a Saxon looking for towns to pillage, what path would you take?"

Arthur's eyes widen when he realizes I expect him to answer in front of everyone, but he rises to the challenge with only a moment's hesitation. He studies the map briefly before tracing a path from the coast.

"I would follow the swamp on the right, avoiding hill marches when I could. I would attack the villages within sight on my path. When I reached the river here, I would follow it up. Southern towns are often on rivers, and this river looks large." He swallows and looks at me. "King Marcus' base is on the river."

I nod at him and turn to address the group at large.

"Arthur is right. I've traveled those lands a number of times in the past, and last summer stayed in Lord Gethin's villa on the coast, only a couple of miles from where the Saxons landed. There are a few ways the Saxons might go, but the path Arthur described is by far the most likely. If I may suggest a course of action?" Uther nods and I continue. "They'll be moving slowly. Setting up camp, organizing raiding parties, moving inland—it will be a week or more before they come near Marcus' base, which gives us a little time. If we move quickly, we can sweep around the hills here," I push the map to the center of the table and point. The lords all lean in for a closer look. "Then we can catch them on their flank, hopefully without much forewarning."

"What of any scouts they might have?" A chieftain with a scraggly beard and loose, flowing lauvan asks.

"We'll send our own and kill them before they can scurry back to the Saxons," Uther says. "Thank you, Merlin. That was most enlightening. Does anyone have objections to Merlin's plan?" There's a shaking of heads around the table. "Then assemble what men you have here tomorrow, and on the following morning we march south to beat back this plague of Saxons once again."

The nobles mill about for a few minutes longer to say their goodbyes and call for their horses. It will be a dark ride home, but the moon is bright and the sky clear. None live more than an hour's ride from Uther's villa. There will not be many men in this little army when we depart, but they will be tough fighters and will likely prove formidable against a simple raiding party.

Arthur stays quiet at my side while I look over the map, and ruminate on the few months I spent climbing the low-lying hills of the region and swimming along the frigid coast with its stony beaches. I snap out of my contemplation and nudge Arthur with my shoulder.

"Advising the war council now, are we? Why, it's almost like you'll be one of them someday."

Arthur flushes and tries not to smile. Then he looks at me, worried.

"I hope I said the right thing. What if the plan doesn't work?"

"It's exactly what I would have advised. Don't worry. If it weren't a sound plan, your father wouldn't have agreed to it."

Uther joins us then, the last of the lords finally departed. He claps Arthur on the back.

"So, Merlin, it looks like you're teaching something to Arthur after all. We'll make a warrior out of him yet." He gazes fondly at Arthur, who smiles self-consciously under the attention. "Speaking of which, you'll be coming with us, Arthur."

Arthur's face lights up.

"Really? Truly?"

"Don't get too excited," Uther laughs. "You'll be squiring for me. No battles yet for you, my boy." He sighs. "Your time will come soon enough."

Arthur droops a little, but perks up when a thought occurs to him.

"But I'll be near, so I can watch the battle?"

"We'll see. If there is somewhere you can stay out of the way."

I can't help smiling at Arthur's excitement. He has heard battle stories of the invaders all of his life, and much of his education is centered on fighting and war strategy. Every year the Saxons and Angles that have settled in the east push farther and farther west, and even more arrive on the coast to take whatever they can carry, hampered only slightly by our defenses. Arthur wants to change that, and as his father's son he is well-positioned to play a bigger role in the defenses if he so wishes.

But first, he has to earn his way, and that includes squiring for his father. As a squire, he will take care of Uther's armor and weapons, feed and saddle his horse, and prepare Uther for battle. It's an important role, but for a boy itching to bloody his sword it is a weak substitute for the real thing.

"The Saxons that landed, do you know their tribe?" I ask Uther.

"No one has spoken to them, but they bear the mark of a yellow spear on their shields. I don't care who they are—if

170

they invade our lands, they deserve our wrath."

I suck in my breath. I know that sign.

"The yellow spear is the mark of Aldwulf's tribe. I spent last summer on the mainland and passed through his lands." I did more than that—I played my harp for one of Aldwulf's men for a month in exchange for my supper. Uther doesn't need to know that, though. My wanderings take me many places, and that's my business. I bear no allegiance to any lord or master, only ties of friendship. Many find that hard to understand, especially when it involves Saxons. The man I stayed with, Penda, was solemn, but fair and wise. The rest of Aldwulf's men, as far as I could tell, were grim and pitiless. "Aldwulf leads a terrible people, cruel and hard. He will show your men no mercy, so be warned."

"Wise advice." Uther looks grim.

"Are you looking for another sword?"

"Always." He looks at me with narrowed eyes. "Are you offering?"

"I fight for whoever feeds me." I flash him a smile. "That would be you right now. I'm a fierce fighter. You won't regret having me along."

"I would never turn down an able-bodied warrior. Thank you, Merlin."

"It will be my honor, and my pleasure."

Uther moves toward the kitchen. Arthur gazes at me enviously and I push his shoulder.

"Don't look at me like that. Now I'll be able to give you a blow-by-blow account of the battle. You know your father isn't likely to give you that."

Arthur huffs.

"I guess. I could fight, though. I could."

"Ha. Your father isn't going to put his only son into battle until he's sure you can avoid getting killed. Maybe if you disarm me one day, we can petition him."

"Disarm *you*?" Arthur looks at me, dismay written across his face. "How can I ever do that? You cheat."

I shake my head.

"Arthur, what do I always say? There's no cheating on the battlefield—everything is fair game. In battle, winning means you live, so you do whatever you can to survive. The other man is doing exactly the same thing. Fair play will only get you killed." I grin. "Besides, if you can beat me, you can beat anyone."

***

We depart for the south two mornings later in a noisy caravan of shouting men and huffing horses, and ride for two solid days. It's been a while since I've been on horseback for this long at a time, and I'm not sorry to see the familiar hills of the south coast region when they appear on the horizon. The outriders find only one scout, and dispose of him quickly after they discover the Saxon camp's whereabouts. They've progressed just as Arthur predicted. We make camp and prepare for battle in the morning.

The next sunrise, Arthur wakes me where I sleep, rolled in a blanket in front of the dead fire. The camp stirs, and men begin to rustle armor and sharpen weapons. Boys run around with saddles and swords.

"Here." Arthur hands me some dried meat and hard bread. "Breakfast."

"Mmm. Thanks." I take the food and sit up, yawning until my jaw cracks. "Shouldn't you be helping your father get dressed?"

"I'm going now. I left your sword and a shield behind you."

172

"You're taking your squiring duties seriously." I nod in approval. "But I won't need the shield."

"What do you mean? You use one in practice."

"That's because it's good for you to practice against a shielded opponent. But in battle, I never use one."

"Isn't that foolish? How do you defend yourself?"

"The best defense is a good offense." I grin at him and wiggle my fingers. "I need my hand free."

Arthur stares at me and then laughs.

"You are such a cheater."

"Tell me that when I come back alive with the Saxons beat. Then we'll see what you have to say about my so-called cheating."

***

The battle is swift and furious. We thunder down a grassy hill on our horses to the camp, where our war cries alert the unaware Saxons to our presence. The surprise attack doesn't faze them for long and they range out to meet us. The shrieking clash of metal on metal mingles with the shouts and grunts of men and the screams of horses.

I leap off my horse at the earliest opportunity and send it flying back up the hill with a slap on the rump using the flat of my sword. I don't have hands enough to fight and ride as well, and the horse's lauvan only get in the way. I'm an anomaly among the horsed warriors I arrived with, who slice powerful sword-blows from atop their mounts at the foot-bound Saxons. I'm not concerned. On the ground I'm sure-footed and ready to meet my enemies. It doesn't take long for one to find me. A huge Saxon with a tremendous frizzy beard and battle-madness in his eyes rushes toward me and hefts a massive spear in both hands. I raise my sword in one hand to greet him. It's much smaller and lighter than the swords of Uther and his compatriots. I favor a *spatha*, similar to swords used by the Roman legions before they left our shores. It's meant to be wielded in one hand only, which gives me much less power, but the metal is strong and it thrusts and cuts efficiently. And I have a weapon that most others don't.

With my free hand, as the mighty spear thrusts toward my unshielded chest, I grasp the flailing lauvan of the warrior before me and pull hard. I'm not concerned with accuracy here—speed and force are much more important.

The warrior stumbles over nothing and his spear skims past my left arm a scant finger-span away, stabbing ineffectually at the ground. I'm ready for my opening and slice his arm cleanly. The big man roars and swings wildly at my legs with his overbalanced spear tip. I parry the weak blow with a shout and yank at another handful of his lauvan. The man twists as if given a blow to his side and gasps. It's my turn again, and I thrust my blade into his ribs. The sharpness of my sword gives me only momentary resistance against his ribcage before slicing and crushing straight into his chest. The man screams and falls on his backside, writhing away from my blade. I twist it with a practiced motion. The man screams again and slumps backward. Blood gushes from of the wound when I jerk the blade out of his body. My heart pounds in my chest with fierce vitality and I release a wordless yell of triumph.

My shout is hardly noticed above the clash and din of battle. Thirty paces to my left, Uther defeats his opponent handily, and I turn to find another Saxon to conquer. Uther can manage on his own. I expect Arthur will have his father come home to fight another day.

I'm ready for my next opponent. My teeth are bared and my breath comes quickly. I'm tense and on my toes, looking for an opening. I wasn't boasting when I told Uther that I'm a good fighter. Some skill with the sword, matched with exposure to different techniques in my travels and my secret weapon of lauvan manipulation, make me difficult to beat. Battles—and I have seen a few by now—give me a chance to use my skills in a way that is urgent and necessary and powerful and liberating all at once. I was built for this.

I cut down an opponent charging at me from the fray, dodge an errant spear, and turn to face another Saxon. This one has ripped off his helm and his dark blond hair whips its length around his face, giving me the impression that it is tangling with his light-brown lauvan. He is dressed in a typical Saxon leather jerkin and short mail shirt, his body slighter than his compatriots. Blue eyes meet mine.

I freeze. It's Penda, the man who took me in last summer. I played my harp for him and his family during their midsummer festival. I played tafl with him in the long sunlit evenings, teased his wife about her baking, taught his son how to skip stones in the river. The rest of his people may be ruthless, but he showed me only kindness. In the fraction of a second that I have while I stare at him, I wonder what drove him and his people to pillage our shores. I knew times were tough over on the mainland—Sighard's tribe was pressuring them to pay tributes of grain and meat that they didn't have— but I didn't know it was bad enough to try their luck over here.

Indecision plays over Penda's face, just as I imagine it does over mine. The noise of battle doesn't allow us to speak. I don't know what I would have said, even if I could. I can't kill him. I could—if we fought I would win, I know that. Arthur calls it cheating—I call it survival. But I can't repay trust and friendship with a sword in the gut.

"Go," I shout in the Saxon tongue. He can't hear me, but

175

he sees my lips form the word. I lower my sword tip and step to the side, jerking my head. He looks at me for a moment more, his face unreadable. Then he nods and charges to the left, into the fray and out of my sight. I wonder who I've doomed to die now that I've let Penda live.

***

It's not long before Uther and the lords push the little Saxon horde into a run to the south. We give chase on our horses, harrying the survivors and herding them toward their camp. They have no extra men, no reinforcements from the camp, and we stop a few hundred paces away to watch the Saxons hurriedly pack gear and drag it to their longboats.

Uther rides up to me.

"Merlin, you can speak the Saxon tongue, can't you?"

"Yes," I say. I look at him curiously. "Why?"

"Tell them that they must never return, that they will never be welcome here. That they must leave us alone or die."

I nod and ride toward the beach. The crashing surf is loud, but I raise my voice to bellow Uther's message. The Saxons stare at me with bitter eyes but say nothing. Penda is on the second boat, frustration flooding his face.

I wait until they push off from the beach, put their oars in the water, and pull out from land. I ride back to Uther, and his men give a great cheer. I look back at the Saxon ships whose sails sprout from the masts. Their billowing tan fabric catches the wind and bellies out to pull the Saxons away from our shores.

Uther claps me on the back when I approach him.

"Thank you for fighting by my side, Merlin. It was a good battle, a successful battle. King Marcus will reward us richly,

I have no doubt."

The cheering and Uther's commendation warm me from the freeze of my heart at the fear and bitterness of the Saxons and of Penda. We won, after all, against an enemy that was killing innocent farmers and stealing their crops and goods. I smile broadly at Uther.

"I fight for the joy of battle, but I'll never say no to a reward."

Uther laughs heartily and we turn to head back to camp.

***

Arthur and the other squires run to us when we come out from the trees along the path from the battleground.

"Well?" he says to his father, panting, his eyes bright and high color on his cheeks. "You won?"

"We did indeed." Uther reaches down to ruffle Arthur's hair. "It was a rout. The Saxons ran from us with their tails between their legs like whipped dogs." He smiles, then sighs. "I fear there may be more this year. The winter storms have not yet come, and the Saxons may use that opportunity to pester us once again, this time with greater numbers."

"But you'll beat them off again," Arthur says, confident in the might of his father and his people.

"I hope so, son. I hope so." Uther digs his heels in and trots his horse over to one of the other lords. I consider Arthur's profile.

"So, do you want to hear what really happened?"

"Yes!" He grabs my reins and puts his hand on my horse's cheek. "Tell me everything."

I grin at him.

"Tonight, after supper. I'll give you the full story, every dodge and blow. I promise."

"How many did you fight? How many did you kill?"

"Oh, I lose track of numbers. In the thick of battle, all you can think about is your next move. I didn't stop to take a tally."

Arthur rolls his eyes at me. I flick the ends of my reins at him.

"Cheeky little squirt."

Uther joins us once more. Arthur rubs his shoulder where my reins smacked him.

"Can you please stop calling me 'little squirt?'"

"Why should I do that?"

Arthur wrinkles his nose, thinking.

"I'm almost as tall as you now, so I'm not little anymore. I've seen fourteen summers, so I'm not a child anymore. And father trusts me enough to squire for him."

I nod slowly.

"Okay, no more 'little squirt.'"

Arthur looks taken aback. I've been calling him that for four years now.

"Really? Just like that? I've been asking forever."

"Well, it's true you are older. When I was your age I was living on my own and fending for myself. And you are certainly more responsible. But do you know why I changed my mind?"

Arthur shakes his head.

"It's because you argued your case with calm logic instead of pestering me with a child's whine."

Uther lets out a huge, rolling belly laugh that causes nearby men to turn their heads curiously.

"Well said, Merlin."

Arthur looks thoughtful.

"But you're still a little gangly," I say from my perch on the horse. "You remind me of a growing tree. From now on,

I'll call you 'sapling.'"

Arthur makes an exasperated sound in his throat.

"How do I lose this name?"

"When you're ready, you won't have to ask. It's not something you can cheat."

Uther laughs again. Arthur glowers at me and drops my reins, stalking off to join a gaggle of other young squires walking back to camp.

I grin broadly and Uther chuckles.

"It was a great win today." I roll my tired shoulders. "We really made them run. They'll be rowing back to the mainland faster than the wind can push them."

"Yes, but there will be more. There are always more. And we won't be able to stop them every time."

"Cheer up, Uther. Enjoy the win."

Uther shakes his head.

"You are wise and have traveled much, Merlin, that sometimes I forget you are still a young man. Battles are a young man's sport and I can see you revel in them. But we cannot forget to remain vigilant against the invaders, lest we rest on our laurels for too long and let our enemies sneak up on us unawares. They will be back." He gives me a sad half-smile. "I had hoped that Arthur might someday live in a world where he didn't have to constantly look over his shoulder for the Saxons. Unfortunately, that day seems like a long time coming." He nods to the approaching camp. "Come. Eat supper, rejoice in our win, but don't be fooled that this battle was the end. There will be more, you can be sure of that."

I watch Uther on his horse trot away, frowning. His words fill me with a deep foreboding I can't shake. Unbidden, Penda's face floats in my mind's eye, frustration and fear plain on his face. Whatever is driving the Saxons here is worse than the perils they may face at the end of our swords.

CHAPTER XIX

My arm shakes.

"Merry. Merry, wake up."

I blink blearily awake. The television is yammering quietly in the background about something called the SonicAb 3000. It's the only source of light in the otherwise soot-black room. I look to Jen who has a hand on my arm. Her hair is tousled and she looks sleepy but concerned. I rub my hands over my face and sit up.

"Ugh, I guess I fell asleep. What time is it?"

"Four in the morning," Jen says. She sits up as well. "We both fell asleep. I was just so tired after my stressful day. I don't even know what we were watching when I crashed." She looks at me carefully. "Merry, are you okay?"

"Hmm? Why wouldn't I be?" I yawn hugely, my jaw cracking. "Besides being awake at four in the morning, that is."

"It's just—" Jen bites her lip, as if unsure what to say—or how to say it. "Your sleep was really restless, like you were having a bad dream. And then you started talking." She looks at me fully, her warm brown eyes worried. "And the other night you were crying in your sleep. Are you okay? What's wrong? Is there anything I can do?"

I look away, toward the flashing television. Now a well-muscled man so oiled he's practically dripping is demonstrating the use of the SonicAb 3000. I look down at my hands instead.

"Sleep's overrated," I say, flashing a quick grin at Jen before looking back to my hands. "It's probably just my body telling me I'm getting too much."

Jen heaves a sigh much larger than I expect from such a

slight body.

"Merry, if there's something wrong, you can't keep it cooped up inside. It isn't healthy. And if you don't talk about it with me, that's fine, but you need to talk to somebody. But the problem is, I don't think you've got many other people, do you? You never talk about other friends, and I don't even know if you have any family." Out of the corner of my eye I see her run a hand through her hair. "You know what, Merry? I think I know more about my roommate's boyfriend than I do about you, sometimes. I don't even know your middle name, or where you were born. You're one of my best friends, but honestly, you have to open up. That's what friends are for. I can take whatever you want to dish out."

Be careful what you wish for, Jen. There's more in this world than you can imagine.

I'm still silent, unsure of what to say. Jen fills in the pause.

"I guess I just wanted you to know that you can talk to me, okay? I'm sorry, I didn't mean to make you feel bad. Just know I'm here for you."

It's my turn to sigh. I wish I could tell her about my dream. I would love to talk about my memories with someone. Maybe then they would get out of my head and not haunt me so frequently. But the truth is, I'm afraid. Jen's right—beside Braulio, ninety-six and in a care home in Costa Rica, Jen is the only friend I have. And I'm terrified that I'll lose her if I tell her everything. It's happened before, more often than I like to remember. The knowledge of my life shakes people's worldviews, and some can't handle that. I don't want to push Jen away, but the only way I know how to do that is to keep her at arm's reach. It's a tricky balance, and now I wonder how long it can last.

"Thanks, Jen. I appreciate that." I wait a moment before

standing up. "I should let you get to sleep. We both have a long trip tomorrow." I look back at Jen, whose face is a mixture of disappointment and resignation. I give her a half-smile which she only barely returns. I turn to go.

"Wait, Merry."

"Yeah?"

"When you were talking in your sleep—you spoke very clearly, but I couldn't understand the words. But they sounded so familiar, like a strange hybrid of Welsh and something else I couldn't place. What was it?"

It's getting harder and harder to keep Jen out. I turn and try a laugh.

"It was probably just dream gibberish. Who knows?" I shrug. "Night, Jen."

I leave her frowning after me, lit by the flickering blue of the television.

***

I drift down the corridor in the direction of my hotel room, my mind roiling in a foggy, unkempt way. It's not surprising that I can't keep a straight thought given the time. Jen's warnings of keeping my secrets bottled up echoes Braulio's words too closely. I scowl. It's very easy for them to say, with their shallow experiences of only one lifetime. The problem is, I've seen it all before and I know how spilling my guts often ends. A memory pops unbidden to my mind of Claude, a man I thought was a friend. That is, until I floated his spoon in midair to prove myself. He landed a blow right on my nose, a hard punch strengthened by his fear, and ran out screaming for the *commissaire*. I fixed my nose using my lauvan, grabbed my cloak, and left town immediately.

I approach the door to my room. At the threshold, I realize

how little I want to sleep right now. I don't want to descend into the world of my memories again tonight. I don't want malingering feelings of dread from warnings given by long-dead warriors. I just want to sleep—for just one night I wish I could go to bed and dream about absolutely nothing at all. I was in such a good mood last night. The volcano was dealt with, I spent a relaxing evening with my friend—everything was as it should be. Then my ghosts raised their heads, bringing anxiety to my mind and driving a wedge of distrust between Jen and me.

I squeeze my fists tight, suddenly angry at nothing, at everything. I pace past my room and continue down the hall where I pass a swaying man opening his door. He gives me a drunken glare.

"What are you looking at?" I snarl, and twitch his lauvan. He stumbles, gives me the finger—I don't think he's coherent enough to vocalize—and slams the door shut behind him. I stride to the window at the end of the hall, my bad mood quickly falling from anger to melancholy. I lean against the wall beside the window and sigh deeply. The hours before dawn are always so dark. I hate being awake and alone at this time. It's too quiet—my thoughts roar loudly and my emotions are easily awakened. Normally I'm excellent at keeping my cool, but at this hour I feel raw and exposed. I rub my arms reflexively even though the hotel is well-heated. I fight a sudden irrational impulse to run back down the hall, burst into Jen's room, and tell her everything. Maybe then the dark emptiness of the night wouldn't feel so oppressive.

But what if she can't take the truth, and kicks me out of her life for good? Then I truly would be alone in the dark. A strained friendship is still better than no friendship at all.

I press my forehead against the glass to cool my fevered anxieties.

184

"A new day will come soon enough," I say out loud. "Darkest before the dawn, et cetera."

I'm not very convincing, even to myself.

I stand like this for a few minutes, holding myself together, until I feel it. The ground beneath my feet shivers, like the skin of a horse when a fly lands on it. I raise my head and my heart sinks.

"No. No, this can't be happening."

I look to the sky and the dark silhouettes of the Three Peaks. The leftmost one has a cap of cloud around its top. Another tremor shakes my knees and a picture on the wall behind me thumps on its hanger. The cloud grows bigger.

Mt. Linnigan is awake, and is angrier than ever.

I'm rooted to the spot. How the hell is this happening? I fixed the situation yesterday. I spent all damn day waltzing around the mountain, fighting my nausea to weave the endless sick lauvan together. Everything was calm and controlled yesterday, the mountain wrapped up in a beautiful lauvan package.

I don't even know what to think. My tired brain revs up out of necessity. Perhaps Anna did something? She's not skilled enough with the lauvan to change what I did, or even to sense it. But the spirits she is in contact with—could they have undone my work? I'm suddenly cold with the thought. I know next to nothing about spirits. How powerful are they?

My thoughts are interrupted by the nearby wail of a police siren. Blue and red lights flash down the street, and uniformed men and women leap out of the vehicles and start knocking on front doors. They deliver a message to the bewildered people answering the doors and move quickly to other houses. Lights flicker on one by one in the dwellings of Wallerton. The floor trembles again.

I jolt upright when the hotel's fire alarm begins to bray.

185

Muffled thumps and bangs precede the emergence of the hotel guests in their sleepwear and robes, looking tired and confused.

"Whereza fire?" a teenage boy mumbles as his parents usher him down the stairs.

Wallerton is being evacuated. That means that the scientists at base camp have measured something drastic on their instruments, something that scared them enough to give the order to move the entire population to safety.

I have to get to the mountain. I have to figure out what's happening. And now it seems my timeline for dealing with this explosive disaster is drastically shortened.

I swing myself down the stairs, barging past the family with the teenage boy who is taking its sweet time maneuvering the steps.

"Hey, watch it, buddy!" the father yells at me. I ignore him and barrel into the lobby, past the front desk where the night attendant and manager hastily pull on reflective vests, and out into the night. I look wildly around for a quiet place to transform, but the best I can manage is the space between two cars in the parking lot. It's dark enough—it will have to do.

I stop for a moment, indecision warring with my urgent need to get to the volcano. Jen is still in the hotel, without a car to get her out of this ticking time bomb called Wallerton. I have no idea how long until Mt. Linnigan erupts, but the best chance any of us have is if I get to that volcano and try to mitigate this disaster long enough for everyone to escape. I whip out my phone and text Jen.

Get out as fast as you can. Take my car. Keys are in the glovie as usual. I'll hitch a ride. I need to do something first.

That will have to do. I crouch down and fumble for my lauvan. Eventually, I stop what I'm doing and take a deep

186

breath.

"Calm down, Merlin. Getting yourself in a twist isn't going to help anybody." More methodically, I feel out for the correct lauvan. They're in my fingers in a matter of moments—I've done this a thousand times before. It was only my anxiety getting in the way. I flap out from between the cars. My wingbeats take me farther and higher, but before I float out of hearing, someone on the ground speaks.

"Hey, look. Is that an owl?"

No, you idiot, I think crossly. Does nobody know their birds of prey anymore?

CHAPTER XX

The sun breaks the edge of the horizon between two distant mountains in a fierce display of fiery red. I flap my wings harder. My wish was granted—dawn came quickly this morning. But instead of bringing with it the promise of hope and renewal, all I can see in the near future is death and destruction.

Ahead of me, the mountains glow a brilliant orange. They remind me disturbingly of fire, and lava. I banish the thought from my head and fly faster. My tiny heart, already pumping more rapidly than my human one, strains in my feathered chest. The highway stretches to my right. A line of vehicles glints in the rising sun, a miniature robotic snake far below me. I desperately hope that Jen is in one of them, zooming away from this cursed volcano and back to Vancouver, home, and safety.

From up here, there is an incredible view of the whole coastal range—peaks upon peaks, crests upon crests of mountains, snow-covered rows of teeth in a titanic shark mouth. The Three Peaks are straight ahead, sentinels before the army. And now Mt. Linnigan is not alone with its smoke signals.

Mt. Vickers and Mt. Kullen steam as thickly as Mt. Linnigan does.

The rush of the cold, dew-laden air wakes me up more strongly than coffee, and the familiar feeling of wind passing through my feathers calms me despite the circumstances. There's no point in worrying until I get there—I can't plan until I know what happened.

But I can find out what the scientists know. Banking sharply when this thought hits me, I spiral over to the base camp. It's only a few minutes as the merlin flies, and shortly I flap to a perch on top of the white tent in the parking lot.

If I thought there was a buzz of activity at the base camp the last time I visited, it was nothing to the hubbub today. Everyone is shouting instructions, rushing out of the tent into the parking lot, unceremoniously hauling pieces of sensitive-looking and undoubtedly expensive equipment from inside the tent and loading them into the waiting trucks. Some vehicles are already backing up, and their irritating beeping noises produce an unpleasant disharmony. They narrowly avoid the frantically milling scientists and rangers. Another tremor shakes the ground and a few people scream. The shaking causes the tent to sway on unsteady poles. It catches me off guard and my wings flap vigorously to maintain my balance. I click my beak in annoyance and try to ignore the fresh plumes of steam rising from the three mountains just ahead. My keen falcon hearing picks up on the babble below me. Most of it is shouted instructions, but I sift through the cacophonous jumble of voices until I focus on a male voice speaking in the tent directly below me. I recognize the voice—it's the man I spoke to, Dr. Pessimist from the television. I suppose I should rename him Dr. Realist, and myself Mr. Misguided Optimist.

"There's no way I can tell," he says. There's silence for a few seconds. He must be speaking on a phone. "I told you I can't pred—no, just make sure everyone's out. I've only ever seen readings like this right before an eruption. Wallerton's on the lahar flow path, I've told you that before. It's shaping up to be a plinean, as far as I can tell. Worst of both worlds." A pause, then, "As fast as you can. Look, I have to go. I need to get my people out of here before it's too late. I've left some remote monitoring sensors here—they'll have to do."

The call apparently finished, I wait until I see Dr. Realist leave the tent. While he talked, most of the trucks were loaded and left. Now there's just the one remaining. The scientist swings into the passenger seat and the pickup spins with a spray of gravel as it shoots out of the parking lot.

So, that's it. It's just me and the mountain. If it were as satisfying to sigh heavily in this bird body as it is as a human, I would. Another tremor shakes the empty tent and I use the opportunity to take off toward my lauvan ring—if it's still there.

I aim my wingbeats toward the spot where I buried the fire opal. I have to start somewhere, and it seems as good a place as any. Perhaps the grounding has come undone. Perhaps it's an easy fix that I can shore up quickly. Perhaps I'm still a misguided optimist.

I spiral to height in an updraft and flap toward the fire opal. From this height, so close to the mountain, the glistening blanket of healthy lauvan is clearly visible in the morning light. The peak appears to be free of yellow, which puzzles me. Why all the commotion if it's not caused by sick lauvan? I finally fly close enough to get the lauvan ring in my sights. It's still intact and visible from this distance, but upon closer inspection it's fraying, disintegrating into its individual lauvan components. I flap harder to get to the fire opal. The lauvan ring should be holding—there should be no reason why it's falling apart.

As I near the ground, I let my lauvan resume their usual form and land hard in a stumbling run. The opal is only ten paces away. Instead of a neat lauvan cluster descending into the ground, all I can see are writhing strands of lauvan convulsing in a loose pile of earth. I slide onto my knees, push the twitching lauvan aside, and scrape out loose earth in frantic handfuls.

"Where the hell are you?" I mutter. My mind starts to

process what I'm seeing. Only a small portion of the sick lauvan still enter the ground—most flap aimlessly around me in the air and in the grass. But what puzzles me more is that none of the multicolored lauvan of the fire opal are showing yet, even though I've dug far enough to reach them. The depression should be filled with them by now, wrapping around the sick lauvan and twisting between my digging fingers. The hole is conspicuously empty.

My fingers feel a smooth roundness unlike the jagged rocks naturally in the soil. I brush dirt away and grasp the object between finger and thumb. It's not entirely smooth— my fingers feel an edge where they should only encounter polished roundness. I hold my breath and bring the object up into the light.

The rays of the rising sun hit the opal, passing through milky translucency to reach shards of glittering orange and red which glow like fire deep within the stone. Sylvana was right—it really is beautiful in the sun.

But there are two problems. One, I'm only looking at half an opal—this one is clearly split right down the center to leave behind a jagged edge.

And two, I shouldn't be able to see the fire opal at all.

Where are the opal's lauvan?

CHAPTER XXI

The fire opal is lifeless in my hand. Where a multitude of colorful lauvan should twine around my fingers and brush against my own lauvan with a tingle of connectivity, there is only emptiness. There's nothing but the glowing fire of the opal.

I shiver despite the sun on my face. I didn't know it was possible to strip the lauvan off of a spiritually-valued object like that, not so quickly. Once, in the past, I tried to remove the lauvan from a lover's crucifix out of idle curiosity, but the lauvan clung stubbornly. And it felt wrong, somehow—the lauvan belonged on the crucifix. If an object is forgotten or ceases to be valued, the lauvan will eventually fade and drift away. But the fire opal doesn't have even a single lauvan hugging its surface—it's as clean as a lifeless rock at the bottom of a pit.

The spirits that Anna communicates with must have done this. I severely underestimated their power and reach. Somehow they are manipulating the lauvan to disrupt this center and create a volcano where none should be. I tried to tie up the sick lauvan and ground them, and I have no doubt that it would have worked if it hadn't been tampered with.

But no spirits dug that hole. At least the ones I saw wouldn't have—they were made purely of lauvan, and wouldn't have been able to interact with the physical world. And no human stripped the lauvan off of the fire opal. Even I can't do that—it must have been done by the spirits.

"Anna, are you still getting into trouble?" I say out loud. I feel around for the other piece of the opal. It won't do me any good, not now that it's stripped, but I feel bad leaving it in a hole. I put the useless pieces in the pocket of my jeans. Then

I stand up, decided on my course of action.

There's only one way out that I can see. I need to confront the spirits if I can, and either find out what they want or show them who they're dealing with. I don't let anyone walk all over me, ever.

I stride over to the nearest lauvan-cable. My heart pumps and my breath comes in quick bursts. I'm ready for this confrontation. I've skated around the real reason for Mt. Linnigan's activity for days. I need answers, and I need results. And I'm ready to fight to get them if need be.

But truth be told, I'd rather talk. I want to know more. I want to learn what the spirits are, why they talk to some, why they've never come to me. I want to know what Sylvana heard when the spirits mentioned my father. I want answers to questions that have plagued me for centuries.

Pumped up and ready for action, I halt at the surface of the cable. The sick and healthy lauvan are twisted together yet again. I set my jaw in defiance.

"Ready or not, here I come," I say, just in case the spirits can hear me. I doubt they can, but what do I know? The spirit world didn't exist for me until yesterday. I brace myself and plunge both my hands into the swirling mass of lauvan.

My phone rings. Who the hell is calling me right now? The university can shove it, as far as I'm concerned, and Braulio can wait. Telemarketers can stick it up their—I freeze. What if it's Jen? What if she's in trouble? The car hiccupped once last week—what if it won't start for her?

It's time for some multitasking. I keep my right hand in the cable and try to concentrate on feeling for the presence. My left hand fumbles in my pocket across my body when the phone rings for the second time. It's Jen after all—I'll make the call quick.

"Jen?"

"Merry!" Jen practically shouts my name. Her voice is filled with relief that quickly turns to exasperation, anger, and fear with her next words. "Where the *hell* are you? What could you *possibly* need to do? A *volcano* is about to explode. *Please* tell me you got a ride with Anna and are on the highway."

"Umm—no." I try to keep my mind on my exploratory right hand in the cable, but it makes it difficult to think about what to say to Jen. "I just have to do something first. I'll get away safely, I promise. You're out of town, right?"

"No, I've been trying to call you for the past—argh, Merry, what the hell?" She must have called while I was in my falcon-form. My phone was probably a feather at that point. "*Where are you?*"

There's a slight wavering in my fingertips. I'm distracted—is it the presence? How should I communicate with it? Can I send my questions about the spirit world and its intentions through my lauvan the same way I travel along the cable in my mind's eye?

"At the mountain," I say, then bite my tongue hard. I didn't mean to say that. Dammit. I lose track of the wavering as my mind snaps back to my conversation with Jen.

"*What?*" Jen is speechless for a moment. "How did you get there without your car?"

That's another question I don't want to answer. I feel a surge of tingling in my fingertips.

"What the—"

There's a blow to my lauvan so powerful as to give me physical pain. It throws me back, breaking my connection to the cable and making me drop my phone. I sail through the air.

"Fuck!" I'm so enraged at the unknown presence getting the better of me that I let forth every expletive I can muster

194

on the spot from my large and impressive vocabulary. "*Merde*! *Scheisse, godverdomme*! *Satans også, sıktır*!" I crawl back to my phone. The cable twists innocently in front of me.

"Jen? Are you still there?"

"What the hell just happened? Is the volcano erupting?" Jen sounds terrified.

"No, no, everything's fine," I reassure her as best as I can, although my voice sounds strained and tight even to my ears.

"Everything is not fine. I'm coming to get you. Meet me at the main parking lot. Get yourself straight there, do you hear me?"

"No, Jen, don't—"

"Shut up, Merry. Be there." The phone goes dead.

"Jen!" I yell into the phone, but she's gone. I howl and chuck the phone from me in frustration. It flies away in a shallow arc and I panic—what if she tries to call again? I grab the phone's trailing lauvan and it boomerangs back to me. I snatch it out of midair to dial Jen's number. Maybe I can persuade her not to come, that I have Anna here and we're leaving now, any lie that will prevent her coming to the mountain and risking her life unnecessarily.

"This is Jen. Leave a message at the beep!" Jen's voicemail comes on after four rings. I know exactly what's going on—she's already driving and won't pick up the phone. Jen's a stickler for safety rules and won't touch a phone while she drives. She can't stand it when she's in my car and I drive above the speed limit—so basically she hates it when I drive.

I don't have time to babysit Jen. I can't keep her safe as well as deal with the presence and Mt. Linnigan, teetering on the edge.

But she came for me. An eruption imminent and she's

driving to ground zero just for me, even after I held out on her a few hours ago. I swallow hard, suddenly overwhelmed by gratitude for Jen in my life.

I need to keep her in my life, and the only way to do that at the moment is to keep her alive. I need to ground the lauvan again, at least to give me a few minutes to figure out the presence. I worry the phone in my hands and think frantically. My fingers turn the tiny machine end over end. What can I use to ground the lauvan? I need something of power, something with lauvan, something that has a connection to fire and earth...

I start to pace, back and forth alongside the cable.

"Think, Merlin. Think." Nothing comes. I try Jen's number again but only reach voicemail. Fire and earth, power, lauvan...

My head snaps up. Of course. I don't need something—I need someone. I have lauvan. I'm alive, so I have intrinsic power, far more than an inert object. And I am human, and according to the ancient teachings of the druids—teachings I am starting to think more highly of now—all humans are an amalgam of the four elements of air, water, fire, and earth. I can ground the lauvan with my own body. Maybe then I can fight back against the spirit presence that has the nerve to throw me bodily around the forest.

CHAPTER XXII

I shove my phone back in my pocket and race to the end of the cable, where the lauvan disperse and where my ring around Mt. Linnigan lies. Even more lauvan have unraveled from the ring. It appears as a badly frayed rope lying on the ground. The yellow lauvan writhe as if trying to escape their orderly bonds.

I grit my teeth and start to gather the ragged ends of the ring beside the dug hole where the fire opal used to lie. It's difficult, as the ends twitch wildly and erratically. I snatch at them, leaping to grasp the ones that dance out of reach.

"Come—here," I grunt at a particularly energetic lauvan eluding me. I swear if it were alive and had a mouth, it would be laughing at me. I prepare for the jump that will capture it for sure, but the ground trembles again and I lose my footing. I tumble onto my side and don't break my fall to avoid dropping the handful of lauvan I've already collected. Pain shoots through my arm.

"Argh!" I scream, but there's nothing to vent my frustrations on. The only visible enemy here is the mountain, and I'm already doing everything I can to finish that beast. My jaw sets grimly and I stand again. I ignore with difficulty the shooting pains in my arm. I don't have time or hands enough to fix my own lauvan. I'll just have to add it to the nausea on my list of bodily grievances against this mountain.

I continue to collect lauvan, paying closer attention to the tremors to avoid another fall. They come with frightening repetition, and the clouds above the three mountains continue to grow. The clouds are composed not only of steam now— smoke is starting to billow out of the tops.

By the time I have an armful of lauvan, I'm sweating from

exertion and shaking from nausea. Now I need to ground myself and let the lauvan send their energy through me into the Earth, where it can disperse harmlessly and reduce pressure on the center. I keep the sick lauvan under my left arm and bend down. My own lauvan swirl around my ankles, and I gently tease a few strands away from my body. It's not difficult—over the centuries my lauvan have become looser and cling to my body with less tenacity than is usual. The frayed ends are easy enough to spread out on the ground. They slowly extend to feel their way like blind worms hunting for soft dirt. They will eventually turn back and find their way to my body, so I quickly turn my attention to the sick lauvan in my arms. I comb the raw ends into my chest and wiggle with my fingers to promote untangling and connection with my own lauvan. The nausea grows worse when the yellow lauvan wind around my own. But as they attach more firmly to me, my lauvan on the ground spread out purposefully and sink their ends into the soil. The yellow lauvan freeze momentarily, then relax. The nearby lauvan in the ring begin to weave themselves into a tidy rope once more.

I sigh in relief. It worked. I can act as a grounding. Another tremor shakes the ground, forcing me to bend my knees to absorb the movement. I frown. Grounding these lauvan isn't enough anymore? Yesterday this is all I did, and the volcano became a silent mountain once again. Now, smoke still rises from all three summits, albeit slightly less than before. I look down to check my connections but everything looks good. The sickness must be greater today. The spirits must have been angry at my meddling and ramped up their attack on the center.

I smack my forehead. What am I thinking? How am I supposed to feel out the presence and actually end this if I'm

198

stuck in this spot as a grounding? How can I get to the cable?

My phone rings. Damn, it must be Jen. I'm definitely not going to the parking lot now, not that I planned to before. I answer.

"Jen?"

"Merry, where are you?" Her voice is angry and panicking. She sounds close to tears. "I'm at the parking lot."

"Jen, I can't move right now. I'm not hurt, I just—" I sigh in exasperation, unable to come up with the right words. A thought hits me. Jen might be the key to my dilemma, if I can get her here. "Can you come? I need help."

"Oh, Merry. That's why I'm here."

"Take the Eagle Creek Trail, five minutes max. You'll see me in a clearing on your right." I swallow. Why is she doing this for me? "Thank you, Jen."

There's a slight pause.

"I'll be right there." Jen's voice is quiet and husky. The phone beeps and goes silent.

Now I just have to wait. Wait, and watch the mountains puff smoke disconcertingly. I push air through pursed lips and tap my fingers together, fidgeting. A minute passes. I look down to my chest. Through the mess of yellow lauvan attached to my abdomen, I can just see the brown and gold threads that mark the connection between Jen and me. They run in a straight line to my right and into the trees. I stroke it gently and give it a gentle tug. It quivers between my fingers—Jen's fright and tension clearly vibrate through her lauvan. The pull I gave should help her navigate to me. She won't know why, but she'll be drawn in my direction from the influence of the lauvan.

A crashing sound precedes Jen's arrival a minute later. She bursts out of the forest twenty paces away and runs straight for me, almost bowling me over in a crushing hug. I wobble precariously, but manage to keep my footing and my grounded lauvan secure. I return her hug with equal ferocity and surprise myself by how glad I am to see her.

She pushes away quickly and holds me at arms' length. Her face is a war between confusion, anger, relief, and terror.

"What the hell are you doing out here?" She grabs my forearm and turns to drag me away. "Come on. We've got to get to the car."

I hold my ground and cover her hand with mine.

"Jen, stop."

She turns to me, impatient. Her lauvan are electric and their deep golden strands dance frenetically around her body.

"I need you to do something for me. It's very important, but I don't have time to explain right now."

"What is it?" Jen dances on the spot in her agitation. Thinking quickly, I begin to manipulate the lauvan on her hand where our skin touches. I try to make my movements small so as to not attract her attention. She's too wound up to even listen to me, let alone do what I need her to do. I can calm her down using her own lauvan. It's not manipulation of her emotions, not really. It's as if I'm removing unnecessary stress and fear from her body so she can think clearly and act just as she would normally. I hope it's enough.

"Jen, do you trust me?"

She stops fidgeting immediately, mostly in surprise at my question, although my hand gestures are calming her already. She looks bewildered and her lauvan slow to a gentle swirl.

"Yes, of course."

"Truly? Profoundly and truly? Do you know in your heart that I care deeply about you, and would never do anything to harm you?"

"Merry, what is this about?" Jen whispers. She would look frightened if I hadn't calmed her lauvan already. As it is, she just looks tired and confused.

"Please, just tell me."

She stares at me for another few moments, searching my eyes as if she will find answers there.

"Yes, Merry. I trust you. I know you would never do anything to hurt me."

I take a huge breath and release it in a gush.

"Then please stand in this spot and wait for me to return. There's something I really need to do, and I need your help. I can't explain right now." I tighten my lips, immensely frustrated with my inability to tell Jen what's going on and why it's so important that she stay here. "I promise you the mountain will not erupt before I return."

"How do you know that?"

"Please trust me. There's so much you don't know— please, Jen." My voice is shaky and strained. Jen bites her lips, undecided. Then she nods slowly.

"Okay, Merry. I'll stay here. I trust you." She closes her eyes and draws in a deep breath. "But please hurry."

I grab the lauvan from my abdomen and rip them out of my center, trying not to wince when they tear away from my own. I wrap my arms around Jen wordlessly, taking the opportunity to brush the sick lauvan into the ones on her back. She doesn't return the hug, but leans into me nonetheless.

"Thanks, Jen." I pull back. "For the record, I have one other friend, aside from you, who lives in Costa Rica. I don't talk about my family because they're dead. I was born in Wales, and I don't have a middle name."

She looks confused, then gives me a weak smile.

"Hurry up, Merry."

I bend down to ostensibly tie my shoes, but in reality I pull Jen's lauvan out from her feet. They snake into the

201

ground immediately due to her connection with the lauvan ring. I gather as many healthy lauvan as I can reach and pull them up and over Jen, then manipulate a few of the lauvan in a tricky little rendering. I keep my motions small and unobtrusive. Jen watches me but says nothing. The healthy lauvan barrier will help if an eruption actually occurs—the lauvan will trigger into a hard shell from the excessive trembling of the Earth and the disrupted lauvan attached to the troubled center. It will protect her, hopefully enough. I just need to get back in time, that's all. Or, better yet, stop this volcano from erupting in the first place.

"Okay, stay here, right here on this spot, no matter what happens. I will be back as soon as I can. Nothing will happen to you, I promise."

"Go." Jen says, her voice harsh with repressed emotion. "And then come back."

I turn without another word and run into the woods.

***

I run beside the lauvan-cable through the trees until I'm out of sight of Jen. I don't want her to see me waving my hands in midair like a wild man. I grit my teeth, roll my shoulders once, then thrust my hands into the cable. I close my eyes and let my consciousness travel into the cable.

Immediately I feel the presence. This time, I'm ready for it. Before it can send a pulse of energy my way, I speed down the cable toward it with my mind and along the lauvan ring almost faster than I can think. When I reach the presence, contact is swift and explosive. I get no sense of what the presence is—I only know that it's an obstacle in my way.

The presence was clearly not expecting the attack, and after my hit it disappears from sensing. The lauvan ring is

202

empty. I pull back into my body which trembles with effort and the exhilaration of combat. Not that it was much of a combat, but still, I won. And more importantly, I now know where I can find the presence in the physical world. It's not far, and lies at the cross-section of the lauvan ring and a cable, two cables to the east. How convenient. I turn on my heel and run down the path back toward the parking lot. Somewhere past there, the presence waits.

The parking lot isn't far. I burst out of the trees, panting, and stop short. My car is carefully parked in a nearby spot, as if Jen expected the lot to fill up later that day. But it's not alone. Two more cars join it in its silent vigil of the steaming volcanoes. One I recognize as Anna's red Acura, parked neatly in a delineated space. The last car is an avocado green VW van with rust spots along the rim of the door, parked haphazardly across three spots. A woman with short brown hair and heavy bangles on her wrists slams the door and looks around with a frown.

"Sylvana?" I shout.

Sylvana's head whips around to locate the source of my voice. Her eyes widen when she sees me.

"Merry? What are you doing here?"

I lope toward her, stopping ten paces away. Sylvana has her phone clenched in her right hand as if she plans to make a call.

"Trying to stop this blasted volcano," I pant. "I think I almost have it figured out. But I thought I had it in the bag yesterday, and now look at it." I run my hands through my hair distractedly, glancing up at the mountains. They're smoking even more than when I left Jen minutes ago. The center is getting worse, and even Jen's grounding didn't work for long. I need to ground again if I have a hope of finding and finishing off the presence in time. I turn back to Sylvana.

"What are you doing here? Shouldn't you have left town with the evacuation?"

Sylvana sticks her thumb in her mouth and nibbles at the nail unconsciously.

"I was worried about Anna." She looks up at me with her big eyes full of concern. "She was right behind me in her car during the evacuation, but she veered off toward the park at the turn-off. She was in such a strange mood yesterday. I know you said she's into something bad, and I was supposed to be watching her..." A pause, and she adds, "And I think she took the necklace. Last night sometime. Maybe she snuck in—my living room window doesn't lock properly, and she knows it."

"What?" I stare at Sylvana in dismay. That must be how the volcano started up again—Anna gave access to the physical world to the spirits sometime in the night.

"I would have told you, but I didn't know where to find you. And then I saw Anna drive off to the park—I was worried about her." She looks to me as if for validation.

I sigh. This is no place for Sylvana. Her crystals and incense won't do much good here, and now I have someone else to take care of and worry about as this center falls apart, probably literally. I need to find the presence, now.

A tremor shakes the asphalt under our feet. Sylvana throws out her hands and wobbles in place. Her breathing quickens and her lauvan twitch and tense.

The center won't last long at this rate. I start to calculate how long it would take me to fly to Jen, maybe transform her and Sylvana into mice or something small I can carry as a falcon. Assuming I can avoid eating them in my falcon-form, that is.

"Wait," I say. I need more time, and I think I know how to get it. "Sylvana, can you help me?"

"Of course," she breathes. "What can I do?"

"Come on," I say. I grab her arm and run toward the lauvan ring, dragging her behind me. Her bangles clang together with the motion. A path toward a lookout passes through sparse bushes that ring the parking lot, and exits into a meadow at the foot of Mt. Linnigan. The lauvan ring is directly ahead, just before a tiny creek that meanders to the right and out of sight.

We reach the lauvan ring and I stop abruptly. I use Sylvana's motion to swing her around to face me.

"Okay, I need you to stay here and not move." I gather some of the wispy ends of the frayed lauvan ring, enough to attach to Sylvana for grounding. She watches me, open-mouthed. A small tremor makes me drop a lauvan.

"Dammit." I mutter. I yell into the direction of the mountain, "Just hold on, you great lump of rock!"

"Are you touching the energies?" When I look at Sylvana she gazes at me with longing, oblivious to the volcano belching smoke behind me.

"Yes. To make a long story short, I'm collecting the—energies of the mountain, then I'll attach them to you. You'll act as a conduit to release excess energy back into the Earth. That should relieve some of the pressure, at least give me enough time to track down the person—or other entity—responsible for this mess." I pluck the last lauvan in the vicinity out of the air, and lay it under my arm with the rest. "Does that make sense?"

"Oh, yes," she says. A happy smile blossoms on her face.

"You're okay with this plan? You're okay with standing at the base of a volcano while I go off to stop this?" I'm puzzled by her complaisance, but willing to take it at face value. I don't have time to second-guess her.

"You have an amazing gift, and I trust you'll be able to

use it to save Wallerton."

Wow. That's a lot of faith in some unknown man who waves his fingers in midair. I look into her shining face and realize what I'm looking at. It's not faith in me, it's faith in her beliefs, in the underlying interconnectedness of everything, in powers and energies that she can't see but can still perceive, in things she can't explain but knows are there. She believes—no, knows, in her heart—that I can do what I claim.

I hope she's right.

"Okay, great," I say. My words feel inadequate in the circumstances. "Thank you, Sylvana. Stay right on this spot. I'll be as quick as I can. And I promise nothing will happen to you, okay? I'll come and get you if I can't stop the volcano."

She nods, her thumbnail long since out of her mouth and her face serene. Then she frowns.

"What about Anna?"

"The sooner I stop this eruption, the sooner we can concentrate on finding Anna and getting her out of trouble. But the volcano has to come first. We don't have long."

Without further ado, I press the loose ends of the lauvan into her abdomen. I spread my fingers in a pulsing motion and hover them over her stomach. The strands tease apart to mingle with her own. She tenses slightly.

"Do you feel that?" I ask, curious.

"A little," she says. "Mostly from the necklace."

I nod and bend to plant her ankle lauvan in the ground, then draw a makeshift lauvan cage over her body as I did with Jen.

"Okay, all done. I'll be back for you soon."

"Blessings on you, Merry." She brushes my cheek briefly with a butterfly's touch of her hand.

I give her a crooked smile in return, and turn to run along the lauvan ring.

The presence isn't far. Soon, I will confront it. I will solve this riddle, fix this cursed center, save Jen and Sylvana—and Anna, wherever she is—and get out of this town. I think briefly of the hotel room I haven't yet slept in, and my teeth bare in a mirthless smile. I glance to my left at the Three Peaks. Are their smoke clouds a tiny bit smaller? I hope that's not just my imagination. I hope grounding with Sylvana made a difference and bought me some time.

I pass through a rolling meadow alongside the lauvan ring, and slow my pace to approach the cable. I don't know what I'll be facing. I presume there will be spirits in the cables here, but I know so little. Can they come out of the cables and be lying in wait for me? Is there another person here controlling them, perhaps the writer of the lauvan-note from Anna's apartment?

I climb a small hill through some scrubby bushes toward a low promontory. It looks familiar, and I realize that it is the Michelson Lookout where Anna and I shared a coffee and that intimate lauvan-touching moment two mornings ago. It feels so much longer.

I climb up the promontory and stand in front of the park bench. The lauvan ring runs directly in front of the bench, and the cable lies along its left side. I step up to the cable where it intersects with the lauvan ring. There's nothing out of the ordinary here, nothing I can see that would indicate another presence. I look around cautiously, but there's no sign of anyone nearby, nor can I see any strange lauvan shapes that I should be worried about. Where is the presence? Has it left, or is it within the cable itself? Perhaps the presence has moved on somewhere else. It's been a while since I last checked its location, after all. There's a pang in my gut when I think of Jen, standing frightened in a field with a smoking volcano above her.

"Hurry up, Merlin," I chide myself. "Get going."

I prepare, then plunge my hands into the cable to find the presence again. Immediately I feel it—there's no distance between us. The presence is here, right here, and it's ready and waiting for me. A surge of energy races toward me, but I'm ready for it also. I meet it with strength of my own, and our two forces meet. It's a battle of willpower—whoever can force the energy to move to the other will make their opponent suffer. The presence has a wicked psychic punch, as I can attest. I have no idea how my earlier blow affected the presence. If it's a renegade spirit, does it feel pain? Whatever I did certainly made the presence back off, so it worked in some way to my advantage.

One thing is certain, though—the presence is right here, somehow. Either invisible, which I'm pretty sure is impossible, or within the cable itself. Anna's spirits came out of her amulet, as if they were within the lauvan of the necklace itself, or were able to access the physical world through it. Perhaps they live in another plane of existence that can be accessed through the cable? There's so much I don't understand, and it makes me feel helpless in a frustrating way that I haven't experienced in many centuries.

Sweat breaks out on my brow as I concentrate on bending the presence to my will. I don't want to lose. I want the presence to feel my wrath, to understand that I'm not someone to trifle with, that it should think twice about blowing up this mountain. I'm certain the presence is behind this. I don't know why the spirits want to destroy this center, but it's obvious they are culpable.

Suddenly, the presence is not alone. I distinctly feel another join it, right here in the cable. Then there is another, and another, and the cable starts to feel positively crowded. My sweat turns clammy and I fight to maintain my position against the extra force. The presences pile up, all working against me, far more than the three spirits I saw coming out of Anna's necklace. My willpower slips against their sheer numbers. Closer and closer, the spirit force draws near until with a surge it meets my hands and rockets into my body. It pushes me up and away and breaks my connection to the cable. I fly through the air and an excruciatingly hot pain sears my abdomen at my lauvan's center.

I land hard on my side and clutch my stomach. I wheeze there for a moment to catch my breath and try to manage the pain. The skin on my stomach is red and blistered, covered in knotted lauvan. They would take far too long to untangle for me to do now. I'll have to deal with the pain the regular way. I stagger to my feet, massaging one of the knots in a futile effort to relieve the pain.

A tremor throws me off balance. I look up and note with dull resignation that the mountains are acting up again, worse than when I left Sylvana. There's not much time left. I need to ground again. I need more time. But will more time help? I still don't know what to do. The spirits are dead set against my meddling, and getting the better of them is the only way I can see to fix this, since they are the cause of this center's disintegration.

Grasping at straws, I plunge my hand into my pocket and dig out the two halves of the fire opal. Maybe the lauvan have reinstated themselves somehow? I don't know. It might be possible. I've never seen lauvan stripped from an object like that—maybe the lauvan can come back just as suddenly. It's becoming painfully obvious in the past few days that I don't know everything.

No such luck—the opal glistens with its inner fire clear

for me to see. There's no trace of rainbow lauvan anywhere. I shove the pieces back into my pocket, disgusted. Panic is licking the edges of my consciousness, like fire through a sheaf of paper. I swallow hard. I can't afford to let panic get the better of me. Jen's counting on me, Sylvana believes in me, and Wallerton needs me. I have to find a way.

Another tremor shakes the promontory and all three mountains puff out large billows of smoke sequentially. I need more time. I need to ground the center again. The only person here is me—maybe if I ground the lauvan ring right next to the cable, I can act as a grounding as well as fight the spirits.

It's the only plan I have, and it's better than standing here doing nothing. I leap to the intersection of the ring and the cable and feverishly collect loose lauvan. Once I have enough—it's not all of them in the vicinity, but it will do—I squash them into my own center, wincing at the nausea, and force the lauvan to join. A brief combing of my ankle lauvan allows me to act as a grounding. The billows of smoke reduce slightly.

I bought myself time—now I have to use it.

"Okay, spirits." I face the cable. "Prepare to meet your doom." Maybe if I show my strength, they will back off. Ha. That trick might work sometimes on the battlefield, but I have a sense that spirits don't work on the same set of rules as humans do. Suddenly, I long for the simplicity of battle with sword and spear. It was easy to know what my opponent would do, was capable of doing. I grin fiercely at the memories and roll up my sleeves. I always had the advantage, too. That didn't hurt. Now I can empathize with my enemies in the past. It's incredibly frustrating and frightening to face someone who outranks you in abilities beyond your comprehension.

But there's nothing else I can do besides pit myself against my little-known foes. Jen and Sylvana are counting on me to pull this off, or at least get them out of here alive. I take a deep breath that stinks of sulfur from the billowing smoke rolling my way, before I plunge my hands into the cable once more.

Immediately, a backlash of force hits my own, and the mental grappling begins. I grunt with effort, and through watering eyes I see my own lauvan twitch spasmodically as I strain against the pressure forming from the spirits. Heat builds in my outstretched fingers. I pull out whatever strength I have left and scream aloud, pushing everything I have into the combat.

It's not enough. More spirits pile up against me. In the small corner of my mind that is not wholly focused on the battle, I note with satisfaction the number of spirits it takes to subdue me.

But subdue me they do, and with a crackle of static a tremendous, hot pain in my center hits me, aggravating the previous injury that I haven't yet healed. The shock winds me and I have no breath left to shout out. My hands leave the cable as if shot out of a cannon, and I am flung backward. I don't fly through the air this time—my grounding keeps me in place. I merely bowl over and slam with excessive force into the ground, bruising my hip and slamming my head. My torso burns with heat from the spirits' attack. Stars shoot above me as I lay for a moment, stunned.

As my eyes clear, I make no effort to get up. I failed. I can't win against these spirits and I have nothing left to try. I can't even leave my position now, because one less grounding will destabilize the center and bring forth the eruption, I have no doubt. The mountain will eventually explode with fiery carnage, and there's nothing I can do about it.

CHAPTER XXIII

Jen's face swims before my mind's eye, terrified and confused. I have to go back for her, and Sylvana too. I made promises I have to keep. I sit up slowly and my head swims. My hand reaches back to massage the lauvan behind my head. They are more than twisted this time—a few knots also meet my exploratory fingers. I grimace. Hopefully a little massaging will be enough to reduce distractions for my transformation to a falcon. By foot is too slow. If I fly, I might just manage to collect Jen and Sylvana in time.

Billowing smoke makes my eyes water and my lungs cough dramatically. Through my streaming eyes I see a shadow of a figure approaching. My heart clenches. Has Jen or Sylvana left her post? If so, the mountain is liable to go at any moment. It's too unstable to allow for any reduction in the groundings. A small breeze pushes over the promontory and the smoke clears briefly to expose a figure.

"Anna?" I gasp. She's between me and the mountain, which I can now see thanks to the shifting winds. I gulp in the fresher air. Smoke flows down to my right and I'm intensely grateful that Jen and Sylvana appear to be out of its path.

Anna contemplates me, still sitting on the ground where the spirits left me.

"What on Earth are you doing here?" She stares at me for a moment longer, then nods. "No, you know what? I'm not surprised. You felt the changes, didn't you? I bet you wanted to be a part of what's happening here." She raises her arms and lifts her chin with eyes half-closed, as if reveling in the moment. "Feel the glory of the fire all around you. Isn't it incredible?"

Is she high?

"Anna, we need to get out of here. The volcano is about to erupt. We will die if we don't leave now. I can't overemphasize the danger here."

She ignores me and continues on whatever train of thought she's riding to Crazy Town.

"I knew you were different, someone special. I could feel your aura glowing like a beacon in the night. And when I touched it, your reaction was more than I'd ever dreamed of." She smiles at me then, a lazy, confident smile that is entirely out of place in this situation.

"Anna, I know you're in the thick of something here, with the spirits you can summon—"

"How do you know about that?" she interrupts. A small frown creases her brow.

"I just—I know what the necklaces can do. Jackie told me."

Anna purses her lips at the mention of her former friend.

There's no time for this. How can I make her understand?

"You're deep into something, but it's hurting you and everyone around you. I don't know what the spirits promised you, but they're going to blow up the mountain and destroy Wallerton. Along with us, if we don't get moving."

Anna shakes her head at me, a half-smile of knowledge on her face.

"Oh, Merry. You don't understand. I know what the spirits are capable of. The volcano is all in the plan. It will erupt in a few minutes. The spirits will keep me safe here."

I stare at her, horrified.

"You knew? You're content to let your hometown burn?"

Her mouth twitches. She whirls around and sits on the park bench, spreading her arms along its top.

"Unfortunate casualties. I have to think of the bigger

214

picture. Much more is at stake than you can imagine. Besides, everyone was evacuated."

"Jackie is still here, looking for you," I say quietly. I slowly rise from my seated position and turn to face Anna. She looks discomposed. Her eyes drop to the ground for the first time. After a moment, she looks up at me again, her eyes hard.

"Jackie made her choice. I'm sorry for it, but it can't be helped."

"What's the bigger picture, Anna? What are you doing this for?"

"The power of the spirits—it can be ours, Merry. Think of it." She leans toward me with her eyes wide and excited, almost fanatical. Her lauvan spread out from her body as if searching for me. "We'll be able to join with the spirits, make their power our own, manipulate the elements, see the future, read people like books—the power of the necklace is only the tiniest taste of what we could have. The spirits will give us all our desires. The power, Merry—" She sighs with longing. "Think of what we could do. Where we could go."

I misread Anna so badly, yet all the signs were there. I didn't want to see her true nature. The spirit communication, the reveling in the volcano, her rift with Sylvana—and yet I didn't want to put her in the villain's chair. I didn't want to believe that she would go so far as to destroy her hometown and risk the lives of her friends in pursuit of power. I gave that duty to the faceless spirits that were so easy to blame. How could I believe it of Anna, of someone I was so intimate with? I'm intensely angry at myself for being so stupidly blind. I should have known better. What's the point of having an endless history if I don't learn from it?

"Think about it, Merry," she repeats. "The spirits can give us everything and tell us anything we want to know."

I freeze. This is a development I haven't considered. I could communicate with the spirit world, find out more about this unknown plane of existence hidden from me for so long. Could this lead me to my father? My heart clenches with longing. The central enigma of my life, my powers—is this the key? I could find out. The spirits don't tolerate me, but they talk to Anna. She's offering me the chance of a lifetime.

"How does the necklace work?" I stall to buy myself time, in order to calm the turmoil in my head. "Why isn't that enough?"

"I was told that the necklace was made especially for me. A part of my aura was woven into the energies of the spirit world and trapped within the pendant. With it I have the ability to summon the spirits at will, especially at the sacred location." She sweeps her arm around languidly to indicate the promontory. "This is where the spirit world is closest, but only for those with a connection. The necklace won't work for anyone else. I have to be careful with it. If it were destroyed the spirits wouldn't have access to our physical world through me and would be pulled back to their world.

"It's connected to Jackie and Bethany's too, unfortunately." Her mouth twists in annoyance and her purple lauvan twitch. "I don't know why Drew did that. We were supposed to be a team, I guess. Stronger with three. Luckily, they love the powers the necklaces give them, and take good care. Otherwise, mine would stop working. They were supposed to be helping me, ungrateful bitches. They got the necklaces for free. They owe something for that. A little bit of spirit summoning, some lava, and then endless power? I say that's a fair trade." She pulls herself up straight and lifts her chin. "Luckily, I didn't need them. I did it all on my own and I'll reap the reward on my own too."

A tremor rolls through the promontory. Anna smiles at

me.

"Unless *you* want in, of course. I like you, Merry. I think we have something pretty great between us, and I'd love to know you better." She stands and steps up to me, placing her palm on my chest. I look down at it and then into her face. Her beautiful brown eyes gaze into mine, confident and sure. "Join me, Merry. Be one with the spirits, and with me. We can go places, you and me, and the spirits will take us there."

My mind whirls with Anna's suggestion. She's offering me a chance to finally know the truths that have eluded me for fifteen hundred years. And I can't do it without her. The amulet will work only with Anna, and the spirits will only respond to her call. I think of Jen and Sylvana waiting for me in the meadows below. They're protected from the volcano by the lauvan cages. Probably. Maybe. Then I think of the spirits and all the answers I could have. A moment later, I'm decided. I know what I want.

I bend toward Anna slowly, not taking my eyes off of hers. Her face is excited and filled with anticipation. I close my eyes and kiss her mouth. Her respond is immediate and fervent, and she opens her lips to mine and slides her tongue against my own. I press her mouth with mine and push her hips with my hands, forcing her to sit down on the bench when I lean over her. She offers no resistance.

My hands are not idle. I grab the lauvan around Anna's hips and she moans against my mouth in pleasure. It seems that the necklace lets her feel my touch more intensely than most. Quickly, I wrap her lauvan around the lauvan of the park bench. The bench is fairly new and the gleaming wood still has plenty of life in it, enough for my purpose. Once my work is complete, I end the kiss abruptly and step back.

Anna looks confused, her dilated pupils half-lidded and her breathing fast.

217

"What's wrong? Why did you stop?"

I reach around her throat and swiftly unclasp the necklace. She moves her hands to stop me but I'm too quick for her, dazed as she is. Her eyes harden.

"What are you doing?"

"Stopping this madness you created. You may be content to let Wallerton burn and your friends die, but I'm not. I'm going to destroy this necklace and stop the eruption."

"You can't do that, you stupid man," she spits out. "Scratching the surface or crushing it won't break the connection to the spirit world."

I stare at her, my mind working frantically.

"It has to change elemental form, I suppose, to break the connection. I guess there's only one option." I look up to Mt. Linnigan, its roiling clouds bursting forth from the peak.

Anna attempts to rise and snatch back the necklace while my back is turned, but only succeeds in scuffing her feet on the ground. She slams back into the bench involuntarily. My work with the lauvan holds her firmly.

"What the hell did you do to me?" she shouts. Panic gathers in her eyes. "Who are you?"

I don't have time for this. I shove the necklace into my pocket and slip down the promontory to find a place where Anna can't see me. I need to fly.

"Lauvan, don't fail me now," I say when I stop out of sight of Anna. My arms and hip ache, my head spins, and my abdomen pulses with burning pain from the spirits' treatment of me, not to mention the lingering nausea from when I gathered the sick lauvan. I hope I have enough focus to transform. I have to have enough.

"For Jen," I say out loud and gather the necessary lauvan. I take three deep breaths and pull. I can almost taste the relief as my wings unfurl and I take off toward the mountain.

CHAPTER XXIV

The winds are stronger now. They buffet my tiny form and I beat my wings against their might. Adrenaline courses through me, and I need every drop to push through my injuries and stay aloft. I dive to dodge a puff of smoke pushed into my path by the errant wind patterns.

The air swirls, and for an instant the top of Mt. Linnigan looms ahead. My tiny heart in its feathered chest drops to my talon-studded feet. The mountain spits up magma in spurts of fire hundreds of feet into the air. They eject into the sky and fall back down to the slopes, still red-hot and flowing, as liquefied rock burns the trees in its path. Above the mountain, storm clouds gather. The first lightning bolt generated from the massive positive charge of spurting lava strikes the top of the volcano.

I pump my wings harder than I've ever done before. It's not far now. I just need to get there before any more magma is released from the mountain. I know enough about volcanology to know that these spurts are just the start, the warm-up act to the main show. Once the big talent arrives, none of us will have a chance. Deep in my gut a sharp pain emerges. I wonder what it is now.

Faster and faster I fly, and ignore the growing pain in my stomach. My plan is simple—drop the amulet into the heart of the mountain, fly away. Heat from the volcano will melt the metal and change its structure completely, destroying both it and the connection between the physical world and the spirit world. The plan is brilliant in its simplicity.

A lightning bolt sizzles past my left wing. All my feathers rise uncontrollably from the charge and I veer away with a shriek. It's getting harder to control my bird-form. All my instincts want to do is to fly far away from this madness. Another bolt flashes past, its thunderous crack pounding straight through my body. My hearing numbs and blood trickles down my feathered head, indicating burst eardrums.

Another bolt nearly takes off my tail feathers, and I flap my wings with barely controlled panic. There isn't that much lightning around—it's almost as if the bolts are directed at me. My brain ponders this thought. Am I being targeted? Are the fire spirits that Anna called up behind this attack?

There's not much I can do at this point, beyond avoid being cooked into roast fowl. I head straight for the peak, aiming for the hole now apparent in the top of the mountain, when it hits me—the necklace is in my pocket. My human-form's pocket. As a merlin, I have no pockets, no necklace, and no way to drop the amulet into the magma.

I shriek my horror to the tumultuous skies. There's no time to go back to the ground and change form, place the necklace on the ground, transform to a bird, pick up the necklace in my talons, and fly back here. There's just no time. I realize now that the pain in my stomach must be the spirits in the amulet attacking me. It's getting worse and worse, almost incapacitating. I don't know for how much longer I can hold my bird-form.

Think, think, think, I shout in my head. Then I realize what I have to do.

I'm so close now that the heat of the spurting magma dries the membranes of my eyes faster than I can blink. I close my nictitating eyelids and peer through the fuzzy membrane of my protective inner eyelid, thankful for my bird-form's anatomy. I sweep upward as far as I dare, directly above the gaping caldera. The air is thin up here, and there's just no time.

Okay, Merlin, I think to myself. *You can do this. And*

survive to tell the tale.

I hope I'm right.

I let my bird-form melt away. My human-form drops like a rock. Air whips past me and I swallow the urge to scream. I spin downward, wingless and out of control. My hand plunges into my pocket to pull out the necklace which throbs and stings in my hand, shooting sharp pains through my arm and into my shoulder. The necklace snags for a moment on a belt loop of my jeans and my heart nearly stops. I finally yank it free and toss it away from me. It falls beside me and we both plummet to the magma below.

I let out all my breath and ignore the monstrous heat emanating below me. I reach out for my lauvan, like I've done a thousand times before. One hand, two hands, twist, and—yank.

Nothing happens.

Shit, shit, shit. I must have forgotten a vital lauvan. The heat from the volcano sears my skin and my hair starts to dry and crackle. Another lightning bolt skims past and my hair stands on end. I have one more chance, just the one.

One hand, two hands, twist, and—yank.

I stop my frantic spinning by spreading my wings. I shriek with relief and I soar away from the hellhole behind me. There's a pulse of energy from the mountain and I nearly let go of my lauvan in the shockwave. Then—silence.

I wheel about to look behind me. Smoke dissipates from Mt. Linnigan's peak and no spurts of magma leap out of the top. It still steams, but even that is much reduced. The other two mountains, Mt. Vickers and Mt. Kullen, are calming as well, and all three simply steam gently as their heat fades.

I look down to the ground. The lauvan ring is visible from up here with my falcon's eyes, but it is different. It's no longer plagued with sickly yellow, but instead glows with the silvery-brown of healthy lauvan. From here I can even tell that the ring is disintegrating, untangling, and the lauvan are resuming their usual swirling free-forms.

I did it. I actually did it. I swoop in two circles and do a barrel roll to release my feelings. I shriek exultantly, then remember the three women on the ground waiting for me. I aim my flight to Anna, the closest one.

***

I land hard on the ground and let go of my lauvan in relief. I was only barely holding on to my bird-form. I lay on my back in the long grass, gazing up at the dissipating clouds against a bright blue sky. Across my vision, seed heads dip and bounce in a slight breeze that flows over the meadow. I stare up past the grass, focusing on nothing, and let the stress and madness of the past three days flow out of my body in a rushing wave. I'm exhausted, but it's a euphoric exhaustion, the relaxation a body feels after a job well done.

I allow myself only a few moments to enjoy doing nothing before sitting up. My body complains loudly and vehemently. I look down at my bruised and battered figure. Lauvan are tangled everywhere in brown knots that give me a headache just to look at them. I look past them to my physical body— my arm has scrapes up and down its length, my hip is one large purple bruise, and when I lift my shirt my abdomen is pocked with a multitude of reddened blisters from the burning given to me by the spirits. I press my side gingerly and gasp when my fingers encounter what feels like a broken rib. All these injuries made so many knots in my lauvan that it will be the work of an hour or more to smooth them out to their original state. I can't do it now—Jen and Sylvana wait for me. I don't care how long Anna waits for, but I might as well release her so I can get out of this town. I'm done with Wallerton. I just want to go home, work out my knots, and sleep all night without the distractions of Anna or the volcano getting in the way.

I haul myself up the promontory, and wince when my breath expands my broken rib. As soon as I crest the hill and pull myself up and over a large boulder in my path, I see Anna. She's still on the park bench where I left her. Good. I hope she's stewing in her bad decisions. She turns her glare in my direction. If looks could kill, I'd definitely be on my last legs. Even her lauvan are sharp and point their ends in my direction like an angry porcupine.

"Get me off this bench," Anna says through gritted teeth.

I saunter over to her, clearly taking my time just to annoy her. It works—she's practically steaming by the time I reach her and her lauvan tremble in fury. I squat down in front of her knees and contemplate her angry face.

"It's over, Anna. The amulet is destroyed and Mt. Linnigan won't be erupting any time soon."

"You fool." She laughs with disdain. Her face doesn't suit her words. It's difficult to associate the beautiful woman I slept with and this cold bitch. Where is Anna? She sneers at me. "You think this is over? We will find a way to let the spirits into the world. I will have the powers they promised me. This is not over."

I sigh. There's so much poison in Anna. How did she get like this? What lies has she been fed, and by whom?

"Who are you working for, Anna? How did they make the necklaces?"

"I'm not telling you anything. Who the hell are you, anyway?" Her glare is tinged with a trace of fear. Is she worried about what the people she works for will say when they find out that she failed, that I thwarted her nefarious

223

plans to incapacitate this center? Does she need a good story about the man who foiled the eruption? My annoyance and disgust with Anna melt away, and I just feel sad.

"It doesn't have to be like this, Anna. You don't need these powers. You don't have to pander to these people. You don't owe them anything."

"You don't know a thing," she spits out.

I put my hand on her knee. She doesn't move it away, surprisingly, and her lauvan touch mine tentatively. I'm heartened by this. Maybe Anna is still there, under the fear. I try to reach to the heart of what Anna really wants, the real reason she's drawn to these people who promise her power.

"I know how hard it can be to get away and make a new life for yourself. Trust me, I've done it before. But you don't need any powers to do it. You have enough strength of your own, Anna Green—rely on yourself. You won't be disappointed."

Anna glares at me and says nothing. Her jaw is tight and her eyes defiant.

"If you're ever in Vancouver and need a friend, look me up. The name's Merry Lytton." I gaze at her with compassion.

"Don't you dare pity me."

"Whether you want it or not, it's yours. And it's not pity. I just—get it. That's all." I sigh and reach around her hips to unfasten the lauvan. She tenses, and I wonder how she thinks I attached her to this bench.

"What are you doing?"

I don't answer, but complete the untangling and straighten up.

"Good luck, Anna. I hope you find what you need, not what you're looking for."

I turn to walk away but before I take five paces, Anna

speaks.

"They'll come after you, you know. They won't like that you stopped their plans. They'll want revenge."

I turn to look at her. She stands beside the park bench, her face now unsure and devoid of contempt. A couple of her lauvan reach toward me, waving in midair, and the few lauvan that connect us quiver.

"Thank you for the warning, Anna. You be careful, too."

I leave her looking after me, motionless beside the park bench.

***

I hike quickly back to the meadow beside the parking lot where I left Sylvana. It's not far, and I'm at her side in a few minutes. She faces the mountain with her eyes closed and her palms spread, as if receiving a volcanic blessing. I smile. Her lauvan calmly swirl around her body and her face is serene. She clearly had no doubt that I would prevail. Her faith in me is heartwarming, and I feel a tremendous fondness for this woman with her sensible haircut and painted wooden bangles.

"Sylvana." I touch her arm. "It's done."

She turns to me and opens her eyes with a beatific smile.

"I know. I felt it, when you finished it. There was a huge pulse of energy. I felt it here." She pats her chest where the necklace lies under her shirt. "And then there was nothing, and the tremors stopped." She grabs my arm and shakes it gently. "You did it, Merry. You saved Wallerton."

I smile back in the face of her joy. The euphoria of destroying the amulet, put on pause during my talk with Anna, slides back with her praise.

"I couldn't have done it without you, Sylvana. You gave

225

me the time I needed. Without your help, your stabilization of the energies, the mountain would have erupted long before I had the chance to fix this."

"I'm glad I could help, and be a part of this incredible experience. I'm so lucky."

I can't help myself—I laugh out loud.

"There aren't many who would consider almost-certain death by lava and ash to be their lucky day."

"But we had you, and your abilities, to save the day. And I was a small part of that. I'm content." She looks at me with an almost worshipful awe and joy, then looks concerned for a moment. "Would you mind if I told my Aunty Bethany about all this?"

"Be my guest, if you ask her to keep it mum. I don't want to leave my home right now—I like Vancouver. I have a good thing going at the moment."

"Leave? Why?" Sylvana is genuinely perplexed. I shrug.

"If too many people know about me, it never ends well. I don't tell many people about my—abilities, and I never stay in one place for very long, regardless."

"That's terrible." Sylvana shakes her head, then gives a decisive nod. "But you can trust my aunt. She's very discreet."

I nod. A thought strikes me.

"Can I see your necklace?"

Sylvana draws it out of her shirt and over her head. Just as I suspected, the amulet is entirely stripped of its lauvan. I can now see that the pendant is a polished chunk of quartz surrounded by a ring of silver filigree. It's quite beautiful, with a nineteenth-century appeal. I grimace and give Sylvana the bad news.

"About that—I'm afraid your necklace won't work anymore. It won't help you with your aura reading, tea leaves, whatever you were using it for before. When I destroyed Anna's necklace, the access to the spirit world was cut off for all three amulets."

"Oh." Sylvana looks crestfallen for a moment. She gathers herself together and puts on a brave face, but her lauvan droop despondently. "Well, easy come, easy go. If Wallerton is safe because of it, then it was a fair trade. Although, I won't deny that I'll miss the connection and the knowledge." She tilts her head in inquiry. "Did you find Anna? Is that how you got her necklace? Is she okay?"

"Yeah, I found her. She's alive and healthy, if that's what you mean. But I think she needs a friend, someone other than these people she's working for. She's still wrapped up in their business, and I think she's scared. I hope she finds her own two feet to stand on, but I don't know." I give her a tight smile. "I hope so."

Sylvana's eyebrows knit together anxiously.

"I can certainly try to reach out, but I don't know how successful I'll be. She's pretty good at brushing me off these days. But I'll try."

I glance in the direction where Jen waits.

"I should go—I used my friend as a grounding as well, and I need to collect her. She doesn't know about me, and she's probably beside herself right now about the volcano."

"Oh, yes, go," Sylvana says at once, then says, "Wait. I wanted to tell you that I appreciate you calling me Sylvana. Most don't. They think it's silly."

I look at her. Her lauvan are tight to her chest. She's afraid I think she's silly, too.

"Sylvana is who you've chosen to be. I know a little something about reinventing yourself. I wanted to respect your decision. I'm sure it was not made lightly."

Sylvana's eyes are watery, but crinkle in a smile.

"Bless you, Merry. Now, go find your friend."

I turn, eager to follow her instructions.

***

I start to trot when I take the trail out of the parking lot toward Jen. At the lauvan-cable I turn right, running through the forest and out into the meadow. Jen stands with her back to me amid the grasses and wildflowers blooming at this time of year, pinks and yellows and purples. Her long hair is unbound and drifts in the breeze, a direct contrast to her static lauvan, frozen with fear. She looks so fragile. My heart squeezes tightly.

She turns when she hears my running footsteps pounding on the ground behind her. Whatever calm I was able to stroke into her lauvan when I left has apparently long since evaporated. Her face is fixed in an expression of utter terror.

"Merry?" she croaks, but doesn't move. Has fright paralyzed her, or is she still following my orders? I sprint the last few steps and sweep her into a fierce clutch. She's stiff in my arms for a moment, then her body melts and she dissolves into sobs.

I rock her while she cries.

"I thought you weren't coming back." She forces out words in between gasping sobs. "I thought I was going to die."

"Oh, Jen." I smooth her hair, my own eyes misting over. "I promised I'd come back. I promised you'd be safe. I always keep my promises."

She doesn't answer. Her body shakes out all the terror and anguish and adrenaline she accumulated during her ordeal. I feel the shoulder of my shirt grow wet.

"It's okay. It's over. You're safe now." I stroke her head

228

until her sobs quiet into little hiccups. We stand there for a few moments longer, silent, affirming our aliveness and our connection to each other. At least that's what I'm doing. Jen's so quiet and still that I wonder if she fell asleep on my shoulder.

Eventually, she stands upright, pushing off me for balance. She searches my face with questioning eyes. I don't know what she's looking for. I try for a comforting smile, but she doesn't respond. Finally, she speaks.

"Is the volcano safe now?" She shakes her head. "Do you know the answer to that question?"

"Yes, and yes," I say. She just nods, sparing a short glance to Mt. Linnigan to confirm my report. I put an arm around her shoulder and steer her away from the sight.

"Come on, let's get out of here."

She follows my lead down the path to the parking lot. It's tight in places, but I keep a firm grip on her shoulders. She's so shell-shocked that I'm afraid to let her go, in case she keels over without my support.

When we reach the car, I stand her next to it. She leans against the side and closes her eyes.

"Jen?" I say softly. "I need the car keys."

She feels around in her pocket without looking and holds the keys out. Her arm falls to her side as a dead weight after I take the keys. I unlock the door and lead her to the passenger seat. She's unresisting while I buckle her in and shut the door. I slide into the driver's seat and start the car.

"I'm heading back to the hotel to pack up our stuff and then I'm taking you home. Okay?"

Jen nods, the long black lashes of her closed eyes brushing her pale cheeks.

CHAPTER XXV

Jen gives me her key after I pull into the hotel's parking lot, and I head to her room. I snatch her suitcase from the closet and look around the suite. Except for her work clothes carefully hung up in the closet, she's been living out of her suitcase. I haul the case to the bathroom and sweep all of the toiletries into it, then grab her clothes from the closet and stash them hastily on top. A pair of shoes from beside the door completes the packing, and I wheel the case over to my room. There's not much to pack up—I've also been living out of my satchel, and the bed hasn't even been slept in. I wonder what the maid thinks.

At the front desk, I check out then retreat swiftly to the car. I throw our bags into the trunk and jump into the driver's seat. Jen hasn't moved.

"Are you okay?" I say, starting to worry. She's so pale—I don't want her to succumb to shock. Her lauvan look slow but healthy and I relax a little.

"I'm okay. Just tired." She keeps her eyes closed. "Let's go home."

I couldn't agree more, and pull out of the parking lot with a squeal. Out of the corner of my eye I see Jen wince, and this heartens me more than her words. She must be feeling okay if she can still be annoyed with my driving. All the same, I vow to make the rest of the trip smooth sailing.

A half-hour into our drive, Jen stirs and opens her eyes.

"Did I sleep?"

"A little," I reply, checking my rearview mirror before passing a motorhome tootling up an incline. Jen nods, and reaches to turn on the radio. She starts to search for a station that isn't entirely static. I'm glad for the distraction—I don't know what to say to Jen. I have no idea what she's thinking, how she's feeling. Her lauvan don't give me much of a clue. They swirl somewhat calmly, but almost in a careful manner, as if she isn't sure herself what she feels.

The constant stream of static finally resolves into one lone station. The announcer's voice is bouncy and irritating, but it fills the uneasiness in the car and allows us to avoid talking about what happened in Wallerton. The announcer babbles on about some concert we can win tickets for, and then plays a jingle to let us know that it's news time.

"The big news for the Coast Mountain Region is Mt. Linnigan. While scientists say they can't confirm that the mountain is once again dormant, officials have started gathering the evacuees to return to Wallerton."

So much for avoiding the topic at hand. I feel Jen looking at the side of my face. My eyes stay on the road. I don't know what to say, what she wants to know. She lets the announcer prattle on for a minute, then jabs at the button to shut the radio off. I sneak a glance. Jen's lauvan have tensed and sharpened into angles. Uh oh. She's decided how she feels, and is now ready for some answers. Am I ready to give her some?

"Merry." She says my name with no question in her voice, just a demand for my attention. She has it. "What happened back there?"

Here we go. I attempt to probe her to see what she really wants to know.

"What do you think happened?" Her head snaps toward me and her mouth opens angrily. I hastily cut in. "Just so I know how to explain, given what you know."

"I know nothing," she says, repressed frustration in her voice. "For some reason, you come to Wallerton, act all weird for a few days—hiking? Really?—then when the evacuation order comes, you're nowhere to be found. You'd just left my room, Merry. Where the hell did you disappear to so quickly? You couldn't have come found me before you left? I was worried sick about you. Shut up," she says when I open my mouth to answer her accusations. "I'm not finished. Then you don't answer your phone for ages. Meanwhile, I'm sitting in the car while people run around me. Evacuation is in full swing, people are shouting, crying. The mountain is smoking and tremors are shaking the ground every couple of minutes. Then when I finally get a hold of you, you tell me you're at the base of an active volcano. Then you're not at the parking lot when I come to get you."

I'm silent. What can I say? That's what happened. My heart squeezes so tightly at the thought of Jen's anguish that I can scarcely breathe. Jen's not finished yet.

"Then you ask me to stand like an idiot, watching an erupting volcano, while you run off to do who-knows-what. And I seriously figured that was it. I mean, there was no way I wasn't going to die." She gives a shaky sigh and turns to look out the side window.

"Why did you stay?" I ask quietly. There's silence for a moment.

"I guess I trusted you. You promised me you'd come back, and I believed you." She shrugs incredulously. "You've never let me down before, and you seemed really serious." She turns so her whole body is facing me. She even tucks her left leg under her bottom and adjusts her seatbelt so she can lean against the door and look at me fully. "So tell me, Merry. Why was I right to trust you? What could you possibly have to do with this volcano? What's the connection?"

A few moments pass while I gather my thoughts. Jen stares at me, waiting.

"What if I told you I could see things differently from everyone else?" I choose my words carefully. This is a dance I've done many times before, and I haven't yet found the best way to broach the subject. My odds are fifty-fifty on whether they join the club, or run.

When they run, they run fast. Usually I have to run, too, when they call the witch-hunter or the men in the white suits.

"So, what, you're insightful?" A heavy note of sarcasm threads through Jen's voice.

"No. Well, yes, but that's not what I meant." I sneak a glance at Jen's stony expression and wish I hadn't. "I mean that there are layers of energy around everything, and I can see them and manipulate them."

Silence from the other side of the car. I start to sweat. The words are not coming out right. I plow ahead, trying to make her understand.

"Mt. Linnigan had a major problem with its lauv—its energy—and I was the only one who could tell that it wasn't natural. And thanks to your help, I was able to fix it, to keep the volcano dormant."

I peek again at Jen as we drive down a straight stretch of highway beside a river. She's staring openly at me, her big brown eyes filled with a mixture of alarm and pity.

"Is that what you believe happened?" she asks in a carefully neutral voice. Wow. She's afraid of me now. She either thinks I'm high or have gone off the deep end.

A little laugh escapes me. It probably doesn't help my status as a crazy man.

"Yeah, that's exactly what happened."

"Okay, Merry. That's great." She tries to make her voice soothing, but I can hear the strain. "Why don't you just pull over here and we can talk about it?"

She's really frightened. I sigh and pull over on the

shoulder, crunching a few dead branches along the way. I don't want to distress her, not more than I have to.

I turn my body to look at her fully. She stares back at me, her eyes wide and unsure.

"Have you ever talked to a—therapist or someone?"

I smile wryly.

"Yeah, I'm seeing a shrink, but not for this." I lean my head back on the headrest, trying to think of what I can do to prove to her I'm not crazy. The car, now that it's stopped, is a minimal lauvan zone. Jen has plenty, most of them standing out from her body like the fur of an angry cat, but I don't want to frighten her further by playing with her lauvan. I open my door.

'Step out of the car for a sec. I want to show you something."

Jen looks like she wants to say no but doesn't dare. She silently climbs out of the car and stands with one hand on the frame of her open door. I nod encouragingly.

"Okay, good. I want to prove to you that I'm not crazy. That I'm telling the truth." Jen doesn't answer. I cast my eyes around for a good subject.

"Do you see that hanging branch, just beyond the car?" She nods. I say, "Watch it carefully. I'm going to break it off from the tree, while still standing here."

"Oh, Merry," Jen whispers. She looks distressed and puts her hand over her mouth.

"Just watch. After I snap it from the tree, I'll swing it around three times, and place it on the hood of the car."

Jen shakes her head silently. I look into her eyes.

"Just watch. Then we can talk."

I turn to face the branch and raise my hands. I don't need to do that, but it will help me find the correct lauvan more quickly, as well as look impressive to Jen. A car whizzes by, kicking up dust, and the diffuse lauvan of the tree drift through my fingers.

I grab lauvan from the tip of the branch in my right hand, and the base of the branch in my left. I can almost feel Jen's consternation when I wave my hands and wiggle my fingers wildly through the seemingly empty air. Once the lauvan are secure, my left hand closes sharply.

The branch snaps off the tree. I hear a gasp from the other side of the car, but my job is not yet complete. I promised her a specific sequence of events. My right hand twitches, and the branch—still hanging in midair—rotates once, twice, thrice. I pull both hands slowly back and the branch floats gently toward us. It lands on the hood of the car, rocking slightly when I release its lauvan.

I look at Jen. She's half-crouched behind her open car door. Her face is fearful and disbelieving. My heart contracts, but I keep my face calm. I don't want to lose Jen.

"It has to be a trick." Jen shakes her head, and pulls herself out of her crouch using the car as support.

"Jen. We're in the middle of nowhere. How on Earth would I have set up a trick? More to the point, why would I?" I swallow, trying to stay calm as I perch on the edge of this cliff. "I know it's hard to take in, I'm sorry—I didn't tell you before because I know it's hard to accept, and I didn't want to burden you with it."

Jen looks at me for a long while, her face unreadable. I hold her gaze as long as I can, but eventually turn my eyes away to stare along the road.

"Okay." Jen's voice is rough and unsteady. "You've got some crazy abilities that shouldn't be possible, but are." She exhales slowly. I keep my eyes on the road until a car door slams. I look over, and then bend down to the car window.

Jen sits in her seat with her seatbelt on. She turns her head when I peer in.

"Let's just—drive back to Vancouver. You can drop me off at home. Then I need to think."

I nod and she breathes deeply, turning back to the road. Her lauvan are still pointing outward, and now they twitch in occasional spasms. I grab the branch and toss it into the woods. Jen doesn't look at me as I sit down, put my belt on, and start the engine. Before I take the car out of park, I turn to her.

"Jen, I—"

She holds up her hand.

"Don't, Merry. Please don't—say anything. Just drive."

It's a very long, very quiet ride home.

CHAPTER XXVI

Dreaming

My aunt stirs the morning porridge in its big blackened kettle hung over the fireplace. Her nose and mouth are pinched as if something stinky wafts by her face. She always has that expression. The baby on her hip reaches for the spoon and almost falls out of her arm. She smacks the little hand away impatiently. The baby lets out a surprised wail.

My mother sets out wooden bowls and spoons onto the table, the table which is the pride and joy of my uncle and the envy of the neighbors. Its massive wooden slabs are hewn out of an oak that fell in the forest nearby, years before I was born. My grandfather claimed it as first finder, and together with his son, my uncle, spent two whole weeks fashioning a mighty table. Now it stands in my uncle's house—my grandfather long since dead and in no need of a table—the dominant furniture in the small, windowless hut. Its reputation is such that it, and our house by extension, is the recognized gathering place for neighbors living in the nearby dwellings.

I bend down to stoke the fire. I'm accepted as the best fire-builder in the family, although no one except for my mother likes to acknowledge why. I kneel on the dirt floor and spread my fingers, searching for the correct lauvan. I can see them, the bright, blazing orange lauvan that spark and twist out of the flames and spread like water over the rocks that surround the fire pit. When they extend past the rocks, however, they mix and mingle with the other lauvan swirling nearby from my aunt and from me, making them difficult for me to distinguish. They do feel different, and I'm learning to discriminate lauvan based on feel alone. It's tricky, though.

I half-close my eyes to better concentrate, and through my eyelashes I see my aunt turn away in distaste. She can't stand me. She's afraid of me, of what I can do.

She likes the result well enough, though. I finally feel out the warm vibrancy of the fire-lauvan and pull slowly. The flames rise in height to lick the bottom of the kettle.

Wordlessly, my mother comes to stir the porridge, letting her hand rest briefly on my head. I smile up at her. She smiles back, her one good eye filled with warmth but ringed by a dark shadow above her pale cheek. She holds herself carefully as if a sudden movement will hurt her.

My fist tightens and I look down, swallowing. It's hard to see my mother so ill.

My cousin, Rian, enters the one-room hut with my uncle. Rian may be my eldest cousin at twelve, but I still have two years on him. Rian was a tractable-enough playmate when we were both children, but he feels the power of his advancing years keenly. Years of being bossed around by me at our games has resulted in a well-honed desire for supremacy, now that he is treated more like a man by my uncle. And now that he's older and understands more, he knows how to gain the upper hand over me.

My uncle moves to his wife to tickle the baby who gurgles with delight at the attention. Rian squats down beside me in front of the fire where my mother still stirs the porridge.

"Father took me with him to visit the other elders to discuss the summer pasturing," Rian says in a conversational tone. "Very important, the timing of the pasturing. All the local men were there with their sons. I didn't see you there, though." He pauses for a well-timed moment. "Oh wait, I wouldn't, would I? Because you don't have a father."

I stare into the fire, my cheeks burning with anger. Rian knows exactly how to needle me in the most efficient way possible. In the past few months, I've had difficulty controlling my temper. My mother says it's because I'm growing up, but I know her sickness weighs on my mind with an antagonistic heaviness. It doesn't take much of Rian's ill-natured ribbing to push me over the edge. My mother watches me nervously.

When I don't speak, Rian continues.

"It must be terrible to not have anyone claim you as a son. It's like no one wants you. Maybe your father is embarrassed of you."

My anger boils over, as I knew it would as soon as Rian joined me. This is not the first time he's goaded me past endurance. It doesn't take much, these days. I shift around to face him and push him back into the dirt, my hand on his chest. I'm still the elder and have the advantage of weight and height. He flails ineffectually and tries to pry my hand off his chest. I lean my body into it and plunge my free hand into his lauvan's center. He stops flailing immediately and looks at me with wide eyes, gasping like a landed fish. My teeth bare in a feral grin. I slowly squeeze. His eyes roll back in his head and his breathing becomes shallow.

The only sound I can hear past the blood pounding in my ears is Rian's frightened gasping. All I can think of is how much I want to hurt Rian, wipe the smug superiority off his face in the only way I know how. Show him that he has no reason to raise himself above me.

Eventually, sound returns to my ears when strong hands grab me by the shoulders and throw me bodily aside. I try to get onto one knee but my uncle cuffs me with a backhand blow that contains all the fury of his fear. My mother lets out a scream that she quickly stifles. I try again to rise but am forced back to the ground by another powerful blow.

"Don't you dare touch my son," my uncle roars. I'm still

slightly stunned and don't attempt to rise from the floor again. My uncle looks as if he would like me to try, so he can cuff me again.

My aunt shoves the baby into one of my younger cousin's arms and drops to her knees beside Rian. She helps him to a sitting position where he coughs sporadically. She glares at me with all of the considerable venom she can muster.

"You keep your unnaturalness away from my children, demon-spawn."

Gentle hands grip my arm and tug upward. My mother pulls me to my feet. It obviously costs her a great deal of effort, and as soon as I pull out of my half-stunned state enough to notice, I support my own weight.

"Come on, love," she whispers in my ear. "Let's go get some air."

We leave my uncle's family staring after us, daggers from my aunt's and uncle's eyes and wide-eyed confusion from my cousins.

Past the threshold, my breathing is loud and harsh in the still morning air. Anger pumps through my veins, but it is now tempered by fear. How much longer will my uncle tolerate me in his house?

My mother threads her arm through mine and leans heavily on it.

"Take me to the river, Merlin. It's a beautiful morning."

We direct our steps south. It's not long before I speak.

"I'm sorry, mother. I just—I just got so angry." I swallow, feeling the fury ebb when I acknowledge it aloud. She pats my arm.

"I know. I heard what Rian said. But you must remember that we owe your uncle for giving us a home. With no one willing to marry me," she gestures at her face with its taut scars and drooping right eye, "your uncle was kind enough to

240

provide for us. And now that I can contribute so little, well, it's important to remember our place." She rubs my arm consolingly. "Those are not the words a young man wants to hear, I know. Nevertheless, they are true. And when I am gone—"

"Don't say that," I whisper. She squeezes my arm.

"When I am gone I want to know you'll be well. And the best way for that to happen is if you stay in your uncle's good graces."

"It doesn't matter how much I try," I say at once. "As soon as you—" I can't finish the sentence. "One day they will kick me out. They're afraid of me."

"Oh, Merlin, can you blame them?" She sighs deeply. "You need to learn when to use your abilities, and when to hold back. Promise me you'll be careful who you tell in the future. Some people, like your aunt, will never be ready to know."

I'm silent, pondering both her words and the injustice of the scene at the house. The path leads us to the river. It has no name—it's simply known as "the river." There is none other nearby, and we don't see enough travelers in our forgotten corner of the world to bother with a name. The river is brown and muddy from the spring rains and snow melt from higher in the hills. Thick trees shade most of the bank where a few scraggly wildflowers bloom, but the slanting sun illuminates a patch of moss under an ash tree. I lead my mother there—it's her favorite spot.

I guide her to the ground carefully. She tries not to show how much the movement pains her, but she clutches my arm and remains tight-lipped until she settles on the moss. She's so slight these days, and I know it's not simply a function of my emerging strength as I grow. I sit next to her and pick up a stone within arm's reach to fiddle with. My mother sighs

241

with something approaching contentment.

"I always meant to travel with you, Merlin. Someday, when you were older." She gazes into the swirling water.

This is news to me. She always appeared content to live her life in our tiny, nameless cluster of huts, helping with the harvest, aiding my aunt with her many children.

"Really? Why—I mean, where did you want to go?" I've never been farther than the fort of Caernarfon, a two-day walk through the mountains. Exciting possibilities blossom in my mind of the unknown world beyond these hills.

"I've watched you grow over the years, Merlin, and my heart nearly breaks every time you have to hide your abilities or are punished for them. I wanted to find somewhere you belong, somewhere you could be yourself without fear or judgement. I thought that if we found the land your father came from, perhaps you could finally feel at home."

I stare at my mother's wistful expression as she follows the progress of the river with her eyes. I never considered that there might be a whole land of people like me.

She catches my eye and smiles regretfully.

"I'm sorry I couldn't make it happen before I go. Perhaps one day, when you are older, you can leave here and find your way in the world. You are so special, my darling." She touches my cheek with her hand. "Especially to me."

My fist tightens around the stone and I look down at my mother's abdomen, swallowing hard. Her center is a mess, a terrible lauvan cluster above her stomach. In some of our rare quiet moments together I've tried to smooth away the knots, but whatever I try never works and every day it gets worse.

"Let me try again," I say, reaching for her center. She intercepts my hands and clasps them in her own.

"Merlin, my darling boy." She sighs and squeezes my hands. I can't meet her eyes. "Please, just sit with me. Talk to

242

me."

"About what?" My voice is raspy with repressed emotion. I can't fix her. I don't know how to fix her.

She leans against the tree and holds out her arm.

"Tell me again about the owl nestlings you found last week."

I look for a moment at her closed eyes in her tired face, then I lean back into her arm. She pulls me close and rests her cheek on the top of my head. I fight to control my emotions. After releasing a deep sigh, I speak.

"I was walking north down the trail, twenty paces past grandfather's oak stump, when I heard a shrill shriek to my left..."

***

"He'll have to go."

My aunt doesn't realize I'm right outside the door. Or maybe she does, and she doesn't care. Both are equally likely. I hang back and lean against the wall of the hut to listen. I know they're talking about me.

My uncle replies, his voice weary and strained.

"He's still family."

"Hardly. His mother may have been your sister, but what of his father? The one we know nothing about? The one he obviously takes after, with his unnatural ways and those intense eyes. And his temper? Your sister was such a sweet, mild woman—may the goddess be gentle with her."

My uncle sighs but says nothing. My aunt must sense her advantage because she presses on.

"You took her and her child in for all those years, fed her, clothed her, protected her. You helped her despite her deformities, the mark of the goddess' displeasure. You have

243

done more than enough, and owe her boy nothing. Why, he's not much of a boy anymore, practically a man. He would be out supporting himself soon enough—a year or two early won't kill him. It might even be good for him. Teach him to take some responsibility for his actions for a change."

"There is that," my uncle says. "He's almost of age."

"That's perfectly true," my aunt says, eager to foster her agenda in my uncle.

"But I promised my sister I would look after him."

"What about your promises to me? Only last month he pinned Rian to the ground at breakfast. I honestly thought he would kill Rian. Do you remember his face?"

This seems to awaken my uncle.

"Yes, I remember."

"You have a duty to your children, to protect them. I don't see how you can do that as long as we harbor that boy in the house. For the safety of our children, the boy has to go."

There's a pause, and then a deep sigh.

"You're right. The boy must go."

I am stricken. My knees would give out on me if I weren't frozen in place. So, this is it. My mother's body is scarcely cool in her earthen grave and already I am abandoned, bereft of mother and home and place in the world all at once. Anger simmers deep within, but my mind is covered by the dull, numb blanket of grief laid on at my mother's deathbed.

I can't stay here, not in this house anymore, and not on this mountainside where no one trusts me or likes me. My mother was all I had.

Through the haze of loss and fear I remember my mother's words. *I thought that if we found the land your father came from, perhaps you could finally feel at home.* Is there something else out there? Somewhere else I might truly belong? Someone else who might care about me?

My aunt and uncle walk toward the door and I quickly scuttle around the corner. Once they leave, my aunt leaning on my uncle's arm, I slip into the house. It is dark without the fire lit, but I know my way. In my blanket I bundle the bread my aunt made this morning and some smoked meats hanging from the ceiling. I swing my cloak over my shoulders and adjust the pin holding it shut. A moment's hesitation, then I grab my uncle's hunting knife. It is a prized possession that my uncle has owned for years, well-oiled iron with a carved wooden handle. But he's on good terms with the blacksmith at the nearby fort of Dinas Emrys. He can get another one. I have nothing. Besides, he'll probably think it's a good trade, the knife in order to be rid of me for good. I grit my teeth and kick a stool over. It hits the wall with a solid thud. I take one last look at the room I grew up in—the only home I've ever known—and leave forever.

CHAPTER XXVII

I push open the turquoise-painted door with my hip, grimacing at the force needed. When the door pops open, I stumble with the sudden lack of resistance. A jangling dissonance from the disturbed wind chimes reminds me of my visit with Jen for our free palm reading. Was it only a week ago?

The door needs a shove to close, and leaves me blinking in the dimness. A voice floats out of the corner.

"Good afternoon."

The voice comes from the middle-aged woman behind the counter. Her silver lauvan drift gently around her, in the breeze from another world. I clear my throat.

"Is it Bethany? Aunt of Jacqueline Appleton?"

Bethany's lauvan tense and she stares at me closely. A wide smile follows, and she comes out from behind the counter with her arms outstretched.

"You must be Merry." She reaches for my unresisting hands and grips them firmly, shaking them for emphasis. "Jacqueline told me all about you and what you did for Wallerton. Words cannot express my gratitude for saving my lovely girls." She beams up at me. The hand-holding lasts for longer than I'm comfortable with before she releases me. She says, "I had no idea it was *you*."

"You remember me?"

"How could I forget? That intense reading—I knew immediately that you were different, but I never guessed how."

"Out of curiosity, what did you see?" I wouldn't mind knowing exactly how much Bethany knows about me. She ponders my question, her forehead wrinkled in thought.

246

"It wasn't visions that came to me, so much as feelings. There was a sense of time, of endless waiting, of sorrows and disappointments beyond number."

"Sounds about right," I mutter.

"But then a sense of relief, of future joy and reuniting, of the bonds of affection between two friends." She looks at me with earnest eyes. "It will occur, and soon, that reunion you long for. The spirits do not lie. Take heart."

I stare into Bethany's eyes, letting myself believe for just a moment that she knows what she's talking about. I wonder what "soon" is to Bethany. Do the spirits go by her clock or by mine?

I give her a wry smile and break eye contact.

"Thanks, Bethany." I remember one of the reasons I came to the shop today. "Oh, I wanted to tell you—your necklace won't work anymore. I destroyed Anna's, and it seems to have stripped the connection to the spirit world from all three necklaces."

"Yes, Jacqueline told me as much." She sighs and smiles a little sadly. "I won't pretend I won't miss the spectacular insight, but I'm more grateful that the volcano did not erupt. And if that is what was needed to be done, then so be it."

"It was. About the necklaces, do you have any more information on the man who gave them to you? I think Sylvana said his name was Drew?"

"I wish I had more to tell you. He came in claiming to be an acquaintance of a good friend of mine, who just so happened to be on a month-long yoga retreat in India, with no contact to the outside world. Of course, when she arrived back two days ago I asked her, and she'd never heard of Drew."

"When he gave you the necklaces, did he do anything strange?"

247

She looks at me and nods slowly.

"When he gave me the necklace, he placed it around my neck and kept his fingers above my collarbones for a while, with his eyes closed. I couldn't see what he was doing, but I felt a strange sensation of too much familiarity with the stranger. It was unnerving. But when his hands left me, oh, I could feel the world open up to me. It was intoxicating, that sense of revelation."

Bethany touches the nape of her neck absentmindedly, and closes her empty fist above where her necklace used to lie.

"Is there anything else you found out about Drew? Anything he mentioned?" A first name and a vague description aren't much to go on if I want to know more about these necklaces and the spirit world.

"He didn't say much else, but after Anna spoke with him on her own, the night she and Jacqueline had their big row, Anna mentioned the name of the organization Drew was part of. She called it Potestas."

I frown. *Potestas* is Latin for power or opportunity. In light of Anna's shenanigans at Mt. Linnigan, I'm starting to guess what the name means. But what, oh what, is their game? Unfortunately, I think I've found out all I can here. Bethany says she has no more to add, and her openly flowing lauvan conceal nothing. Potestas will have to stay a mystery for now.

I dig into my pocket for my wallet and pull out a card.

"Can I give you my card? If you hear anything more about Drew and Potestas, I'd appreciate you giving me a call."

The card is simple, with MERRY LYTTON on the top in capitals and my cell number underneath. I acquired the habit of having a calling card in the seventeen-fifties, and found them so useful that I've had a version at all times ever since. I especially like the simplicity of name and number. They're both things that I can change easily, to disappear without much of a trail.

Bethany takes the proffered card and holds it in both hands.

"I will ask my friends in the community if anyone else has come across Potestas." She thinks for a minute, then her eyes brighten. "I can ask the spirits as well."

I look at her askance.

"I'm confused. I thought the necklaces didn't work anymore."

Bethany smiles conspiratorially.

"There are many other ways to contact them. Messages from the necklace were incredibly clear and obvious, but I can gain insight through other channels."

Okay, I'm less hopeful about her innate abilities to summon spirits, but what do I know? Spirits didn't exist in my mind until last week.

"Thanks, Bethany." I turn to go.

"Wait," she says. Her face is pensive. "Can I ask—how is it you have these abilities? Who are you?"

I look at her thoughtfully. I have a feeling I could trust Sylvana and Bethany with my secrets, if I wanted. Both their minds are so open, so willing to believe the inexplicable— after an initial shock, I expect they would take it in stride. And their lauvan show no sign of deception or subterfuge— both aunt and niece are open books, so different from Anna.

Still, I hardly know them. And what purpose would it serve? It's a risk to divulge. I'm wary after the recent debacle with Jen. I could be reading them both wrong, although it is unlikely. I'm still undecided when Bethany speaks.

"No, don't answer. I don't need to know. I felt your intentions were good when I read your palm, and your actions in Wallerton confirmed my feelings. I trust you are on the side of good, and that's all I need to know."

A short laugh escapes my lips. I've lived long enough to know there is no good or bad, no black and white, only the murky grays through which every human flounders.

"I try my best. It's not always good enough, but it's all I have to work with." I nod at her. "Goodbye, Bethany."

"Be well, Merry Lytton." She stumbles over my last name, slurring the t's, and to my ears it almost sounds like my true name. She nods back graciously and I turn to leave. The jangling wind chimes echo in my ears long after I close the turquoise door.

CHAPTER XXVIII

I'm in my office, aimlessly swiveling my chair. Papers to be marked sit in an untouched pile on my otherwise sparse desk, a red pen at the ready but as yet unused. I turn around and around, staring at nothing.

I can't concentrate. It's way past lunchtime, but the thought of food sickens me. I can't stop thinking about Jen, her face after I manipulated the lauvan, the overwhelmingly loud silence in the car, the quiet goodbye at the sidewalk. Was that the last time I'll see Jennifer Chan?

I groan and slam my elbows into the desk. My hands cover my face. I don't want to lose Jen. It feels to me that we aren't finished yet, that our story together has more pages yet to fill.

What else could I have done? Could I have said it better, at a better time, in a different place? Should I have done something smaller and more subtle like making the wind blow, or should I have done something drastic like shape-shifting? Why have I done this so many times and still I don't know what to do?

A voice from the open door jerks me upright.

"Head too heavy for you?"

Jen stands in the doorway, a tentative half-smile playing on her mouth. Her eyes remain cautious.

I jump up. My first instinct is to leap across the room and give her a hug, but I refrain. She exudes all the placidity of a frightened deer, ready to bolt at the slightest whiff of the wrong scent. I stay by my desk.

"I'm giving my neck a break. All these brains, you know."

Jen chuckles quietly. I breathe again. So far, so good. She moves into the room and perches on the edge of my spare

251

stool. I lower myself into my office chair slowly and smoothly to avoid startling her.

"Merry." Jen stops, sighs, and speaks again. "Was it all a trick or a dream?"

I force my mouth into a smile that I'm sure doesn't hide the concern in my eyes.

"Sorry, Jen. It was all real."

Jen nods, slowly at first, but then finishes with a decisive head bob.

"Okay. The world just got a lot weirder. I can handle that. I think." She straightens her shoulders and sits up taller. "You know what you're going to do now, Merry?"

"Anything," I say. I mean it, too. If something I can do will keep Jen in my life, I will gladly do it.

"We're going to go out. You're going to buy me a mocha and a very large doughnut. With sprinkles. Then we're going to a quiet park bench by the ocean and you're going to tell me everything." She nods again and gives me a look as if daring me to contradict.

"Mocha, doughnut, sprinkles, bench. Absolutely." And I will tell her everything I can about the lauvan without going into my history. Maybe one day. But that's another very large burden that she doesn't need to bear, not today.

We stand and Jen moves to the door.

"Jen?"

She turns and waits. I try to formulate my thoughts into words.

"I just want to thank you. For trusting me, at Mt. Linnigan. Asking you to stay there was an impossible request, yet you did it with hardly any hesitation. Thank you for your faith in me, even though I haven't really done anything to earn it."

Jen frowns, puzzled.

"Honestly, I'm not sure myself why I stayed. It was a very big ask. But," she smiles and it lights up her face in the way that only a Jen-smile can. "I do trust you. Crazy, I know, but true nonetheless."

I return her smile. My throat is tight.

***

Jen absentmindedly tears the paper bag that formerly held her doughnut. I just finished answering her questions about the lauvan, and now she looks like she's turning everything over in her head. Or else trying not to think about it at all.

"So," she says after a long pause. "Let me get this straight. Everything you look at is covered with these—lauvan. Like some Italian chef has gone crazy with the spaghetti."

I laugh in surprise at the analogy.

"Something like that. If the spaghetti were alive and multicolored."

"Isn't that distracting? All these things are squiggling around, adding so much noise to your vision."

I consider her question.

"I've never thought of it that way. It's always been like this for me, so I'm used to it and can't compare to whatever it is you see. But it seems to me that you and everyone else are missing out on a world of information. Sometimes I wonder how you cope." Jen punches my arm. "No, really. It'd be like losing one of my senses."

"You're like Superman with his X-ray vision."

"Daredevil except with super-sight instead of hearing."

"An X-man whose mutation gives him extra eyespots and floaties."

"Hey," I protest.

"Well, it's a dubious superpower."

Instead of answering, I feel out for the lauvan of the nearest seagull. It swoops toward us, shrieking with indignation at its loss of control. I wrinkle my brow in concentration and twitch my finger.

The bird gives a final squawk and sails off, leaving behind a wet splatter on the grass a hand-span from Jen's sandaled foot.

"Yuck!" Jen moves her feet back instantly. I start to laugh. She looks at me suspiciously.

"Was that you?"

"Dubious mutant power indeed. It's all in the imagination. The sky's the limit."

She stares at me for a long moment, and I wonder if I've made light of this too fast. Then her face releases in a slow smile, like petals opening on a flower. She laughs briefly and leans back into the bench.

"Wow. I'm going to have to get creative with you."

We sit in comfortable silence, gazing at two sailboats fighting the stiff breeze in the distance. Jen seems calm and composed now and her lauvan are back to their usual bouncy swirls. Still, I sense that the dynamic in our relationship has changed. I hope it's for the better.

"Merry?"

"Hmm?"

"Why do you call them lauvan?"

Uh oh. It's the first question I can't answer fully. Normally, I'd say it's Welsh. Most buy that, if they even ask. But Jen has taken Welsh.

"I, uh, kind of made it up." Smooth, Merlin. Smooth. "I was studying Cornish and I think I misheard the word for rope, which is *lovan*. I liked the sound of lauvan, and it just stuck."

"Huh." Jen thinks about this. "It's so close, but yet not."

She tilts her head to one side. "It sounds right, somehow. You know how etymologists trace back to reconstruct what ancient languages sounded like, like Proto-Indo-European? Lauvan sounds like, I don't know, proto-Cornish or something."

Damn, Jen is too clever for her own good. I steer the conversation back to safer waters.

"I can't tell you how relieved I am that you're taking this so well. I've told others before, and they often run as hard as they can in the opposite direction."

Jen puts a hand on my arm and looks me in the eye.

"I'm not running. Don't get me wrong, I think you're really weird, but I can deal with that." She gives me a small smile. "And thanks for telling me. That was a lot of trust you showed me."

I smile back. I know it's a long road to reacquaint ourselves, but my shoulders feel considerably lighter. It's amazing how great it feels to have someone in your court.

"You've more than earned it." I pat her hand and stand up. "Come on. I'll take you home."

***

I wait until after six o'clock Central Time to make the call. Braulio's nursing home serves dinner from five to six. He'll be free now. I want to thank him for his advice, and let him know that a disaster was averted thanks to his help. I'm eager to recount the events, especially with someone who understands. He'll be happy I called.

A pleasant but brisk voice answers in Spanish on the third ring.

"Happy Valleys Care Home, Maria speaking. How can I help you?"

"I'd like to speak to Braulio Fernandez, please. I'm his friend Merlo Nuanez."

There's a brief hush on the end of the line. I hear the crackle of the long-distance echo in the silence.

"I'm so sorry, Sr. Nuanez. Braulio left us late last night. His passing was peaceful, in his sleep. Please accept my sincerest condolences."

I hardly know what to say. I stammer out some thanks, goodbyes, and Maria hangs up. I slowly take the phone away from my ear and press "end." I'm hollow, devoid of feeling. There is a limit to how many times one can get bad news and still be able to process it.

I don't make too many friends, as a rule. Not deep, lasting friendships. Not ones where I tell the friend everything.

Braulio was one of those few. He and I had rollicked around Central America for years together in the forties. He was my best man when I married Josephine in a dusty little church in Georgia in 1951. He eventually settled down and had a family, but we had kept in touch all these years.

And now, gone. Another friend disappears, and I'm still here.

Underneath the hollowness, emotions gather like storm clouds. Grief, of course, that cloying, familiar bugbear that I never get used to. There's also anger. Anger that I'm still here, that I am going through this song and dance again. Anger that I've waited for fifteen hundred years and Arthur has never shown.

But there's also something else. It takes some time to identify it. When I do, I'm surprised to feel jealousy. Braulio took the journey that it seems I never will. He lived and loved and aged and died.

I'm so tired. I grind the heels of my hands into my eyes, wiping away the tears that will not come. I don't want to be alone right now.

I briefly consider sex, going to a club tonight and finding someone, anyone, to touch and hold and pretend I'm not alone, to bring the mindless oblivion of lovemaking. I dismiss that notion quickly. I want to talk, and the wordless voicings of coitus are not what I have in mind.

I could talk to Jen. I reach for the phone before reconsidering. I only just laid the knowledge of the lauvan on her. I don't want to get into my whole history, not now, if ever. It's too soon and our relationship is still fragile. I could try to tell her about Braulio, but mostly everything I tell her would be a lie. I don't have the energy to keep my story straight today.

There's no one else, really. Not in this place, not in this time...

...except one. I hesitate, then pick up the phone and search for a number. There is someone I can talk to, someone who won't need explanations, who will just listen.

CHAPTER XXIX

Dreaming

Boys run out to meet us, stable hands and sons of the other warriors, laughing and skipping and grabbing our reins. Women wait at the gate of the villa, Guinevere central among them with a smile on her face. I glance over at Arthur who answers Guinevere's smile with one of his own, eyes only for her. Their connecting lauvan are clustered in a thick rope of shining flax and leaf green, the product of their many years of love and life together.

I let him trot forward to greet his wife in a few moments of privacy, but it's not long before Guinevere calls me over.

"Merlin! Will you not greet me?"

I smile broadly and slide off my horse, passing the reins to a nearby stable boy and striding over to two of my favorite people. When I reach Guinevere, I lean over and kiss her cheek.

"I brought your husband home safe and sound, my lady. Are you satisfied he is in good health and in one piece?"

Arthur laughs.

"I'm in one piece, certainly. But my shoulders ache like nothing else. I'm getting too old to fully appreciate the hard earth as a bed and enjoy battle as much as I did."

I clap my hand on his back.

"You'll feel better in the morning. Perhaps you're getting soft. I feel fine, and I have thirteen years on you. Don't worry, I'll get you out tomorrow for practice with the squires."

Arthur punches my shoulder lightly.

"Very amusing. If you dare to make me rise early tomorrow, I will show you exactly how adept I still am at swordplay."

I laugh, and notice Guinevere looking at me critically. I raise my eyebrow.

"Don't worry, Guinevere. I won't disturb your slumber tomorrow. Arthur's earned a rest before we battle the hordes on the northern borders in a few days. We all have."

"No, it is not that. It is only—I never noticed, but you look the same as before." She shakes her head in puzzlement. "The same as when I first met you, I mean. How do you look so young when Arthur has gray in his hair already and I have lines on my face?" She touches the outside corner of her eye.

Arthur looks at me with narrowed eyes, considering.

"He hasn't really changed, ever. Merlin, you've always looked like you do now." He grins. "Do you use the lauvan somehow? I think you might share your tricks with your friends. It's only good manners."

I frown. I very rarely see a representation of myself. I have a burnished copper disk the size of my palm that I use to shave, but the image is fuzzy and distorted. Occasionally, Guinevere will leave her polished mirror where I can pick it up and have a look, but that is a rare occurrence.

"I don't do anything, I swear." I look down at my hands, strong and unblemished as always. Even the scars on my left wrist I received only last year have almost disappeared.

"Maybe you sprang from the Earth fully formed. You were a child once, weren't you?" Arthur hasn't picked up on the change in my mood, and still speaks in a joking tone.

"Yes, of course." I run my hand through my hair. "I was born—" I count quickly. "Forty, forty-five years ago? Can that be right?" That sounds old, far older than I feel. What am I, that I can no longer feel the passage of time?

Guinevere must sense my distress, because she lays a hand on my shoulder.

259

"Never mind, Merlin. You are a little different, that is all."

***

I pull my sword out of the gut of my twitching opponent, and my eyes flick over to Arthur. Time slows to a crawl as a blade slides out of his abdomen. Arthur sways, blinking. The other warrior watches Arthur to gauge the effect of the killing blow. Slowly, so slowly in my vision, but quicker than a snake in reality, Arthur's sword whips up and with a blow too powerful for an injured man slices the warrior from the groin up. The other man drops without a word. Arthur sways once more, then clutches his gut and drops to his knees.

"No!" I scream. Time speeds up once more and I lunge toward Arthur. I grab every lauvan that passes me and pull with a vengeance. Men fall around me and shout in alarm and pain when unseen forces incapacitate them. I have eyes only for Arthur, who slumps over onto his side.

I fall to my knees beside him and roughly turn him over so he lies on his back. He hisses in pain but I focus on his lauvan above the terrible gash in his gut. The sword thrust sliced through the leather jerkin and found a soft path into glistening intestines, now exposed to the air. Arthur's lauvan are tangled beyond recovery, layers upon layers of knots that would take me weeks to sort out. But I don't have weeks, only minutes at the most.

I press Arthur's wound hard. Blood leaks out from between my fingers. Arthur lifts his hand and places it over mine on the wound in his abdomen. It's clearly a great effort. His already gray face blanches even more.

"Don't move," I say, frantic. The mess of his lauvan twitches and spasms around my hand. Because we are so close, every touch of his lauvan with mine opens me to his agony. Sweat runs down my temple. My free hand searches for his lauvan. Arthur's eyes roll back in his head before they stabilize on my face.

"Arthur, I can't—I can't fix this. Oh goddess, I don't know how to fix this."

Arthur pulls his lips back in an attempt at a smile. His graying hair is streaked with crusted blood from the battle.

"Merlin. Merlin, it's too late. I'm dying."

Tears begin to flow down my face in an unending stream. Arthur closes his eyes briefly. When they open, I see acceptance and peace.

"Take care of Guinevere. Please, Merlin, promise me."

"Of course." I force the words through my thickening throat.

"And Merlin?" His eyelids flutter.

"Yes?"

"Thank you for being here. You're always here when I need you. If—" he gasps for air briefly. "If I ever have the chance to come back, I promise I will. Your people believe in rebirth of the spirit, and why not? There's so much more I want to do." His head lolls to the side. "I will find you."

With his last breath, Arthur's lauvan loosen from his body and float through the air like dandelion seeds in the breeze. As they leave, they fade from the familiar spring green I've come to cherish to a translucent gray that quickly disintegrates into nothing, leaving only a few pale strands lying limp on his torso, lifeless. Arthur's lauvan disappear, and my lauvan that were connected to him flutter untethered between us. An aching, overwhelming sense of emptiness rips at my insides. My tears drip onto his chest.

"Don't leave me alone, Arthur." The blood leaking through my fingers from the wound on his abdomen slows, and then stops. I start to sob, pressing my forehead into his chest. "Don't go where I can't follow."

CHAPTER XXX

"It's good to see you again, Merry," Dr. Dilleck says when I enter her office. She's dressed in a matching pink sweater and blouse combo that suits her midnight-blue lauvan. She tucks her hair behind an ear in a gesture I recognize from last time—it must be a nervous tic. She smiles on my approach to the couch, but the smile falters when she sees my face. Huh. I didn't realize I looked as bad as all that. She asks gently, "Is there anything you'd like to talk about in particular today?"

I sit heavily on the couch. I don't play around this time. Braulio's death weighs too profoundly on me for games. I sigh, wondering what to say, wondering why I'm here again. It seemed like a good idea yesterday after hearing the news about Braulio. Now I feel dull resignation settle over me like a deep muffling snowfall. I just want to sleep, to lose myself in memories if I can't have oblivion. At least my memories are old wounds, familiar bruises that I know how to deal with. Braulio's death is still too sharp.

"I don't know why I came," I say. My voice sounds slow and heavy. "This was a mistake. I should go."

"Merry, please." Dr. Dilleck leans forward as if she will get up and force me back down to the couch, although I haven't yet moved. "Please stay. Please tell me what's troubling you."

I stare at the fruit bowl. Today it's filled with green apples, all perfect and gleaming except for one with a small wormhole near the stem. It's been turned on its end to hide this imperfection by some zealous receptionist, but I can still see it. The room is quiet, almost muffled-sounding.

"A friend of mine died yesterday," I say into the silence.

It's horrible to hear the words out loud. In my peripheral vision the psychologist shifts in her chair, but she remains silent. I'm grateful. I don't want to hear empty platitudes, no matter how much she may mean them. "He was my best friend. I'd known him for so many years. He was best man in my wedding…" My throat closes up and I look to the ceiling, feigning an interest in the crown molding while I focus on keeping the tears in my eyes where they belong. How many more times can I do this? I vowed after Josephine's death that she was the final woman I would let into my heart. I didn't anticipate that I would have as much trouble with friends. Am I destined to be alone forever? Is that the only way to keep my splintered heart intact?

"I'm so sorry, Merry," Dr. Dilleck says, her voice filled with warmth and compassion. She sounds like she really means it. I wonder if she could ever understand the depth of my aloneness. She probably has loving parents, an extended family of aunts and uncles and cousins, friends she grew up with, maybe even a dog. She might have been to a few funerals, perhaps her grandfather's or a great-aunt's, but has loss ever really touched her life? Loss, without the safety net of a support network of friends and family that love her? Would she ever understand what it means to be truly alone?

"Everyone I've ever loved has left me," I say to the ceiling. "Sooner or later, they leave me. And I don't think I can keep doing this. I don't know how to keep loving and losing over and over again."

I bring my face into my hands and sit on the edge of the couch, in an attempt to control myself. What am I doing with this woman, this child who knows nothing? What did I think this would accomplish? It feels as if gravity is much heavier than usual.

"Have you ever seen the Grand Canyon? It's like that. I'm

264

standing on the cliffs and everyone I've ever loved is on tiny rafts, a mile below me. I can barely see their faces anymore, and they're drifting further and further away. And I'm afraid that one day night will fall and I won't see them ever again. I'll be all alone in the dark without even my memories to cling to."

My eyes are closed, and I sense rather than see Dr. Dilleck come around the table to sit next to me on the couch.

"Even now I'm standing at the edge of the darkness. I'm alone. I'm always alone."

A hand touches my shoulder. Its gentle pressure grounds me. I lean into it slightly without meaning to.

"You're not alone," she says. Her voice is quiet in my ear, compassionate and sure.

It should have felt like hollow comfort. Why do I believe her?

EPILOGUE

Time marches forward as it always does. Braulio's death reminded me of that all too sharply. His last words to me still echo in my ears. *You need to let someone else in, Merlo my friend.* But how can I do that when they will only leave me again? My relationship with Jen is as fragile as a spiderweb—the bonds are strong, but one sweeping hand of revelation could brush it all away. I'm glad Jen knows one part of me, but I don't know if I can give any more. I don't have much left to give, these days.

The crisis at Mt. Linnigan took Jen and me to a whole new level, but it brought with it far more questions than I'm entirely comfortable with. Anna's actions and her fearful reaction when I thwarted her plan puzzle me. Who is she working for? Drew and the mysterious Potestas promised her power beyond imagining, and gave her the tools to get it. What do they want? I wish I had more to go on, but the name "Drew" isn't enough to search with. And Potestas handed out three of these lauvan-necklaces like they were candy. How many more do they have, and how are they making them?

Then there is the small matter of the spirit world. All this time, all my long years, I've been convinced that no such realm exists. It's disturbing and unnerving and exciting all at once, and I feel a pang of sympathy and understanding for what Jen must have gone through at my big reveal. My whole perception of the world and how it works is turned on its head, and now I have to figure out what's up and what's down all over again.

And then the hints about my father, those tantalizing morsels the spirits let drop. They know something, and anything is a whole lot more than the nothing I know

266

currently. My father may be centuries dead and gone, but if I know more about him then I might know more about myself. I've had time to come up with a lot of questions, and I think it's high time I got some answers.

So I'll explore the lauvan-cables more, and study what legends, myths, and religions can tell me about the spirit world. I have time to kill before Arthur comes back, after all.

And I will wait. He made me a promise, and I have all the time in the world to hold him to it. Who knows, maybe it is possible. Spirits are real, after all. If he needs me, I'll be here, waiting. I'm good at that.

HISTORICAL NOTE

King Arthur is one of the best known legends in the English-speaking world. Centuries of storytelling have turned what may or may not have been a historical figure—or possibly two figures—into the myths that ground so many books and movies and cultural references. But is there any truth behind the stories?

During my research for *Ignition*, I read many books about King Arthur, Merlin, and the knights of the round table, both fictional stories as well as anthropological and archaeological texts. At the end of the day, however, I came to the conclusion that King Arthur is the ultimate enigma, and hardly anyone knows anything for sure. Even the time period he may or may not have lived in, 5th century Britain, is often referred to as "the Dark Ages" mainly because the historical records of the era are so sparse. The decades after the Romans pulled their forces out of Britain were tumultuous and full of upheaval, and record-keeping was likely the last thing on most people's minds.

I wanted to give a real flavor to Merlin's backstory, and to follow the "truth" as much as possible. All of this historical uncertainty left me bewildered, until it dawned on me that I had been given an opportunity. If nobody knew anything concrete, I could make up my own story, just the way I wanted to. I used this freedom to take what parts of the legends I wanted to take, morph the fantastical into something approaching reality, and ground everything in as much historical context as I could find about life in 5th century Wales. The result, I hope, is a realistic source from which our modern-day legends could have arisen, given enough time and creative storytellers.

ACKNOWLEDGEMENTS

A lot of people came when I called for help, and magnificently rose to the challenge. Editors I relied on include Gillian Brownlee, Judith Powell, Wendy and Chris Callendar, Diana Monks, Linda Powell, and Kathryn Humphries. Their fresh eyes and diverse perspectives were invaluable. Help with foreign languages was graciously provided by Kathryn Humphries, Kirsten Kooijman, Danielle Baines, Mathias Middelboe, and Selim Dost. Christien Gilston undertook the glorious cover design for the book, and Melissa Bowles contributed to logo design. Maggie Claydon generously reviewed Merry's therapy sessions for authenticity. Duncan Johannessen kindly discussed volcanology with me, which I interpreted in the context of the story—any transgressions against science are my own.

ABOUT THE AUTHOR

Emma Shelford enjoys experiencing different countries and cultures. She has traveled widely, including crossing the high seas of the Atlantic during her doctorate in earth and ocean sciences. Her inspiration for *Ignition* came from her abiding love of English literature and Arthurian legends, which she has cultivated over the years with extensive reading and far too many literature courses for a science major.

When she sat down to write *Ignition*, Merlin practically scrambled to get out of her brain, so eager was he to make his voice heard. He will be returning, as *Ignition* is the first book in the *Musings of Merlin* series.

Emma is also the author of *Mark of the Breenan*, the first in the *Breenan* series for young adults, published in 2014.

42569323R00169

Made in the USA
Charleston, SC
31 May 2015